A Dangerous Passion
The Hellion Club, Book Eight

by Chasity Bowlin

© Copyright 2023 by Chasity Bowlin
Text by Chasity Bowlin
Cover by Dar Albert

Dragonblade Publishing, Inc. is an imprint of Kathryn Le Veque Novels, Inc.
P.O. Box 23
Moreno Valley, CA 92556
ceo@dragonbladepublishing.com

Produced in the United States of America

First Edition July 2023
Trade Paperback Edition

Reproduction of any kind except where it pertains to short quotes in relation to advertising or promotion is strictly prohibited.

All Rights Reserved.

The characters and events portrayed in this book are fictitious. Any similarity to real persons, living or dead, is purely coincidental and not intended by the author.

ARE YOU SIGNED UP FOR DRAGONBLADE'S BLOG?

You'll get the latest news and information on exclusive giveaways, exclusive excerpts, coming releases, sales, free books, cover reveals and more.

Check out our complete list of authors, too!

No spam, no junk. That's a promise!

Sign Up Here

www.dragonbladepublishing.com

Dearest Reader;

Thank you for your support of a small press. At Dragonblade Publishing, we strive to bring you the highest quality Historical Romance from some of the best authors in the business. Without your support, there is no 'us', so we sincerely hope you adore these stories and find some new favorite authors along the way.

Happy Reading!

CEO, Dragonblade Publishing

Additional Dragonblade books by
Author Chasity Bowlin

The Hellion Club Series
A Rogue to Remember (Book 1)
Barefoot in Hyde Park (Book 2)
What Happens in Piccadilly (Book 3)
Sleepless in Southampton (Book 4)
When an Earl Loves a Governess (Book 5)
The Duke's Magnificent Obsession (Book 6)
The Governess Diaries (Book 7)
A Dangerous Passion (Book 8)
Making Spirits Bright (Novella)
All I Want for Christmas (Novella)
The Boys of Summer (Novella)

The Lost Lords Series
The Lost Lord of Castle Black (Book 1)
The Vanishing of Lord Vale (Book 2)
The Missing Marquess of Althorn (Book 3)
The Resurrection of Lady Ramsleigh (Book 4)
The Mystery of Miss Mason (Book 5)
The Awakening of Lord Ambrose (Book 6)
Hyacinth (Book 7)
A Midnight Clear (A Novella)

The Lyon's Den Series
Fall of the Lyon
Tamed by the Lyon
Lady Luck and the Lyon

Pirates of Britannia Series
The Pirate's Bluestocking

Also from Chasity Bowlin
Into the Night

Author's Note

The Liberty of the Mint was a real place. Across the Thames from the City of London, the Mint was a lawless area that answered only to the High Court. In the 17th and 18th century it was a bastion for debtors. Debt collectors had no authority inside that area and thus would wait outside the gate that separated the Mint from the rest of the city on the Old Kent Road. This resulted in those who owed debts being virtual prisoners there. The law at the time prohibited the collection of debts on Sundays which meant that on that one day, the inhabitants could come and go freely from the Mint.

In 1722 The Mint in Southwark Act was passed in Parliament, revoking the protection afforded to that area and to the debtors who had sought refuge there. Through the remainder of the 18th century and well into the 19th century, the Mint and its surroundings were home to some of the worst slums and rookeries in London. The area was also home to the Clink Prison, the Marshalsea Prison and many others. The residents of this region were often desperate and destitute.

I've taken a few liberties with the timeline of when this book occurs and when the legislation that changed the Mint's status was enacted. But it's a fascinating subject and there is a wealth of information available online.

Part One
One Fateful Night

Chapter One

1826

IN HIS STUDY, surrounded by volume after volume of ledgers, Vincent Carrow, better known as the Hound of Whitehall, was in his element. Some of those books contained simple accounts, others tracked favors done, favors repaid, and those who still owed him things much more valuable than mere money. And yet, nothing within those leatherbound tomes was illegal. Suspect, certainly, but not illegal. *Those* transactions were kept elsewhere, far from his home or any place where he might be incriminated by them should the local constabulary choose to stop turning a blind eye to his misdeeds in spite of his *generosity* to them.

"You can come out now," he called out. All traces of the accent he'd used during his meeting were now gone from his voice. The moment Viscount Seaburn had left, he'd shed it much like removing a coat.

When Annabel stepped from behind the ornate and ridiculously ostentatious screen in the corner, he let his gaze roam over her freely. Her beauty was undeniable. With her auburn hair, porcelain perfect skin, and seraphic features, she might have been an angel. But then she wore only the thinnest of chemises—and not in the typical white. No, she favored sheer black with deep lace to trim the neckline. He ought to know—they'd all been charged to him. Of course, as he watched the way that nearly transparent fabric moved over her lush curves, he found himself hard-pressed to be irritated by her expensive tastes.

Without a doubt, she was one of the most beautiful women he'd ever seen. And yet, he was not so awed by her beauty as he had once been. Because now he understood that it was only skin deep. He didn't mind a woman with a fiery nature. In truth, he preferred them. But Annabel wasn't simply a firebrand. She was a spoiled, petulant child with no feeling for anyone but herself. At the slightest hint that she would not get her own way, the tantrums—for they could be called nothing else—would begin. Those would be followed by tearful apologies and desperate clinging. The cycle had become tiresome.

She stepped farther from the screen and into the pale light that poured through the window. It was a calculated maneuver to draw his attention to her greatest assets.

"Why do you do that?" As she asked the question, she pursed her lips into a pout that was designed to make a man think of only one thing. It might have worked had he not seen her use that particular trick many, many times.

"What do I do?" He forced himself to look away from her and the way the light gilded her curves beneath her chemise. He had work to do. No man reached the level of success that he had by being lazy or distracted by a pretty face and a pair of breasts.

"Speak in that horrible cockney accent when you and I both know that your natural way of speaking is as perfectly enunciated and articulate as anyone in society. In fact, I daresay it's better than most!"

It had been said in a teasing manner, but there was something in her tone, some hidden nugget of truth that she did not want him to see. It embarrassed her, he realized. She liked his fine house. She certainly liked the lines of credit he'd created for her at various stores. All the pretty gifts, all the luxuries—and she certainly liked the way he fucked. Either that or she faked it better than most. But she was still ashamed to be associated with a man from such humble beginnings. It seemed that no matter how high he climbed, he would still be the bedraggled urchin from the rookeries. If she only knew, he thought, that the man who'd fathered him was a duke.

His mother had tried to teach him to speak properly, and she'd laid the foundation, he supposed. But it had soon become clear to all of them that he had a better chance of survival if he looked and sounded like everyone else in the den of hovels where they'd lived. So, he'd fallen into the habit of speaking in that manner when out and about and reverting to more modulated speech when home with her. When it had been time to divest himself of that street accent, he'd worked long and hard to eliminate the last vestiges of it. But it still would never be enough. All the noble blood and perfect diction in the world would never truly make up for the fact that he was born in the gutters.

As if he was speaking of something as simple as exchanging pleasantries, he explained, "Because it does not suit my needs for Lord Valentine Somers, Viscount Seaburn, to know that I am anything more than a grubby, cockney street rat who made good."

Annabel sidled toward him, hips swaying in a manner that was almost hypnotic. She perched on the edge of his desk and leaned in close enough that the scent of her perfume, something he had gifted her, wafted to him. But it wasn't her perfume that held his interest. It was the lush breasts now perfectly displayed and so close to him that her intent was unmistakable. She was bent on seduction.

"Why don't you come back to bed, my love? It's so early when we've had such late nights," she whispered suggestively. "And it's so terribly lonely there without you."

For just a second, he considered it. But in the end, his duties and obligations won out. After all, he wasn't just taking care of his business but all the people that were involved in it. If he let things slide, others suffered for it. Everyone in his employ counted on him for their livelihoods and he could not simply shrug off the weight of those responsibilities. Besides, Annabel knew the hours he kept, that the club owned his nights for the most part. To be with him meant she would have to content herself with the few hours he had left, usually just before the dawn. But Annabel was not one to ever content herself with anything. Demanding was the kinder term he might use to describe her nature.

"I cannot, Annabel." It was uttered with genuine regret, as much because he wanted the pleasure and release her body could provide, but also because the burden he bore was growing heavier with time. Since he'd been a young man, less than sixteen, he'd been building an empire. Smarter than most and a good fighter, he'd recognized that he possessed a skill others would pay for—protection. That was how it had begun. With a small crew of only four, they had begun to offer protection to certain businesses for a fee. Security for brothels came first and then the gaming hells. After that, other illicit businesses had started seeking out his services. Fences. Smugglers. For twenty-three years he had been at the helm, and it was growing old. *He was growing old.*

Her expression went from amorous to angry in a heartbeat. The pout was no longer an affectation, but quite sincere, and her brow furrowed with anger. "You know I have to leave soon!" Agitated, she got up and began to pace the room, working herself up into a typical tantrum. "I have to go back to my wretched husband and that monstrosity of a house in the countryside! But you don't even care! You never cared. You're just like all the others!"

Her much-maligned husband. In the beginning, he'd felt a bit sorry for her—a pretty young thing married off to an old roué. But the man she'd married was not a monster at all. After Annabel's many complaints about her husband, he'd looked into the man and discovered that her husband was a young man, quite well liked, and apparently deeply in love with his straying wife. If anyone had been wronged in their marriage, it had been

Annabel's husband. "It's not a house in the countryside, Annabel. It's an elegant if somewhat gothic-inspired manor on the seashore." Guilt was a wasted emotion and one he did not bother with, but he could certainly admit when he'd been party to an injustice. If ever there was a reason to end things with Annabel, that was it. "And I do care, but I have work to do."

The account books were waiting and needed his attention. *And unlike Annabel, numbers didn't lie.* Numbers always gave him the truth. He didn't love Annabel, but he desired her. In fact, he wanted her as he'd never wanted another woman. Or so he'd thought at first.

She was like a fire in his blood in the beginning, one that gave him a fair bit of sympathy for the opium eaters and those bedeviled by the ruination of gin. But that wasn't love and it never would be. Love wasn't something that could grow and flourish in his very dark corner of the world, much less in the hardened black recesses of his miserable heart. And Annabel's shine had begun to dull—her temper and her childishness were wearing on his nerves.

She grabbed the account book he'd been working on and flung it across the room. Ink spilled across the surface of his desk, some of it dripping onto his shirt and trousers. It was not the first time he'd seen such outbursts from her. Annabel could go from throwing things and shouting obscenities at him to crying piteously and begging his forgiveness all in the space of seconds, it seemed. It was the way of things with her. Unpredictable and often dangerous in her temper, there was a volatility in Annabel that had only increased during their acquaintance. Even their passionate bed play and her loveliness could not counteract the difficulty inherent in being with her. He was a man who liked order, and she was a creature of chaos and temper.

"Do not do that again," he warned.

"Why not?" The words were tossed out as a challenge, even as she bared her teeth at him in threat—like a she-wolf.

Pushed beyond reason by her temper tantrums and childish

antics, he snapped, "Because I'm not your husband. And I'll toss your naked arse right into the street, scandal be damned!"

She shrieked at him, a wild sound that was half crazed. Then she came at him, hands clenched into claws as her nails raked over his chest where his open shirt had parted, leaving a burning trail of blood in her wake. Abruptly, he shoved her away from him and her screeches turned to sobs as she collapsed, sprawling to the carpet. She laid there and wept like a broken child, as if she were the victim rather than the attacker. It would always be that way, he realized. There was something inside Annabel that was so irrevocably damaged she hadn't a chance. He didn't believe in happy endings or love—those were myths fools used to justify their behavior—though contentment was possible. A peaceful and pleasant existence could be had, just not with Annabel.

The desire to end things with her had been in his mind for a while and with every one of her tantrums had only grown stronger. But this was more than a tantrum—it was an attack. She'd drawn blood from him. Men had died for less. He wouldn't hurt her. That wasn't his way. But he would send her packing and reclaim the peace she'd taken from him.

Reaching into his desk drawer, he retrieved the red leather box that had been delivered the day before, and he tossed it to her where she remained, crumpled by her own grief at his imagined slights. Perhaps the diamond and emerald parure would soothe her clearly overwrought sensibilities. "That was to be your parting gift. Take it and go. I'll have Stavers send for the carriage."

He didn't look back but walked out of his study and retreated to his chamber. Temper was a liability, something that almost always put a man at a disadvantage, and he typically avoided it at all costs. But she'd managed to stoke his. Pressing his fingertips to the deep gouge on his chest, he drew them away covered with his blood. He'd never struck a woman before in his life. Even pushing her away, he hadn't intended for her to fall. His only intent had been to protect himself from further injury.

At first, he'd enjoyed the unpredictability—the fire and ice of her had been a challenge to him. Living in a world where every person he encountered kowtowed to him, it had been a refreshing change in the beginning. But he could find some other way to alleviate his boredom than dealing with a spoiled woman-child who shrieked like a fishwife.

"And 'er 'usband is welcome to 'er," he whispered as he tugged his soiled shirt over his head and discarded it in favor of a fresh one. He needed a brawl, something to get out his anger and get his mind right again. Right and free of the vicious witch whose weeping still echoed through the halls. There was only one place to find such a thing in the middle of the morning—Whitechapel. The very place that had spawned him.

Chapter Two

HONORIA BLAYLOCK STARED at the group of men surrounding her. With her heart in her throat and a blade extended in front of her, she knew she stood no chance against them, but she'd be damned to hell before she simply gave in without a fight. That was not in her nature. *Not anymore.*

"You ain't never used a sword in your life," one of them spat.

Honoria gripped the hilt more tightly. "I'll happily prove you wrong, sir." She was hardly an expert in fencing, but she wasn't a true novice. After her husband's death, when she'd made the choice to start doing her charitable work in the rookeries where it was most needed, she'd begun educating herself. Self-defense had been part of that. Though there were very limited opportunities for a woman to learn such things, she had managed to find a few individuals who were willing to train her despite the many societal rules broken in the process.

Her driver, who had been knocked to the ground and was nearly unconscious, groaned as he shifted on the dirty pavement. She didn't spare a glance at him. Not because she didn't want to or because she had no concern for the loyal servant, but because she knew that one never took their eyes off a pack of wild dogs. And the men before her could easily be classified as such. Angry and snarling, lean and hungry—they were more terrifying than dogs. Dogs might rip her to shreds out of fear or hunger—but it wouldn't be for their pleasure. The men before her would want her humiliated, and they would enjoy it. They would want to hurt far more than simply her flesh.

One of them lunged forward. Honoria immediately slashed out with the rapier, slicing the man's arm from his wrist to his elbow. It was enough to make the others in the group pause to consider whether she'd been bluffing or not when she threatened to slash them to ribbons if they dared touch her.

"You ain't got no right coming down 'ere," one of them groused. "Don't need no *ladies* down 'ere telling our women they don't got to lift their skirts to earn their bread. It's 'onest work, even if the likes o' you look down on it."

Honest work. Honoria had a very practical view of prostitution. Women had few enough options open to them if they had to support themselves. Working as a seamstress, a laundress, or a maid—if you lacked education—was the best one could hope for in terms of truly honest work. Prostitution was more profitable, without a doubt, but it came with significant risks.

And not every woman who wound up in that profession did so by choice. Sometimes they were forced into it by the men in their lives. That she would fight tooth and nail to prevent. If she'd learned anything in the course of her marriage, it was that women should have more opportunities to govern themselves, and entrusting a man with one's well-being was a guarantee only of disappointment.

"Is it honest work when it spreads the pox to everyone they service? When they bear children so ill from it they cannot survive?" Honoria snapped back at him. "If you think it's such honest work, perhaps you should be the one doing it!"

The other men laughed, clearly enjoying the jab at their friend. But he didn't. He didn't enjoy her retort, and he certainly didn't enjoy their laughter. The hot fury in his gaze only intensified.

"Spread out boys. We'll get 'er yet and 'ave our fun," he said with an ugly threat ringing in his voice.

Her heart was racing, and she could feel the cold sweat of fear prickling her skin beneath her heavy clothing. She'd been coming to these neighborhoods—Seven Dials, St. Giles, Whitechapel, the Devil's Acre—for nigh on two years. She'd been distributing baskets of food, providing direction to clinics where free medical care would be given to those in need, helping to find employment for those who wished it. It was the sort of charitable work her mother had engaged in when Honoria was younger, though perhaps at a greater distance. It was the same sort of work her sister now did, as well, though Henrietta restricted most of her aid to those in hospital, her wretched husband refusing to let her do more.

It was the very sort of charitable work that Honoria had wanted to do as a married woman, but her own husband had also refused to let her. He'd refused anything that would bring her a modicum of satisfaction or happiness. Perhaps that was why she'd dived headlong into her current methods, without fully considering the possible consequences.

Each visit brought her more familiarity with all the different types of misery a human being could suffer in London, and yet, she had naively assumed she was safe there. She'd believed that her willingness to help those who lived in such places would inspire some degree of loyalty and therefore safety for her. In short, she'd been a fool.

But fool did not mean coward. She would fight to the death if need be. Her heart in her throat, her body tensed and ready, she took a steadying breath. She might have been afraid, but she also felt something else that the men surrounding her had not counted on. *Resolve.*

Never again would she be a terrified victim, cowering before any man. Lifting her sword higher, adjusting her grip just so, she was as ready for battle as she would ever be.

"Whatever you take from me," she said, "know that you will pay for it in blood."

Chapter Three

BLOODIED, A LITTLE battered, his knuckles split and swollen, Vincent walked out of the warehouse and into the chilly night air with a sigh of relief. The worst of the cold fury had abated, pounded into the faces of his opponents. No one would dare hit him on the street, but once he stepped into the ring, it was a different matter altogether. He shook off the heavy yoke of his identity then and became what every other man there was—a bettor or a brawler.

The crowd was still cheering and jeering his fallen opponent as he stepped deeper into the darkness. Flexing his hands, the strips of cloth that had bound them were horribly stained with sweat and blood. But he didn't unwind them. Not yet. He'd wait until he was home and Stavers could do it. The former pugilist turned butler knew what to do for bruised knuckles. Stavers had been the one who'd taught him to fight all those years ago. Closest thing to an actual father he'd ever known.

The sound of raucous laughter drew his attention. It was an ugly sound—mean and bullying. He knew it well. It was firmly fixed in his memory from childhood. The scene was as fresh in his mind now as it had been when it occurred. The little girl curled in a ball on the dirty street, a group of boys hovering on the brink of being men, all gathered around her poking at her with sticks and hurling stones. Why? Because she was different. Because she didn't belong in the ugliness of that world. He'd tried to intervene then and had failed. Beaten to a pulp for his troubles, he'd watched those boys drag her away and that little girl had never been seen again.

All the anger he'd dispelled came rushing back. His gaze slid to the scene across the street, and he squinted in the darkness to see it clearly. It was disgustingly familiar.

The woman was surrounded by a gang of ruffians. But there was no weeping or begging for help. She did not curl into a ball and pray for them to get tired of their abuse. No. Not the Valkyrie before him. She'd die before she begged—that much was obvious. With her dark braids coiled about her head and a sword in hand, he could think of no other apt description for the woman. She was fierce and determined, but, even from a distance, he could see she was not fearless. She'd have been a fool not to be afraid. Exquisite as she was, she was also doomed. Standing against such a group she had no chance, regardless of how remarkable he found her.

One lone woman with a sword against six men who had her flanked. Even if she did manage to escape them, another group would set upon her soon enough. It was the nature of the place they were in. Death lurked around every corner, hiding in shadows and waiting to snatch the unwary in its gaping maw.

Why the devil was she here? One of the leering men kicked at a basket that lay upon the refuse-strewn street. Loaves of bread spilled from it, and he understood instantly—she was a reformer. A bloody do-gooder fulfilling her sense of *noblesse oblige*. Someone who thought herself better than all the wretched souls that lived in that hellhole.

Part of him—that small and petty part that resented anyone who had not suffered a beginning as impoverished and miserable as his own—was tempted to leave her to her fate. *She should have known better.* Another part of him recalled his mother taking their own meager food and sharing it with an old woman in the room next to theirs who could no longer work. That food had not been purchased by his mother who hadn't a ha'penny to her name. It had come from someone not unlike the woman before him. Charity.

It wasn't that people didn't deserve help here. It was that so many of the people here simply didn't want help. They would attack any who dared to infiltrate their filthy, impoverished kingdom. It was the place where hope, charity, and kindness came to die. She'd be nothing more than a bit of diversion for them, but she'd become a cautionary tale to others. And another mark on his soul, if he believed in such things. His mother's voice was in his head then. That gentle tone that sometimes whispered in his ear and resulted in a rare good deed.

"That's enough," he said. He didn't shout. He didn't have to. His voice carried anyway, as did the note of command in it. "You'll leave her be."

One of the men turned to sneer at him. But then recognition registered in the man's gaze, and he quickly changed his mind. The man simply turned and fled. Another followed suit. But four remained. Those were tolerable odds.

"We don't answer to you," one of them said. While his tone was challenging, there was fear in his voice. It lacked the conviction of one who was truly committed to their current course.

"No," Vincent agreed, the calm tone of his voice doing nothing to conceal the menace behind his words. "You do not answer to me, but you will."

"And just who the fuck are you to be ordering us about? Don't take orders from no toff. Never 'ave and never will," the shortest of the group answered. Even as he said it, he was clutching his bleeding arm.

"I am the Hound of Whitehall," Vincent replied, his tone conversational, but no less threatening for it. "And I own this street and every street like it. Nothing happens here that I do not approve. And six men—four, now that your cowardly brethren have fled—attacking a single woman... that I would never approve. So you can walk away now, or you can pay the price for your insolence."

It was his name, the nickname that he'd been given as a boy, that sent two more of them running. They scurried away like rats, and he walked toward the woman. The fifth man, seeing the odds in his favor had dwindled considerably, bolted. Only the blowhard remained.

Vincent closed the distance. A few feet from him, the man drew a knife. Vincent slipped one of his own from the sheath at his side, neatly concealed inside his trousers. "I always come prepared," he said.

The man's gaze drifted toward the gleaming blade then to the rapier the woman still held. Without another word, he scurried into the night.

Vincent turned to her, "You may put down your sword. You are safe now."

With her chin jutting forward stubbornly, she replied, "If it is all the same to you, sir, I shall keep it just where it is."

His lips curved into a smile. Of all the expressions that could cross his face that night, it was the one least expected. After all, it was the quicksilver moods and anger of another beautiful woman that had sent him out in search of a brawl, where only violence had been able to set him to rights. But where Annabel was all petulance and pretty pouts, this woman would simply demand what she wanted from him and expect to be obeyed as her right. Her dignity would never permit childish fits.

"Keep it as you choose, then," he conceded. Pursing his lips, one soft whistle had his driver emerging from a nearby alley. His black coach and pair of matched stallions were at odds given the poverty of their current surroundings. But it was a well-known vehicle, one that no one would dare touch. "Timmons will see you home ... and your injured driver, as well. Your coach will be delivered to you tomorrow."

"You do not know my direction to make such a promise of delivery, sir," she replied.

"I will," he said. "I will know all that I need to know by the dawn."

She was frowning as he escorted her to the carriage. Even in the dim light he could see that. His words had both puzzled and intrigued her. It was quite fitting since that was precisely how he felt about her. Puzzled and intrigued. Opening the door, he held out his hand to help her inside. It necessitated lowering her sword for a moment. That opportunity was not one he would pass up.

Vincent stepped closer to her, as she levered herself up on the single step into the carriage. It brought them eye to eye. It was impulse—a thing he rarely gave in to—but he was impossibly drawn to her, and perfect moments came around very rarely in a man's life. This was one of them. He'd likely never see her again, and he was nothing if not an opportunist.

His hand lifted, coiling about the heavy mass of her braided hair that had begun to escape its pins. No doubt the tidy bonnet that had covered it had been lost in the fray. It was like silk, so soft and fine that all he could imagine was having it wrapped around them, feeling it on his skin.

He might have let her go if she'd offered a single protest—even a hint of one. Instead, she simply froze, her eyes widening in something that might have been either anticipation or fear. He hoped desperately that it was the former rather than the latter, because it would have been easier to sacrifice blood and bone than to resist the urge to kiss such a magnificent creature.

Tugging slightly on her hair, he tipped her head forward until their noses were nearly touching . . . and then he waited for just a split second. She did not pull away. When her lashes fluttered and her eyes closed in acquiescence, only then did he touch his lips to hers. He instantly wished he had not.

Mistake. Terrible, terrible mistake.

There were kisses and then there was the thing that suddenly bloomed between them. Heat, need, desperation. It was born in an instant, that simple touch of their lips giving it life and altering him forever. No single kiss had ever affected him so. Making love to a woman had never rocked him as deeply as one relatively innocent kiss.

His blood raced, his heart thundered. He'd gone seven rounds in one boxing match and five in another. Neither of those fights had left him as winded. The force of it—the force of her— had knocked the breath right out of him.

The softness of her lips, the sweet and clean scent of her— lemongrass and lilacs—penetrated his senses, blocking out everything else. The need was overwhelming. He wanted nothing more than to push her into that carriage and let the heat of that kiss carry them toward its natural conclusion.

From the street, the injured driver groaned. It was enough to pull him back, to let the dirty and dangerous nature of their surroundings penetrate the haze of desire. The spell was broken, but it would never be forgotten. Like a soldier on the battlefield, he'd know the precise place, the exact moment, where he'd been marked for life.

Releasing her abruptly, he stepped back. It was the only way. Like ripping off a bandage. Fast. With no time to consider it. She stumbled a bit but caught herself on the carriage door before she fell from the step.

With an arm's length of distance between them once more, Vincent recognized one irrefutable truth. The woman before him was not—would never be—just a diversion. She would be, if he allowed such a thing in his life, a weakness.

"Restrict your reform activities in this neighborhood to daylight hours," he said. "And you will be safe. No one will dare touch you here. Not now. Not ever again."

He turned and walked away, disappearing into the night and leaving her to stare after him.

Leaning back against the carriage seat, Honoria placed a hand to her heart. The rapid tattoo thrumming beneath her palm was not unexpected, given the dark turn the night had taken. But she had to be honest with herself. The fear she'd felt facing off against her would-be attackers had not sent her into such a state. It was him. *The Hound of Whitehall.*

She knew who he was, of course. No one who spent any time at all in the neighborhoods she did could remain ignorant of his existence—of his dominion. While he was not necessarily involved in every criminal enterprise occurring in those shadowy corners of London, he had been right—nothing occurred in them without his approval. If you wanted to trade stolen goods, you needed his blessing. If you wanted to run a house of ill-repute, it was with his permission and to his standards. Smuggling, gaming—even the opium dens had to function within the purview of his very strict rules.

It would be a lie to say that things were not better. While there was still a criminal element that functioned on the periphery, and outliers such as the band of miscreants she had encountered that night, such things did not go unpunished. He was law where previously there had been none.

It had been providence that he had arrived on the scene when he did. She wasn't so foolish that she couldn't recognize the fate from which she had just been saved and appreciate that deliverance. But she was honest enough with herself to admit that what had come after—that kiss—had been perhaps the greatest mistake of her life.

Honoria had learned one lesson from her late husband and their nightmarish union—men were not to be trusted. And from the women whose lives had been wrecked by them, she'd learned something else. The more handsome they were, the more capable they were of making one forget oneself, the more dangerous they were. And given what that ridiculously handsome man with his dark hair, bruised knuckles, and permanent air of danger, had made her feel, she could not afford to ever cross paths with him again. He was the sort of man that could lead her to ruin. Not simply socially, as she didn't care about that. He could ruin her right to her very soul. He was temptation personified. *The serpent in the garden.* Any fruit he offered would bring consequences—terrible consequences.

Part Two
Debts and Obligations

Chapter Four

Six months later

VINCENT STARED AT the notice in the paper with an unfamiliar and rather uncomfortable feeling growing inside him. *Guilt.* Lady Dumbarton—the passionate and wildly unpredictable Annabel—was missing and presumed dead. And he had banished her to that fate. Despite how they had parted, he would not have wished such a terrible end on her.

That the memories of their bitter parting were inescapable was, perhaps, the source of his overwhelming sense of responsibility for her apparent demise. She might yet have lived had he not forced her to return home to her husband. Then again, it was Annabel, and it was not without question that she might have faked the entire thing. She was not a woman to be trusted, after all, and she was certainly both capable of and willing to manipulate the feelings of anyone around her.

He could feel Ettinger's sharp and all-seeing gaze on him. "I'm not going to have a fit of the vapors and require smelling salts," he stated with an infinite amount of sarcasm. "My delicate sensibilities can withstand the shock."

"I didn't think you would go to pieces," Ettinger agreed. "But I also know you well enough to know this won't stand at face value. I've already been looking into some things—poking my nose where it doesn't belong."

Vincent grinned in spite of the grim news he'd just received. "That is what you do best, after all."

Ettinger shrugged, his massive shoulders lifting like Atlas. "Did you know she was married before Dumbarton and that the man she married was still alive? Significantly poorer but alive."

He'd suspected, based on little things Annabel had said, that she had been involved in some rather unscrupulous dealings. It was one of the things, aside from her beauty, that had first drawn him to her. She may have been a terror about other things, but he liked the notion of being with a woman who wouldn't be missish about his work.

"Find out," Vincent said. "Find out."

"What, precisely, would you like me to find?" The younger man asked the question pointedly.

Vincent shrugged, "First, I want to know that this is not all some overly dramatic attempt to get her husband's attention, punish him, or punish one of her other lovers—an attempt that happened to go wrong. It would be just like her to try to teach someone a lesson and wind up paying the ultimate cost for it. And if that isn't the case . . . then find out if he did it, or if someone else did it, and then do what is necessary."

"This isn't murder for hire," Ettinger protested.

"I never said it was. I said do what is necessary. If this person can be arrested, then arrest them. If they cannot be arrested, take the next logical step. But whatever happens, someone needs to be held accountable. She may have been maddening—a spoiled and reckless child—but that's not a crime which warrants a death sentence." Even so, he hadn't pulled himself out of the gutters by being a trusting fool. Nothing, in his experience, could ever be taken at face value. "But be damned certain she is dead before we ruin someone's life. I wouldn't put it past her to fake it just to make her poor cuckolded husband pay for some imagined slight."

"No body," Ettinger stated thoughtfully. "Hers would not be the first death faked by being lost at sea. But there were vicious storms that day in that part of the country. I've had word from a local man there I trust. If anyone had gone out into the water during that weather, they couldn't have survived it. The only question now, assuming she did go in, is whether she took herself into it or if someone else made that choice for her."

Vincent said nothing further. He simply grew quiet, thinking what a waste and shame it was. Not simply her death, but also her life. She'd known pleasure, but always fleeting. She had certainly never known contentment. If there was one thing that Annabel had wanted in life it was simply more. The ability to be content was not something she had possessed. Given a gift of pearls, she would have bemoaned that it was not diamonds. Whether it was a tangible gift, the passion of a lover, social cachet, or wealth, she'd always been reaching out for more while letting go of what was already in her grasp.

"There is another matter," Ettinger said. "Your other troublesome woman."

Vincent stiffened, his spine going rigid. "I do not have another troublesome woman."

"Oh, but you do. Mrs. Honoria Blaylock. She's got herself arrested—again."

Outwardly, he didn't react to that. Inwardly, he was fuming. He could keep the street rats and other human vermin from troubling her, but Bow Street and the constables were another matter altogether. There was something about an outspoken woman that always seemed to rub those sorts the wrong way. "What was it this time?"

Ettinger did something so rarely seen that it was a shock. He smiled. "She marched into a brothel and told everyone present that Lord Ardwell had the pox and was about to give it to their favorite prostitute. The other patrons scrambled like cockroaches in the light."

Vincent let out a deep sigh. "I'll take care of Mrs. Blaylock. You focus on this business with Annabel."

Ettinger nodded and then rose from the chair he'd occupied.

The man positively dwarfed the furniture with his hulking frame. But Ettinger wasn't the clumsy lummox most men of his stature were. He could move as silently and gracefully as any dancer. He could slip in and out of places without ever being seen. There was an almost preternatural stillness about him at times that—even though he'd known him since he was a boy—Vincent still found unsettling.

When the Bow Street Runner and sometimes private inquiry agent had left, Vincent scrubbed his hands over his face. It was a gesture of frustration. *Of exasperation.*

He'd done all that he could to ensure Honoria Blaylock's safety. But she would have to meet him halfway. He could only protect her to a point.

Getting up from his desk, he shrugged into his coat. Leaving his office, he found his "butler" waiting by the door. "Stavers, I'm going out . . . I'll need a carriage."

"I'll see to it."

<hr />

HONORIA TRIED NOT to think of what was making her skin itch as she sat in the damp and odorous cell. Several other women occupied the disgusting space, as well. While a few of them were familiar to her, others were not. Regardless, they all gave her a wide berth. Her widow's garb set her apart from those women with their tucked up skirts and plunging décolletés. One woman wore only her petticoats and stays. In short, it was quite obvious that, whatever her charitable inclinations and connections may be, she was the odd one out in that particular setting. Every single person in that dank little room recognized her as being somehow different from them. Sadly, she'd probably seen the inside of a cell more often than most of them.

Honoria prayed it was only her own nerves that made her itch so, or the fact that her wool gown had gotten wet from the rain and was now drying. Trying desperately not to claw at her skin, she closed her eyes and tried to force herself into a state of calmness. She'd learned that particular trick during her brief but not-brief-enough marriage. It would have worked had the cell doors not clanged loudly.

"You . . . the bloody crow," the guard said.

Honoria opened her eyes and leveled the man with a quelling stare. He coughed, sputtered, murmured something under his breath, and gestured toward the now open door.

"He means you, Mrs. Blaylock," one of the girls familiar to her said. "'Cause of your widow's weeds."

"Of course," Honoria offered the helpful and perhaps not overly bright young woman a smile as she rose to her feet. "Thank you."

"You're out," the guard said. "Bail has been paid, and you're to stay out of trouble."

"Who paid the bail?"

The guard shrugged, his large mustache and large belly bobbing with the movement. "Don't know. Don't care. One less problem to worry about with you gone. Now walk."

Not at all chastened but unwilling to risk any more of the man's unpleasantness, Honoria exited the cell and followed the guard out of the building. He ushered her directly to the door of the jail, gave her a nudge through it, and slammed it forcefully behind her.

"Mrs. Blaylock, ma'am?"

Honoria looked up to see a carriage bearing a noble but unfamiliar crest on the door. The footman who had spoken her name somewhat hesitantly was wearing black and gold livery. "I am Mrs. Blaylock."

"We are here to see you home, madame."

Honoria stepped forward but she didn't immediately accept his hand to be helped inside. "Who sent you?"

"I am not at liberty to say, ma'am."

"Then I'm not at liberty to get in your carr—"

The curtains parted and a familiar face appeared. "Get in the damned coach," he growled.

She knew that voice. Instantly. And just as easily, she recognized the trouble that came with it.

Chapter Five

AT THE SOUND of his voice, it was far more than just recognition which jolted through her. It was him—his presence, the air of power that simply emanated from him and the fact that just being near him was enough to leave her breathless. It made her want to run away in the opposite direction, not from fear but from self-preservation. He made her feel things that her current life and goals simply did not allow for.

The Hound had come to her rescue and there would, without question, be a price to pay. The urge to flee was deep and instinctive, but she fought against it.

He would only come after you if you ran.

Reluctantly, Honoria climbed inside and seated herself on one of the well upholstered banquettes. "Whose coach is this?"

Most of his face was in shadow, but she could see the sneer on his lips. "Are you assuming that I cannot afford a vehicle so fine?"

"No, I'm assuming that the crest on the door is not yours. Or am I mistaken? Have you suddenly joined the aristocracy without the gossips reporting on it?"

"It's Seaburn's," he said. "The man owes me a favor. Or several. And now so do you."

Honoria laughed, though it was a humorless sound. The very idea was infuriating. "I do not owe you anything, sir."

"Need I remind you that I saved your life and spared you terrible indignity at the hands of others?" He demanded. The carriage began rolling forward then, heading back toward Mayfair and her home.

"Yes, and you exacted payment with a kiss—a liberty, I might add, that I did not grant you permission to take!" The man was absolutely intolerable. It wasn't the first time they had interacted with one another since that night. There had been other times when she had encountered some small danger, and with a word he'd made it go away. There had also been times when he had required her assistance, and she'd given it because in those instances their purposes had aligned—to help the vulnerable. But always, he put her on edge. Her normally calm and stoic demeanor failed her when it came to him.

Those slashing black brows lifted in surprise at her answer, and he laughed bitterly. "I wasn't referring to our first meeting Mrs. Blaylock. I was referring to this one!"

"I did not ask for your help," she snapped back at him. "I did not require your aid. I could have handled spending a night in a cell until I could go before the judge!"

"A night in a cell," he repeated in disbelief, shaking his head. "Do you know what they do with women they arrest in brothels?"

"They send them to jail," she said.

"To start. Then they are 'examined' by a doctor to determine whether or not they have the pox. I do not think I need to give you the details on how that diagnosis is obtained."

Honoria shrugged with the appearance of far more nonchalance than she actually possessed. She knew about that, of course. But she was not a prostitute. "As I am not a prostitute and can prove that my financial situation does not require me to engage in such work, it hardly signifies."

"Do you think your protestations of innocence—your denial of plying the oldest profession would make a damned bit of difference?" he asked. "The *examination* is performed prior to the hearing. All it takes is one single well-paid person to tell one single lie—that you are carrying the pox. That alone would determine what the judge would do with you."

"No, I suppose my denials would not matter then." she agreed.

"You walk into a bawdy house and guilt is presumed," he said. "And here's the thing, Mrs. Blaylock, the bawds and abbesses will pay the necessary fines—"

"Bribes!" she interjected. "Let's at least call them what they are."

"Fine . . . bribes. They will pay for the girls who actually work for them because there is money to be made off of them. You are not an investment for them and, the truth of the matter is, they hate you. Oh, not the women you help, of course, but those whose profits you diminish by *rescuing* their product? You better believe they'd let you rot here . . . they might even pay to have you locked up indefinitely."

Silence fell in the carriage, thick and heavy between them, laden with all the things that had been said and all the things that had not.

Finally, out of desperation to end the unbearable silence, she protested, "I am not a pauper—I have funds of my own to get myself in and out of trouble." The words rang hollow. They both knew that her money would mean nothing in a jail cell because she would be on the wrong side of the bars to have any sort of power.

"Are you truly that foolish?" he asked. "If you are, perhaps I ought to let them lock you up. Miserable as the prisons are, a well-greased palm could at least ensure your safety there. And your safety, I might add, is something that you certainly play fast and loose with."

"I do not need you to save me! I do not need to be rescued!"

His only response was to once again lift a single dark brow in mocking disbelief, his derision for her obtusely naïve protests evident in his gaze. "Fine. Then know this, Honoria Blaylock . . .

this is the last time I save you without requiring payment."

"I can repay the bail," she snapped.

A bark of laughter escaped him. "Is that what you think this is about? Money? I do not deal in money. I deal in favors. And you need to think long and hard about the types of favors I might demand of you."

Honoria couldn't speak for a moment. She couldn't even think. And it was impossible to know if what she felt was threatened . . . or tempted.

Trying very hard to hold onto her pride, a difficult thing to muster after a night in jail, she glowered at him. "That is hardly a thing to be proud of!"

"It is," he insisted. "Everything that I possess I have earned in this way. My methods may not be ones you approve of—I doubt there is much about my business that would meet your exacting moral standards—but it is work and I have done it. Meanwhile, the men of your acquaintance either inherit their money or marry it. You tell me which is more or less honorable."

"What does any of that have to do with the fact that you would demand liberties in exchange for providing aid to a woman—even when it was not requested?"

"It's an advantage, Honoria," he said. "And where I come from, every advantage must be exploited. It gets me what I want. And in this case, that distinction belongs to you."

"Is this simply a way to humiliate me? To punish me for interfering in affairs that you think are none of my business?"

Vincent laughed. "Do you think I care that you have championed your causes loudly and passionately? You've shouted about everything from the vote to property rights, temperance and better housing of the poor, even about the poor Bedlamites. There is no underdog that you will not champion, and so long as you do not get in my way in the process, I could not care less. But there will always be some poor sot willing to take the work—on their backs or breaking their backs. It's the way the world works."

He made it sound as if her efforts were some self-imposed

Sisyphean task. As if nothing she did would ever make any sort of lasting difference. "Your own bleak experiences have colored your perception. You haven't the ability to see good in others because you lack it within yourself!"

The moment she said it, she regretted it. To say that the air in the small, tight space of the carriage positively crackled with tension would have been a gross understatement. She could feel his anger.

"You are very free with your opinions of my character."

"I shouldn't have said what I did," she admitted. "You have offered your assistance both today and in the past and I am grateful—"

"Save your gratitude. It's worthless to me," he snapped. "Do you want to know what I think of your activities, Honoria?"

"No," she said softly.

"You'd be a more effective champion if you weren't looking down your nose at the lot of them." The accusation was uttered coolly, dispassionately. It wasn't said in anger to insult or hurt her. It was, instead, stated with conviction. There was just enough truth in it to put her on the defensive.

"I do not!"

"You do," he said. "Without even realizing it, you do. You, my dear Honoria, are the very picture of *noblesse oblige*. But it's not your ideals and prejudices that interest me."

"No. You've made the source of your interest quite apparent." Her tone was icy and her words clipped.

He nodded. "So I have. So ask me to stop the carriage. Ask me to let you out right here. Hell, ask me to get out of the carriage! I will. I'll leave you here to be safely escorted to your home by the servant of a respectable gentleman. Is that what you want, Mrs. Blaylock?"

No, but she couldn't answer the question. Even knowing what the answer was, she lacked the courage to say it. Being in his presence made her feel alive in a way nothing else ever had. She was reluctant to let that feeling go.

"I thought not," he said after a moment.

They settled into silence then. Like two fighters in a boxing match who happened to actually detest one another. Except she didn't feel very much like she detested him. And try as she might to tell herself otherwise, the heat that suffused her was not due only to anger.

HIS TEMPER WAS in check by the time they reached her house. Seeing her again had only served to remind him how much he wanted her—and how far out of his reach she was. For six months, his awareness of her had never lessened. Every day he was given a report on her activities, on her safety and well-being. Every single day, he knew whether she was working in her Mayfair home or whether she was tending to the sick and poor in the rookeries. That awareness of her was like an illness he could not shake—a disease that would be with him forever. Destructive, eating away at him, and ever-present in his mind.

None of that altered one very simple and irrefutable fact. *She was not the kind of woman for a man like him.*

Annabel, with her quick temper, her selfishness, and possibly even her tendency toward madness had been far more suitable for him. But a woman who followed her conscience and whose conscience was so clearly on the side of right? And if they'd succeeded in labeling her as a loose woman, locking her up and subjecting her to their brutal exams, it would have destroyed her.

If he was in the devil's own mood—and he was honest enough with himself to own it—it wasn't because he was angry. It was because he was afraid, afraid for her and equally afraid of her. There remained only one solution that would see her safe.

"From this point forward," he said, "We work together . . . if someone needs help or someone wants out—or needs to be removed from working the streets or a house—you tell me. Between the two of us, we can certainly manage to put these women in respectable positions."

She blinked at him in surprise. "Why would you do that?"

"I'm not a monster." He was. But he never wanted to be one in her eyes.

"Yet you made your fortune on the bodies and souls of these women!"

His temper flared again. "I do not peddle flesh, Mrs. Blaylock. I never have and I never will. What I sell is protection. I can't stop prostitution. No one can. The city runs on it. But what I do keeps as many women safe in that line of work as I can. They aren't beaten by the abbesses, the pimps, or their clients if I can help it. And if they are, those responsible are dealt with. I make sure they keep a significant portion of what they earn, as well."

It was something he'd never put into words. Something that harkened back to the darkest days of his childhood when his mother had been working in the dark alleys of the rookeries, selling her soul one small piece at a time. How many times had she come home bruised and battered? How many times had she come home with fewer coins in her pocket than when she'd left because one of the men who was to pay her had robbed her instead? No, prostitution was a force that could only ever be held in check. Halting it altogether would be like stopping the tide.

His gaze roamed her face, taking in the confusion in her eyes, the way she chewed her lower lip in confusion. But she hadn't replied. And then her eyes widened, with shock at first. And slowly her features settled into an expression that he could only describe as pity. It was not what he wanted from her. "Do not. Do not look at me that way!"

"It's not about money at all, is it?"

"Money helps," he replied sharply.

"Who was she? The woman who gave you such a startlingly compassionate viewpoint for those most pretend they cannot even see?" She asked the question so softly, it was barely more than a whisper.

"My mother, Mrs. Blaylock. And I will say no more on the

matter." He paused before continuing. "Now that you have unearthed one of my secrets, I will have one of yours in return. Equal footing."

"Very well," she agreed.

"Why do they matter to you?"

"Because I am them. My father traded me to my husband, along with a great deal of money, for something that he felt was more valuable—connection, social position. We might have been bought and sold in a different manner, but we are all commodities by virtue of being women," she replied.

It was not the answer he'd expected from her. It was certainly one that he would be looking into further. "We do not see one another again, Mrs. Blaylock. Not without payment due. Anything we need from one another can be communicated in writing. Any of the street lads will know my direction. And I have known yours for some time."

"Since we met that first night . . . after your brawl?"

He chuckled. "It was a match. Not a brawl. And no. I did not know who you were, but I knew this address long before then. Your late husband and I had some dealings together. He was not a very good man, your husband."

"No, he was not," she agreed. "What sort of business did you have with him?"

"He owed money to some very good people . . . and had failed to pay them. The protection I provide to those who pay for my services is not limited to the brothels and hells, Mrs. Blaylock. Whether they are shopkeepers, tailors, bookmakers, or even apothecaries—anyone with a trade has patrons that cannot be trusted to meet their obligations. I encouraged your late husband to meet his."

"You beat him until he paid."

"Not personally," he said with a shrug. "I'm beginning to regret that, however. He seems like the sort I would have enjoyed beating to a pulp."

"I think I should have liked to see that," she said softly. "He was certainly a man who inspired one to violent urges."

It was such a bloodthirsty sentiment expressed in such a prim tone that he could not help but be amused by it. By her. She was the sort of woman who, if he allowed it, could coax him into smiling like a fool. That was the danger of her. That was why he constantly brought up their differing circumstances and lifestyles. He needed to remind himself not only that she was out of reach, but *why* she was out of reach. He could ruin her.

The carriage had stopped before her house, and he could hear the footman approaching. Their time had come to an end.

She glanced at him with a cool smile, "Good afternoon, Mr. Carrow. We shall not meet again, I think. But I look forward to your correspondence."

And with that perfectly polite dismissal, she climbed down from the carriage and disappeared into her proper home. Once again he was left to the streets. They might be the streets of Mayfair this time around, but just like any other street in London, they were still covered in horse shit.

Tapping on the roof, he signaled the driver to go on. All the while, he resisted the urge to look back. Watching her walk away would only prolong the sting of it.

Part Three
A Promise Fulfilled

Chapter Six

One Year Later

Mrs. Honoria Blaylock finished handing out the last batch of pamphlets to some of the younger members of their reform society. Many of the ladies were widows, like herself. Others were spinsters and the much-maligned bluestockings. They did not prohibit gentlemen from joining their society. Unlike the social clubs of men, they refrained from such blatant sexism. Barring a few exceptions, however, most men had no interest in what they were doing.

True, the occasional group of young men would arrive for a meeting from time to time. Some of them were studying to become clerics, but others she suspected were there for much less godly reasons—they were simply dedicated to being wherever ladies were. If some of those ladies were unmarried, wealthy, and possibly desperate—all the better.

The pamphlets, promoting good hygiene and listing the dangers of "loose and immoral" behavior, had been delivered by the printers just that morning. Those words had been chosen carefully and with great consideration. That care was a necessity, as the same government that willingly turned a blind eye to prostitution and the exploitation of women and children would see her jailed as a pornographer for distributing literature that advised against promiscuity and prostitution in plain language. And given what had occurred the last time she had been arrested, and who had come to her aid, she definitely needed to avoid further interactions with law enforcement.

Still, the pamphlets worried her. The wording of the literature had been chosen for ease of reading. While not every poor person was illiterate, a large number of them were. It wasn't due to lack of intelligence and often it wasn't even a lack of desire to learn. Education was simply out of reach for most of them—either because their family had no money to pay for it or because there had been no family at all. Many went from the orphanages or poorhouses straight to the brothels. Sadly, those who lacked the support of a family were the most easily exploited. The rookeries were filled with the discarded, the unwanted, the orphaned, and those who simply wished not to be found.

Now, in the early afternoon, all of the pamphlets were well on their way to being distributed through the poorer and working class neighborhoods of the city. Only a few bundles remained. She had stopped attempting to pass them out in Mayfair or such places. The upper classes, of which she was still a member despite her reform activities, had no desire for change. They were, for the most part, quite content with the status quo—or at the very least, so bound by tradition they could not see their way out of it.

"You do have such a lovely home, Mrs. Blaylock. Are those chairs Hepplewhite?"

The question had come from Mrs. Walpole, an aging matron who was much more a slave to fashion than most of the ladies in the society were. As a general rule, they were more interested in charitable works than in wearing the latest designs. Yet, at every meeting she attended, Mrs. Walpole wore a different gown. Honoria had yet to see her in the same thing twice.

Her son, Maurice, was much the same. While gentlemen's clothing tended to be a bit more subdued and somewhat interchangeable, his waistcoats were always glaringly different. And often just glaring. But he also wore his hair dressed in a way that could not be natural. She imagined that it took his valet the better part of the day just to complete the coiffure. The thought of the man sleeping in curl papers had her lips trembling slightly as she fought to control her laughter.

Oddly enough, Maurice Walpole, was one of only two men in their little group who attended regularly. Most men did not see that the reforms they were seeking were as necessary as the status quo benefited them. The other man in their group was an aging vicar who had been fighting for rights and reform all his life. Mr. Walpole, however, had simply turned up one day, stating that he wished to offer any aid he could in helping the poor and downtrodden. It had rung false then just as it rang false at present, but he had become very attentive. So attentive, in fact, that she had determined he had less interest in the cause than he did in her. While she had never confronted him about it, she had been circumspect in her interactions with him, not wishing to encourage what she viewed as simply a young man's (hopefully) fleeting infatuation.

She'd been quiet for too long. Mrs. Walpole was staring at her expectantly, her guise of patience quickly fading. "I believe they are, Mrs. Walpole. Alas, they, along with most of the furnishings, were already in the home upon my marriage to Mr. Blaylock. I had little say in the decor, but it suits my needs," Honoria answered. Turning back to the other young woman who had stayed behind, Honoria instructed, "Those go to Seven Dials, Clemmie. There will be someone waiting for you at the column to pass them out. John will take you in the cart. Once you hand them off, rush home to your mother. She doesn't like you out after dark."

"Yes, Mrs. Blaylock," the young woman answered. The youngest and shyest member of their group, it was often speculated that she had only started coming because her mother, who was also a member, made her attend. Regardless of her reasons, she worked hard and was eager to please. Her mother had come into the reform movement out of religious fervor, but she and her daughter had been swayed to other causes through practicality and common sense. They had become Honoria's most trusted compatriots as they campaigned for changes to the laws that left women so vulnerable to the vagaries of men.

Property ownership, the stated right to vote freely, and the requirement of an independent assessment of a female before a male relative could simply banish her to Bedlam or other hellish places—those were all things that Honoria was working toward. There was certainly a comingling in her society with individuals who were also part of the Temperance movement, but she had no faith-based aversion to spirits. Her wish was simply to see moderation in the consumption of intoxicants, as intoxicated men often succumbed to violent urges and injured those who were most vulnerable to them—women and children.

With Clemmie now gone, Mrs. Walpole rose to her feet, as well. "I should go. These meetings are always so lively and informative, Mrs. Blaylock. What a champion you are for the underprivileged."

The praise made her uncomfortable, mostly because it sounded patronizing and false. She had the distinct impression that, whatever pretty compliments she might offer, Mrs. Walpole did not like her at all.

"Hardly a champion," Honoria denied with an instinctive humility. Her efforts were not about any perceived heroism. She only desired to do something that was just and good and to remove self interests from the equation. "I simply do what I believe is right and what I see as my duty. Being born with the privilege of wealth ought to inspire generosity and compassion in us rather than disdain and cruelty."

There was something in the older woman's expression that shifted. For just a moment, the mask slipped and the contempt was visible. Then the moment passed and the matron once more wore a falsely bright smile. "So it should, Mrs. Blaylock. I bid you good day and will look forward to next week's meeting."

Honoria watched as the older woman swept from the room.

Alone, she rose to her feet to stretch and relieve the aches and pains from sitting for so long. As she did, she noted the very fashionable gentleman's hat that had been left on a side table and immediately grimaced. At every meeting of late, Mr. Walpole, who arrived in the company of his mother but always sent her home alone, had left his hat or some other item behind—a thinly veiled excuse to return and have a few moments alone with her.

No sooner had that realization occurred than a knock sounded on the drawing room door. Mr. Walpole poked his head in with a too-friendly smile. "Mrs. Blaylock, my apologies. I am always forgetting something, it seems."

Honoria forced a smile in return. Maurice Walpole was not an unhandsome young man. But young was the key word in that description. He was barely twenty—or appeared to be—and at five and thirty, Honoria was nearly old enough to be his mother. It made his admiration of her somewhat uncomfortable.

And he was the worst sort of admirer a woman could have. Obvious in his affection, timid in his actions, and constantly *there*. He and his mother had joined the society just over six months ago and since then he'd been ever present. Honoria could see that he had little interest in the matter of reform and doubted he felt his mother's safety was in jeopardy enough to require escort. Rather, she thought he was the force behind their attendance and it was Mrs. Walpole who insisted on accompanying him. But why? Because she feared he would take up with some rabblerousing reformer? Surely the woman had to know by now that his interest in the group was simply a ruse to be close to Honoria. "Indeed, Mr. Walpole. You need not have troubled to return. I would have had one of the servants deliver it to you."

He stepped into the room and retrieved the hat. His hands smoothed nervously over it. "It is no bother to spend a few more moments in your company, Mrs. Blaylock. In truth, I've been hoping to have a moment to speak with you privately."

A feeling of dread settled in her stomach. "Mr. Walpole—"

"Mrs. Blaylock, you have to know that I have developed a

fondness and affection for you that go beyond simply the respect and regard that your reform efforts inspired," he began. "I realize that, as a widow of your age and given that your marriage produced no children, many men would not deem you a suitable candidate for a wife."

Old and barren. One black brow arched in astonishment. Surely he did not think beginning with such an insult would aid his cause.

Firmly and with complete conviction, Honoria stated, "As I have no wish to be a wife, it hardly matters."

He looked at her blankly, almost as if she were speaking a language he could not understand. Then, ignoring her very direct statement entirely, he stepped closer to her and reached out to grasp her hands. It was certainly the boldest he had been to date. With the heavy, upholstered sofa behind her and him directly in front of her, there was no avoiding him.

With oblivious earnestness, he began once more, "That fate, which you have so bravely accepted, need not be the only avenue open to you. While I had certainly never imagined that my affections would prove so ardent for a woman before a proper courtship could be undertaken—well anyone who suggested such a thing, I would have determined to be quite mad."

Honoria attempted to pull her hands away, but his grasp, for a man who was so slight, was shockingly strong. "It isn't a fate I have accepted, Mr. Walpole, but one I have *chosen*. I do not wish to marry again. Ever. Thus, courtship of any kind is simply wasting time and effort for both parties. Now, please let go of me."

He did not. Almost as if she had not spoken at all, he dropped to one knee before her. "Mrs. Blaylock—Honoria—my admiration for you is such that I simply cannot accept such an answer. You must give me a chance to persuade you. Mother says . . . well, nothing ventured is nothing gained. A drive in the park, Mrs. Blaylock. That is all I ask."

His mother. Good heavens. As if Mr. Walpole did not have

enough strikes against him already, mentioning his mother would have effectively squelched even the most optimistic of prospective lovers. Still tugging her hands to free them from his grasp, Honoria's tone was sharp when she replied, "Then you may reassure her that you have ventured, but there was no return. Get up, I implore you! Mr. Walpole, you must stop this. Do not ask again for my mind will not be changed. If I must, I will ask you and your mother to remove yourselves from the society."

Whether it was her multiple attempts to remove her hands from his clutches or the sharpness of her words, something seemed to penetrate what had to be an inordinately thick skull behind his blandly pleasant face. He blinked at her in surprise. "You cannot mean to refuse me."

"I can mean to. There is nothing, Mr. Walpole, that could induce me to change my mind. I beg you, do not put me in this very awkward situation again."

At that point, he let go of her hands so abruptly that she nearly stumbled. "I see," he said, his tone that of a spoiled boy with wounded pride. "I cannot imagine what you could possibly object to. I am accounted to be a very eligible man, Mrs. Blaylock. Many young ladies have been vying for my attention and would welcome my courtship."

"Then I wish you and those young ladies the best. I think, Mr. Walpole, that you should not attend next week's meeting."

There was something that flashed in his eyes, something dark and perhaps even cruel. Then, like his mother, the mask was once more in place. Superior, condescending, he stated, "One would think a woman in your position would be more amiable. After all, I cannot imagine that you have many men come calling . . . what with your age, your lack of children, and the terrible scandal attached to your name."

The scandal. She didn't care in the least that her husband had died in his mistress' arms. Nor did she care that the world knew it. In truth she was thankful that he'd been enamored enough of the woman to leave her alone. "Good day, Mr. Walpole."

That his barb had failed in its intended purpose, to remind her that she should be grateful for his attentions, had further pricked his ire. "You are an unnatural creature—a woman who does not want a husband is no woman at all."

Honoria's lips firmed. She would not take the bait. Defending herself and her choices to him would only indicate that she cared one way or another for his opinion. And she did not. She would not and could not be under the dominion of a man—never again.

With one final glare, he turned on his heel and departed, his fashionable hat tucked beneath his arm.

On his heels, her sister entered. Henrietta, so like Honoria in appearance, but possessed of a much milder temperament, was staring at her sister with a mixture of curiosity and amusement. Dressed in a charming gown of block printed cotton with a pretty bonnet perched atop her head, her dark curls were artfully arranged beneath it. They were the same height, with similar figures, and yet the differences in them were as obvious as their similarities. Henrietta's light and carefree appearance was clearly a facade. There was a sadness about her sister that had become more apparent with every passing day of her marriage.

"Another conquest, sister?" Henrietta teased gently.

Honoria rolled her eyes. "I know we were supposed to have tea, Hettie, but the day has not gone according to plan. Despite my associates' beliefs about temperance, there is a time and place for spirits. After today, I require a more bracing libation. I am exhausted."

"I'm certain you are! Such forceful and unwanted proposals can be quite taxing, I imagine," her sister offered sympathetically. "I would say we could reschedule and you could get your rest, but I cannot go home. Not just yet."

Honoria felt a pang of sympathy for her sister. For herself, she had the bastion of her widowhood. But Hettie still had her horrid husband, still had to answer to and be controlled by a man who held no love for her at all. Ernsdale was detestable. His habitual gaming had all but paupered them already. Her sister had only managed to survive it as long as she had by avoiding her husband as much as possible. When he was at home, she made certain not to be.

Honoria walked over to a cabinet in the corner and opened it. From within, she retrieved a bottle and two glasses. "Sherry?"

Henrietta smiled. "Oh, yes. That would be delightful. But not too much, I must go to the hospital after I leave here." At the mention of the hospital, her sister's expression shifted—a minute thing that most would not have noticed. But she knew Henrietta very well and could see her sister's distress. Like their mother, they were both heavily involved in charity, though perhaps on a more deeply personal level. Their mother had organized donations and patronages. She had certainly never tended to the sick or delivered food and clothes to the rookeries herself. For Hettie to go to the hospital, not simply for her normal charitable works but to see to a specific patient—as Honoria suspected was the case this time—it must be dire indeed.

"Is it very bad?" Honoria asked. Hettie had not been visiting the hospital as much following her marriage to Ernsdale. It was filled with women who were stricken with poverty, whose bodies had been ravaged by disease or by gin. It was a facility that specialized in treating women who worked the streets. The lowest of the low, in terms of the hierarchy of prostitution in the city of London.

"Sally Dawson," Henrietta said softly. "The landlord had raised her rents and she didn't have the funds to pay it. So she took to the streets again. And . . . oh, it's terrible. He beat her so horribly, Honoria, that she's almost unrecognizable." She drew a shaky breath and continued. "What is truly terrifying is that Sally has said he meant to kill her. That it had been his intent to do so all along."

Sally was one of the women that they sponsored. She was a widow with four children, all of them living in one damp, drafty room in a dirty hovel that they paid a ridiculous amount for. A legitimate position in a dress shop had been arranged for her, sewing and laundering as needed. But it only paid enough to keep the roof over their heads as the rents had continued going up. And unfortunately, housing was so limited that she could not afford better. So for food and other necessities, she depended on their assistance. "How does she know that?"

Henrietta glanced at the still closed door, likely to make certain they were not overheard. "There have been others. He said as much. He said he would make her pay just as the others have paid for being a dirty, disease-spreading—well, I will not say what he called her. Surely, you can guess. Regardless, this man is a predator, targeting women whose deaths would be largely ignored... it seems almost as if he is taking his revenge on them."

A feeling of cold, icy fear washed through Honoria. This was not something that could be ignored or left to others to take care of. Many of those women depended on them and she would not fail them as so many others in their lives had done. "There is someone—well, he may be able to get to the bottom of all this."

"Who?" Henrietta asked, bewildered at what sort of connections her sister might have to see to such a matter.

Honoria would not answer that question to her sister's satisfaction. There were some things she would not discuss with her sister, among them the fraught relationship she had with a man most feared. "I cannot say. Do not ask me anymore. It may be for naught. He can be somewhat unpredictable."

In a low whisper. her sister asked, "It's him, isn't it? The Hound?"

Honoria glanced toward the door then to make sure there were no lurking servants desperate to overhear a bit of gossip. Assured they were alone, she gave Henrietta a single nod. She'd spoken of her sister to him—after their initial meeting and again when he'd gotten her released from jail. But only the barest of details. She certainly had never revealed the more intimate nature of their encounters to her sister.

Henrietta's frown shifted into an expression of concern and

worry. "Is it safe for you to see this man?"

No. No, it most assuredly was not. But it was something he would need to be appraised of and something that only he and his many minions in those rookeries could deal with. It was a risk she would have to take. But for Henrietta's peace of mind, she offered one simple truth, "He would never cause me harm."

"There are more ways to hurt a woman than simply physical harm, Honoria. We both know that," Hettie replied insightfully.

Steadfastly ignoring that bit of wisdom, Honoria answered, "When Sally is well, I will see to it that she has a position that also provides lodging for her and her children. Her oldest boy could easily take on work as a groom or apprentice to a gardener. Sally and her oldest daughter could both work as maids and the youngest boy could be a groom or stable lad. They need not stay in this cursed city that has been so very unkind to them."

Henrietta cocked her head to one side, her assessing gaze quite piercing. "How do you find these positions, Honoria? You are not in society much beyond the people who share your passion for certain charities and causes. Yet you miraculously and out of thin air produce perfect employment placements for entire families. How?"

Honoria sipped her sherry and did not answer. She loved her sister, but if Henrietta knew the truth—that she had often partnered with the Hound over the past year to aid mutual acquaintances or those in particular need—she would be horrified. That he had made the price for more personal assistance for her quite clear—that was something Henrietta could ever know.

Chapter Seven

I T WAS THE wee hours, that last part of the night that was the very blackest, just before dawn pierced the sky. In truth, it was his favorite time. The quiet and solitude, things he so rarely enjoyed at the current juncture of his life, were a welcome reprieve from the noise and chaos that seemed to dog his every step. The party had long since died down, the last of London's most infamous demireps had departed, tentative arrangements with new protectors had been forged. But it wasn't those lovely and quite scandalous ladies that were on his mind.

There had been one amongst their ranks who might have tempted him, but only because she resembled someone else. With her raven black hair and her body swathed in black silk, her appearance had immediately brought to mind another—a different woman encountered on a dark and dirty street in the dead of night. But a brief word with the woman in question had changed his mind. Her voice was not unpleasant but the breathless affectation she favored had been far removed from the light and crisp tones of Honoria Blaylock. The hint of cockney remained. She'd masked it well, but as an expert in the matter, he'd caught it. And then he'd realized that continual unfavorable comparisons would hardly eradicate the lovely widow from his mind, so he'd moved on.

Frustrated, Vincent impatiently tugged at the cravat that

seemed to be choking him. Tossing the silk onto the leather blotter of his desk, the stock came next. He detested the bloody things.

"Like the hangman's bloody noose," he muttered. His diction might have been that of a gentleman, but his vocabulary revealed his origins.

If anyone had ever told him that he would be lonely—that after scrapping and fighting tooth and claw to have the luxury and comforts he currently possessed, it would not be enough—he would have laughed at them. But it was true. He was a man who fit nowhere. The bastard son of a duke, he'd never been welcomed in the rookeries of his birth. Now the man who'd fathered him and abandoned him to the vagaries of fate was dead and the vengeance he had planned and sought for so long had become a moot point.

Of course, none of that changed the fact that he was stuck in a strange sort of limbo, forever on the periphery of society but never welcomed inside. Even if his father had deigned to recognize him before the devil had claimed the old sot, that would not have changed. Society would never have tolerated the gutter-born son of one of their own.

So after years of work, he'd carved a place entirely of his own making, and somehow it still wasn't enough. Ruling London's criminal class with an iron fist, knowing the partnerships and profits to be made from every crime committed by that faction, had allowed him to climb to a place in society that his mother would never have expected—if she had lived. But she had not lived. Instead, she'd died in a squalid room in one of the worst pits in London's slums, desperate, hungry, and in pain.

Those dark memories surfaced from time to time. And as always, they darkened his mood and stirred the bitterness inside him. Cursing softly, he slipped off his waistcoat and left it where it fell. Stavers would see to it, or one of the girls he hired to come in during daylight hours and clean for them.

Pouring himself yet another hefty portion of brandy, he

climbed the stairs to his rooms. The club on Cavendish Street was both the center of his business—a legitimate enterprise to help camouflage the wealth he gained from less ethical sources—and his home. The ground floor and first floor were public areas used for entertaining and for more clandestine activities that his clientele might wish to engage in—gathering rooms on the ground floor and private chambers for more sensual entertainments on the first. But no one ever dared pass the velvet rope that cordoned off his private dwelling, not unless he had expressly granted permission. After all, his success was largely due to knowing the secrets of others without ever revealing his own.

The very second he entered his private quarters, he knew that he was not alone. Someone had dared to invade his private space. He could feel it. The hairs on the back of his neck raised, and his skin prickled with an almost preternatural ability to sense danger.

"I'll cut your throat and your heart will cease to beat before your body touches the floor," he muttered with quiet menace.

"Is that an effective threat on the sort of people you normally associate with?"

The light, feminine voice coming out of the darkness was something of a shock. It wasn't the presence of someone in the darkness, so much as the familiarity. *And the fact that she had just been on his mind.* Though, to be fair, she was always on his mind. He knew that voice as well as he knew his own, though he'd only heard it a few times. Of course, that didn't account for the many nights it had tormented him in his dreams. "How the bloody hell did you get in, and what the hell were you thinking to come here?"

There was a sound in the darkness, that of a match to tinder. A small, soft glow appeared in the darkness, but it revealed almost nothing beyond the tips of elegant fingers. Then the lamp on the table beside her was lit, the wick slowly turned up, and the warm light spread throughout the room, encompassing the black draped figure of the woman before him. Instantly, he wished she'd left them in the pitch darkness. Knowing she was there was temptation enough. Seeing her, being confronted by her undeniable beauty, and being forced to admit that his memory had not done her justice, was a terrible mistake.

For the past year, they'd had a partnership of sorts, even if it had been somewhat clandestine. Furtive notes delivered back and forth through the mews had been their only communication. When people from his world wanted to take on respectable, honest work, he would send word to her and she would help to find them placement. In return, he would make certain that he had men positioned on the streets whenever she and her associates were there to do their charity work, guaranteeing them safe passage through the rabbit warren that was the rookeries. But this quid pro quo had never necessitated contact. They never spoke to one another. They certainly never met alone—and in his private quarters no less.

Against his will, his gaze traveled over her, taking in every last detail. Her dark hair was swept back into a severe style that did nothing to detract from the startling beauty of her face. High cheekbones, wide set eyes that tilted up at the corners, their color some strange shade that seemed to swirl with every hue under the sun. But it was the lush fullness of her lips which drew his eye and stirred his memory. *One kiss. One kiss had wrecked him for life.*

Pulling back from that thought, Vincent corrected course to deal with the immediate issue of why she was there. Whatever temptation she might present, there was only one thing she could possibly bring him. Trouble. The woman before would never be anything but trouble.

He cursed. The four-letter and terribly vulgar word falling from his lips before he could halt it. It had taken little enough effort for him to identify her after their first and only encounter. She was well known. Everyone knew her, particularly men who still possessed a conscience. They knew her and avoided her like the plague. Even the best of men often indulged their baser natures, and her presence—nay, her censure—made that very uncomfortable for them. For that reason, to most men, she was actually rather worse than a plague. She was a bloody-minded woman with a fortune of her own, a backbone made of steel, and a tongue that lashed like a whip as she laid bare all the faults she found with each and every one of them. Honoria Blaylock was a *reformer*. There could be no worse description of a woman according to society.

He wasn't even part of society and just thinking the word was enough to make Vincent shudder. He was never particularly troubled by what others would term his misdeeds, but he had a deep aversion to being preached at by anyone, including—or perhaps especially—a woman whom he routinely envisioned doing far more wicked things with her mouth. But fantasies were just that, and there was no doubt that whatever had brought her to his door would not be pleasant. No, however much he might wish otherwise and however beautiful and seductive she might appear, Mrs. Honoria Blaylock was not there for an assignation. She was there to destroy what blessed little peace he could claim for himself.

"What do you want?" He all but growled the question, his frustration and anger at being disturbed during his private hours putting him in the mood for a fight. *And at being forced to look into eyes that haunted his dreams.*

"I want to hire you ... the infamous Hound of Whitehall," she said, seemingly amused by the moniker.

That almost made him smile. Almost. "Do not be ridiculous! Besides, you could not afford me."

A smirk curved her full lips, drawing his attention to the perfectly sculpted cupid's bow. What would she do if he kissed her? What would she do if he placed his tongue to that little dip in her upper lip ... or nipped it with his teeth? The kiss they'd shared before had been relatively tame, due to their location and the interference of her injured servant. But now they were alone, in a very private space, with no one to see them and no one to interrupt. He could kiss her until he finally exorcised her from his mind.

Forcing his gaze away from her too tempting mouth, he caught a flash of something in her eyes. And he realized that her expression was wrong. Entirely wrong. Tight. Rehearsed. False. *She was hiding something.*

"In case you have forgotten, I am very rich," she informed him primly. "You are quite mistaken."

"I am very rich, as well," he countered. "I can promise you that I am not mistaken. I told you before what the price for my aid would be... and it isn't anything so common as money. Now, as lovely as your arse is, it isn't here for the only reason I would ever entertain a woman in my private quarters. Unless you intend to add cyprian to your list of many accomplishments, Mrs. Blaylock, get the hell out."

She didn't budge. Despite his unwelcoming tone, she remained firmly rooted in the chair. "I do not think I will. It took quite a bit of nerve for me to come here and now that I am here, I will have my say," she insisted.

"You have never held your peace in all of your life. Why should tonight be any different? A more outspoken, outrageous, and overzealous woman I have never met!" He uttered those words to the heavens, almost as if they were a prayer of deliverance. Whatever others thought of her, she was a plague on him, that was of a certain. A beautiful, seductive, and maddening plague. "Incidentally, how did you get in? I'd like to know who I must skewer for such a flagrant dereliction of duty."

"Stavers let me in," she replied. "Appearances aside, I think your butler is more of a gentleman than you are."

"I never claimed to be a gentleman... and you knew that before you ever darkened my door."

SHE DIDN'T RESPOND to that. There was no response, really, that would be appropriate. If she denied it, they'd both know her for a liar. If she admitted it, she'd be acknowledging that her actions were socially unacceptable at best. Not that they were in society together. No, like herself, Vincent Carrow, the Hound of Whitehall, existed on the fringes of society, though for very different reasons.

While her determination to save every wretched soul in the piteous slums of London had resulted in many people of her social standing giving her the cut direct, they clamored—the gentlemen, at least—to curry favor with the man who ruled much of the criminal class of London. From petty theft to extortion in the highest levels of the government, his hand was in it or he at least knew about it, and no doubt some of the coins earned from those enterprises had found their way into his pockets. Their sycophantic toadying did not carry over to the ballrooms and drawing rooms of their Mayfair homes, however. To treat a criminal, even such an uncommon one, as an equal would be to rend the very fabric of their class system.

And yet the criminal behaviors that made him unacceptable were precisely what had brought her to his door tonight. She'd collected and studied every nugget of information she could glean about him for the past year and a half. And in doing so, she'd come to a realization about him that perhaps no one else in all of London had. He was a man of many layers. He was also a man with a conscience, even if it wasn't wrapped as prettily as other gentlemen's.

As for Honoria, what had begun as simple charity work in the rookeries had shifted into something else entirely. Delivering baskets of food and medicine, warm clothing, and blankets was a menial task, yet somehow, in the course of those activities, relationships with the people who lived there had been developed. Many of them had become much more to her than just recipients of largesse. Many of them she considered to be her friends. And among those friends was Sally Dawson.

Launching into her explanation, she was quite fervent as she began, "There is a man preying on the working girls in Soho. Not the ones in the brothels and such, but the street girls. He's targeting the ones who do not have protection either from their—their . . ."

"I believe the word you are searching for is pimp," he supplied, though uttering it seemed to make him angrier.

"Yes. Their pimps," she agreed. "A woman—a friend—was attacked last night. She was badly beaten and would have died in a dirty alley behind her own home had her eldest son not gone looking for her. Surely you are not content to let something like this happen in your domain. Do you not rule Soho with an iron fist? Is such blatant mistreatment of women not against every rule you've instituted in these areas?"

He laughed at that. "No one rules Soho, Mrs. Blaylock. I offer the services of my men to keep the peace for businesses in that area, legitimate and otherwise—anyone who pays my fees. As I told you once before, my clients include as many shopkeepers as abbesses."

"I remember," she answered softly. In truth, she knew more than he'd ever told her. She had asked so many casual questions about him of every contact she had in Soho, Seven Dials, St. Giles, and elsewhere that she'd amassed enough research to write a book on him if she chose—or at least a book about his business dealings with others. He provided protection in exchange for a cut of the profits. The pickpockets could target anyone who didn't live there, but anyone who did was off limits. The brothels that hired him had men stationed inside to prevent anyone from getting rough with the girls. And no one who paid him for protection was ever harassed by Bow Street or any other constabulary. The accounts of his shopkeepers and tailors were settled regularly—no gentleman who wished entrée into his club would be granted it if he was not in good standing.

"Who was the woman?" he asked, walking to a small chinoiserie cabinet. Opening the door, he produced a bottle of brandy and two glasses, pouring one for her.

When he stalked toward her, proffering the glass, Honoria had no choice but to take it. It felt very much like a test. If she refused it, he would refuse her. "Her name is Sally Dawson." She watched his reaction, noting the tightening of his jaw and the way his eyes narrowed. "You helped her get legitimate employment only a few months back. You remember her?"

"I do," he said. "I've known her for years. She was given a position as a laundress or seamstress, if I recall. Why was she back on the street?"

"Her landlord raised the rent on their room. More than doubled it, as I understand it, and with no warning at all. And not for the first time. He continues to raise the prices on even his most humble habitations. She felt she had no other choice. Her children would have been left without a roof over their heads," Honoria explained. She took a sip from the glass he'd handed her, only a small one. The burn was unexpected. She began to cough and he simply smirked at her.

"Is it not to your liking?" he asked in challenge, taking another long swallow from his own glass.

"It is not unpleasant," she said, "But as you are aware, I am unused to such strong spirits. Will you look into the attack on Mrs. Dawson? She has no one, and if we do not take the matter in hand no one else will."

"I was unaware that Mrs. Dawson had been attacked," he answered her. "But I am already looking into the matter for a different reason. Two women are dead already, Mrs. Blaylock. Or did you know that?"

She had not known that. There had been a rash of beatings over the last few months, but nothing so severe as Sally's. And the murders—no one had mentioned them. She wondered if it was because they hadn't known or because they had feared it would end her visits and the much-needed supplies she brought would cease to materialize.

He continued, "Mrs. Dawson is, indeed, very fortunate to have been spared."

Honoria felt a strange mixture of relief and fear. "She and her children need to be away from the city. I'm certain there is some respectable gentleman who owes you a debt of some sort and whose household *requires* the hiring of an entire family of servants."

Silence. The weight of his gaze was heavy on her and, reluctantly, she looked up to meet it.

"Favors are currency, Mrs. Blaylock. I do not need to remind you of that. Do I?"

Honoria blinked in surprise. "We do this sort of thing for one another all the time. How many of your people now have respectable positions that I helped them attain?"

"And how many of your people have been spared attacks or other indignities while they do their charitable works in my territory?" he countered. "This goes beyond the scope of our current arrangement, informal though it may be. Finding such a position would see me utilizing a favor owed. What will you do to make it worth my while?"

Honoria could feel her heart pounding. Neither of them had moved. Nothing had been exchanged between them beyond mere words, and yet it felt very much as if her entire world could shift based on the turn of that conversation. "I assume you have demands?"

He shook his head, a soft chuckle escaping him. As if he found her terribly amusing. Then he spoke, "Not demands, Mrs. Blaylock. This is something I do not typically engage in with others—it is a *negotiation*."

"Then let us begin the negotiation." She swallowed convulsively, her mouth suddenly dry despite the brandy. "What would you have me do?"

His lips quirked in a very suggestive manner, one that, despite her lack of experience in such matters, was clearly flirtatious. "That is a dangerous question, Mrs. Blaylock."

"Within reason, sir. Within reason."

The slight quirk of his lips spread into a grin. One that was, in a word, devastating. Handsome she could resist. Dark and mysterious she could resist. But there was something in that grin which pulled a response from her that she could never have anticipated. Suddenly, she wanted him to ask her for something shocking—because she desperately wished to capitulate.

"I would have you appease my curiosity, Mrs. Blaylock. One kiss. Just to see," he said.

"To see what?"

"To see if it is as I remember . . . earth shattering."

Chapter Eight

AS HE LEANED against the wall, arms crossed over his chest, there was challenge in his gaze. Whether he was daring her to accept or refuse, she could not say. So Honoria considered her options very carefully. A kiss was not so much—not really. Had it been any other man, she would have endured the act for the sake of Mrs. Dawson and the other women who were at risk without a second thought. But nothing would ever be so simple with the man before her. And with him, enduring the kiss would not be the problem. It would be enduring the haunting memories of it after the fact.

One kiss. One slightly heated argument in a closed carriage. Occasionally, in the course of her work, they'd passed one another on the street with a simple nod of acknowledgement. And every time, she felt as though she had walked too close to an open flame—singed by his presence. But that was all they had shared, along with a dozen or so short, perfunctory missives between then and now—missives she had kept tucked carefully into a drawer, hidden from others but always available to her. More often than she cared to admit, she would take those letters out to touch and reread, searching for something in them that did not exist.

He had a kind of power over her that terrified her. Her hesitation was not about kissing but about kissing *him*. The more he took, the more she would want to give. Her independence had been hard won. It wasn't simply about having a man in one's life to answer to, though that was something far more lasting than he was suggesting. No. It was her own emotional independence. It was the idea that she did not need anyone else. Her life was complete as is and just as she had chosen for it to be. He threatened her ability to simply be content with what she had.

And yet she wanted that kiss. She wanted the strange and unfamiliar heat that had suffused her the one and only time she had been in his arms. "One kiss?"

"If that is all you wish." It must have taken great effort to keep the triumph from his voice.

Honoria took a deep breath. It did nothing to dispel the tightness in her chest and the butterflies in her stomach. "Very well. One kiss."

He walked toward her, stopping only when he stood directly before her. Then he reached out offering his hand. It was up to her to take it, to place her hand in his—another sign of her capitulation. But he didn't simply help her to stand. No. He tugged her into his arms. They closed around her firmly, but she wasn't caged by them. She could have pulled away from him if she chose. But she did not. With her heart hammering in her breast, she waited to see what he would do next.

The slow descent of his mouth toward hers was an agony of anticipation. The first brush of his lips against hers had Honoria gripping the fabric of his coat. It was a desperate attempt to hold onto something solid—something tangible and outside herself—for fear of being swept away.

It was beyond strange that when he kissed her, she had the urge to lean in, to get closer to him. When Edwin had kissed her she'd felt nothing, neither desire nor repulsion, at least not until the end. The longer they were married the worse everything about their life together had become, including the marriage bed.

The arms that had been wrapped around her shifted. One of his hands delved into her hair, sending pins scattering. She had enough vanity to know that her hair was her only truly remarkable feature. Long, thick, black as night, and with just a hint of curl—even Henrietta, the beauty in their family, had always envied it.

As he wound the dark mass around his fist, pulling her head back, she felt a frisson of fear tinged with excitement. What was he doing? And why did it feel both dangerous and decadent?

He gave her hair one sharp tug, not painful but surprising. Her lips parted on a soft gasp. Immediately, she knew that it had been a strategic maneuver on his part. It had given him the opportunity to deepen the kiss, to sweep his tongue into her mouth.

Slow. Masterful. Seductive. Every languorous stroke created a maelstrom of sensations which left her reeling. With all of her senses overwhelmed, she could do nothing but cling to him, to lean into the hardness of his body even as that kiss simply swept her away. But through it all, one thought prevailed. She had made a terrible, terrible mistake.

IF THE FIRST kiss had been earth shattering, then the second was simply soul scorching. There was not a part of him that did not burn for her. Physically, he'd never desired a woman more. But it wasn't simply that. No. That would have been too easy. There was an intense desire to possess her, to make her feel as consumed by him as he was by her. Not lust. Not simple desire. *Obsession.*

From the silken strands of her dark hair wrapped in his hand to the press of her soft curves against him—it was certainly not everything he had dreamed of, but it was definitely how most of his dreams of her began. There was no limit to the things he wanted to explore with her.

Even though the haze of his own need, one thing was clear to him, though. While the act of kissing was not entirely foreign to her, it was clearly not the kiss of a woman well-versed in carnal matters. No woman married for a decade should have been so timid, so uncertain and so clearly inexperienced.

He'd thought so the first time he'd kissed her and now he was left with no doubt. Whatever her late husband had been, and he had many opinions on the matter, Edwin Blaylock had failed his wife in one obvious regard. And if kissing was something she was clearly unaccustomed to, what other benefits of marriage had she been denied?

A knock sounded at the door. Stavers. No one else would dare to invade his personal abode. And he would not have done so without reason. Reluctantly, Vincent broke the kiss, lifting his lips from hers. The slightly dazed expression she wore was gratifying to say the least.

Dropping her hair, he let his hand drift to the small of her back, keeping it there as he called out sharply, "Enter!" He couldn't bring himself to let her go entirely. Not just yet. And if he took pleasure in one aspect of their current situation, it was that she made no move to put distance between them either.

Stavers opened the door. "There is a problem, sir. Something that needs immediate attention. I've summoned a hack for Mrs. Blaylock and arranged for an escort home."

Vincent watched her expression shift, watched reality slowly creep back in. He saw her shoulders stiffen, saw the flush of embarrassment creep over her face. And then a thought crept into his own mind—one that was insidious and destructive. *Was she embarrassed because she felt she'd behaved improperly? Or was she ashamed because she'd behaved improperly specifically with him—someone so very far beneath her?*

"Stavers, wait outside for a moment. Then I would have you escort my guest personally to the hack."

"Certainly, sir. I will see to it that she is safe," the butler replied before stepping out into the corridor, the door closing behind him with a soft click.

To Honoria, Vincent said, "This is not over, Mrs. Blaylock."

"You said one kiss," she protested.

"I said one kiss, if that was all you wished. Is it?"

Her inability to answer was answer enough. The sweep of her long, dark lashes as she lowered her gaze told him a truth she might never utter with her lips.

"One kiss . . . just to see if it was as I remembered. It was. Perhaps even more so. And it has shown me one thing with certainty," he stated, tucking one strand of her hair behind her ear.

"And that is?"

Vincent stared down into her upturned face. With her hair loose and flowing over her shoulders, her already lovely features were softened by it. She looked younger. Or perhaps she simply looked the age she was rather than the age she wished to project. "Once will never be enough, Honoria. Go. Now. Before I change my mind."

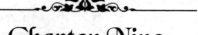

Chapter Nine

"THERE HAS BEEN another... incident."

Vincent was seated in the chair so recently occupied by Mrs. Blaylock. The faintest hint of her perfume lingered. Lilies and perhaps a hint of lavender.

"What sort of incident, Stavers?" Vincent demanded. In the aftermath of her hasty departure, his mood was black and foul. "I'm in no mood for riddles."

"A woman was attacked."

"A woman?" Not just any woman he was certain. Dairy maids and shop girls, so long as that was their only employment, had been safe thus far.

"One of Nell's girls," Stavers replied. "But she was working off the books... taking clients in an alley and cutting Nell out."

Vincent frowned. Personally, he detested prostitution. He'd watched what it had done to his mother—the bleakness in her eyes growing day by day. But he was also enough of a realist to know that it could never be eradicated entirely. Instead, his aim had been to neutralize the seedier aspects of it. He would not provide protection or work with any of the houses that utilized children to serve the disturbed perversions of others, and slowly, many of them were going under because they couldn't get brandy from the smugglers in his pocket. The constables and Bow Street routinely raided those locations while leaving others—

those on his roll—alone.

He'd also made it a point not to work with any houses whose employees were not there of their own choosing. That happened far more frequently than anyone had ever realized. But he knew the truth of it. Which brought him to Nell. She was a good sort. She took care of her girls, and her girls took care of her. Which meant something must have occurred that he was unaware of for them to be working off the books.

"Where did this take place?"

Stavers was silent for a moment. Then he answered carefully, "In a close off Tower Court."

Vincent rose from the chair and paced the room for a moment. That had been where he lived as a boy—where his mother had died and where Stavers had, for lack of a better word, saved him. "Is she dead?"

"Before she hit the ground, sir."

Sir. "Do not do that. We play the parts we must in front of others, but you will not 'sir' me in the privacy of my own quarters, Stavers." The "butler" had all but raised him, after all. Had it not been for the aging pugilist, the rookery of his childhood would have eaten him alive. Stavers had protected him— taught him how to survive, how to fight, how to avoid the pitfalls of gin and opium. The world might see him as an unconventional servant, but for himself, Vincent saw him as a partner.

"All right, Hound," he said, reverting to the name Vincent had been given in childhood. "This one was different. There've been two others, as you know—one strangled, one beaten and robbed. But this one, they cut her throat and left her where she fell. Might be a different killer, but I don't see it as likely. Not with all the attacks happening so close together, both in proximity and frequency. Either way, that's three women attacked, and no one seems to know anything about it."

"Four," he corrected. "Mrs. Blaylock informed me that Sally Dawson, in a fit of desperation, had taken up her old occupation once more. She was beaten and nearly killed in the alley next to her building but one of her children interrupted the attack. How can we know with any certainty that they are all related?"

"All of them were within a quarter mile of one another. All of them soiled doves but not the regular sort. They had no pimp to answer to, since they were taking side work rather than working out of the houses where they were employed. Or not working regularly enough to require one."

Vincent considered what that might mean. "Whoever did this understood that they were without protection."

"Precisely," Stavers nodded. "All of them in alleys, though that's not a surprise really—the women work out of the alleys. But these in particular were very isolated. It's a man who knows the area well to be sure."

Vincent considered that information. Drumming his fingertips on the arm of the chair, he began to organize his thoughts. "We need a plan to expose him. But one that will not involve putting any other women in danger."

"I should also point out that Mrs. Blaylock and her compatriots have been a very visible presence in the area of late. Campaigning against sin and iniquity."

Vincent laughed bitterly. Of course she was. "Well, I wish her the best of luck. All of London could burn and there'd still be sin and inquiry. It springs up like weeds."

Stavers' only response was a grunt that might have been either agreement or dissent.

Vincent was reaching for his cloak. He needed a word with Nell. "There have been no incidents involving Mrs. Blaylock?"

"No. Everyone knows to leave her and hers alone," Stavers replied. "They are off limits and no one would dare defy your orders on the matter."

Except for the man killing hapless women in alleyways. Vincent scrubbed a hand over his face as he tried to make sense of it all. From the night he'd met her, it had been put about that she was not to be touched. In truth, no woman in all of London was likely any safer. But this was a person who didn't follow the rules, so he always felt the need to check. "Are there any other incidents I should be aware of?"

"Nothing to my knowledge."

"Then I guess I'll be talking to Nell," Vincent mused. "The private party for tomorrow night . . . all is in readiness?"

"The tables have been set. Hampers from Fortnum & Mason will be delivered tomorrow by seven. The serving staff are all aware of their duties and the guests should arrive by nine."

The party scheduled to take place the following night had been arranged by Portia Deveraux. It was not her given name, but the one she had chosen for herself. With minimal dancing ability and no talent for singing, the stage had not been an option for Portia. Nonetheless, she'd sought stardom in the only way she could: she had become a notorious cyprian. Currently, she was a notorious cyprian who needed a new protector. Hence the "salon" that would be hosted in his club that night. Lord Whitcomb was technically the host, and Portia, along with the other ladies she had invited, were the entertainment. Nothing could have been further from the truth. The entire thing had been orchestrated by her—like a well-ordered military campaign. He certainly admired her industriousness.

"I'll be back long before it is set to begin."

Leaving his rooms, he made his way down the backstairs and out into the small alley that allowed for discreet comings and goings. From there, he headed for Soho. Nell had some explaining to do, namely he wanted to know why he was providing protection to her bawdy house when her girls were not remaining within the relative safety of those walls.

Chapter Ten

Honoria was up long before sunrise. In fact, it was more accurate to say that she had never gone to bed. She'd returned from the private domain of Vincent Carrow, the Hound of Whitehall, and—after donning her nightclothes—paced the length of her chamber for hours. For a brief time just before dawn, she'd tried to force herself to sleep, but had given up.

In the year and a half since their first encounter—since that kiss—she had convinced herself that it had not been so powerful, so intense. She told herself that it had only been the nature of their meeting and the already heightened emotions of it that had resulted in her unprecedented response to being kissed by him. Alone in his private quarters, she had been proven horribly wrong.

Throughout her marriage, physical intimacy with her husband had been something she endured but never sought. As the marriage had worn on, it became something she actively tried to avoid. Often critical to the point of cruelty, nothing about her had escaped his caustic remarks. From her face to her figure, he'd found fault with everything. And as time had passed and she had failed to provide him with an heir, the cruelty had escalated to that of a physical nature. They'd been married for several years the first time he struck her. And with every passing day, the intensity of his torments had increased exponentially.

Recalling the way she'd gone to her father, pleading for help, and been summarily dismissed, Honoria felt a new wave of anger. But that anger was also tinged with shame and with the pain of her father's final rejection, when he'd turned her away when she needed him most.

But the Hound of Whitehall had not turned her away. He'd met her request with conditions—with negotiations, as he'd put it. But he'd asked for nothing from her that she did not secretly wish to give. Perhaps that was the greatest difficulty she had with all of it. She had to acknowledge that she'd known going there would result in something of that nature, and she had done so anyway. Despite the seriousness of the matter, their business could have been accomplished with a letter. Easily. If she was honest with herself, for an entire year—since the day he'd had her released after her arrest—she'd been looking for an opportunity to put herself physically in his path once more.

Rather than remain in her room, continuing to pace and second guess herself at every turn, Honoria dressed quickly. It was almost dawn. The lamplighters would all be about, extinguishing the gas lamps before the coming sunrise. It was not a fashionable time for it, but the streets would not be so deserted that it would be unsafe. A walk would clear her head. *And cool her blood.*

Dressing hurriedly in the same simple gown and boots she'd worn earlier when she had made her late-night visit to his abode, she donned a dark cloak over it that concealed her braided hair. Honoria hurried down the stairs, but when she opened the front door to step out into the last vestiges of night, she drew up short. She had a visitor. Not the Hound—not the man who had been ever present on her mind since her return home. No, it was her sister who stood there. Even in the darkness, the vicious bruise on her face was visible.

"Did he do this?" Honoria demanded instantly. "Ernsdale?"

Henrietta nodded. "I said something that I should not have."

"Nothing you could say should warrant that treatment."

Her walk forgotten, Honoria ushered her sister inside. They bypassed the drawing room and headed for the narrow stairs that would lead them down into the kitchen.

Settling Henrietta at the table, Honoria went about the process of lighting the kitchen fire to make her sister some tea. The housekeeper and cook would not be in for another half hour at least, and the task gave her something to focus on—something other than her own seething anger.

When at last the fire was blazing and the kettle of water placed on a hook to heat, she felt calm enough to talk about it. "What could you possibly have said to him to warrant *that*? His behavior is inexcusable regardless of provocation!"

Hettie placed a hand to her face, gingerly cupping her bruised cheek. "That I wanted an annulment."

Honoria's stomach dropped. "We had a plan in place, Hettie! If he knows you're thinking of annulment, and certainly if he knows the grounds you will use to seek said annulment, he'll move heaven and earth to prevent it."

"I lost my temper, Honoria. It happens. Even to you."

Honoria laughed. "Oh, I'm well aware—you have no idea! But, Hettie, your husband is a lord. He could kill you and face no consequences! The privilege of peerage ensures that. Do not provoke him and do not allow yourself to be provoked—not when we are so close to your freedom. Two weeks. In two weeks, you will be on a ship bound for the Continent. I will have received another annuity payment from Edwin's estate that will allow you to live quite comfortably if you maintain a modest lifestyle!"

"You live practically as though you are impoverished so you can hoard every groat those wretched trustees dole out to you for my benefit," Henrietta complained. "It isn't fair. Edwin was a spendthrift and a wastrel, yet they all act as if you cannot be trusted to manage your finances. If he hadn't died when he did, he'd have paupered you."

"Then let us thank the good Lord for his weak heart and

enthusiastic mistress."

Silence settled over them. Honoria covered her mouth, horrified at what she had just uttered. "I didn't mean that," she finally whispered. "It's blasphemy to say such things."

"How can the truth be blasphemous?" Henrietta countered. "I am thankful every day that he's gone. I should like to be so fortunate! Widowhood is far simpler than being a runaway wife."

"Widowhood would not help you. He's a lord. All his properties are entailed, and your dowry is now part of that. Those funds which should have secured your future would simply pass to the next Lord Ernsdale barring a small jointure. It's maddening. But with annulment and father's stringent marriage contracts, the money reverts to father's estate and as such would be divided between his heirs—the two of us."

"And will still be doled out to us on the whims of men!"

There was no argument for that point. It was quite true. They would both be at the mercies, or lack thereof, of the trustees to their father's estate. But the trustees had no right to beat them or demand entrance to their beds. It was, in Honoria's opinion, a significant improvement.

"I cannot tarry here too long," Henrietta said sadly. "I will have to return home. If I do not, he will send someone to fetch me, and heaven knows that scandal would be awful! But by the time I return home, his brandy should have him sound asleep."

"His brandy?"

Henrietta smiled coolly. "And a bit of belladonna. Not enough to poison him. Just enough, sister, to make him sleep through the night and give me time to get out of the house the before he awakens the next morning. You need not look so concerned!"

"No more! It is too risky, Henrietta, when you are so close to freedom. Promise me?"

"I cannot promise. I will say that I will only give it to him if I think I am in danger from him. His temper is vile, Honoria. There's a reason he has already buried two wives."

A frisson of alarm rushed through Honoria at that sentiment. It was not an unknown fact. Henrietta was the man's third significantly younger and significantly wealthier bride. Both his previous wives had died from unusual accidents. One had fallen from a moving carriage because of a faulty door latch, or so it was said. The other had drowned in a pond on Ernsdale's country estate—a product of delirium brought on by melancholy. Of the two, the circumstances of the latter's death were infinitely more believable. Who wouldn't be melancholic when married to him?

"Be careful. Do not provoke him. Do not let him goad you into saying anything else damning," Honoria warned again. "And you must come here anytime—day or night—if you need a place to feel safe. You will always have it here, sister."

"I know that. But that is enough talk about my wretched husband and yours, long dead though he may be. What had you up so early this morning?"

Honoria shook her head. "I often have trouble sleeping. You know that."

Henrietta laughed. "I may be ten years your junior, but I am your sister. I can tell when you are lying. You lift your left eyebrow ever so slightly and you shake your head even though a yes or no answer is not required. I've seen you do it a thousand times. Tell me."

"Vincent Carrow," Honoria blurted out. "That is who I saw about Sally Dawson, but you knew that, of course. And . . . he . . . well. Devil take it all! Why is this so difficult?"

Henrietta's lips parted in surprise. After a long pause, she nodded. "I see. The Hound of Whitehall is responsible for your insomnia. And what did our resident King of Criminals have to say?"

"He's looking into it. There were others. Not just Sally. Not just the beatings either . . . two women are dead."

"I wasn't asking what he had to say about Sally, Honoria. There is something there . . . something between the two of you. There has been since the first night you encountered him. And I can see that every time you encounter this man, it becomes more pronounced and infinitely more dangerous to you. Is it worth the risk?"

Honoria considered denying it. As she fiddled with the teapot and its various accoutrements, she wanted very much to refute her sister's observation. But more than that, she wanted to know for herself if it would be worth the risk.

"Have you ever kissed anyone besides your husband?"

Henrietta nodded, as she absently stirred a bit more sugar into her tea. She'd always preferred it to be impossibly sweet. "Of course, I have. Not scores of gentlemen or anything of that nature, and certainly nothing more serious than that . . . but I had a few stolen kisses during my seasons. Didn't you?"

"I never had a proper season, only a terribly abbreviated one. I managed to attend one minor musicale and two parties before father and Edwin shook hands on the *exchange*." It was how she'd always thought of their arrangement to see her married to her late husband—an exchange of money and his eldest daughter for entrée into high society, without anyone ever bothering to ask her how she felt about the matter. Betrothed at seventeen to a man nearly twenty-five years her senior. Was it any wonder they'd been miserable? He hadn't wanted her any more than she wanted him.

Honoria looked away. "So, no. I hadn't ever kissed anyone but Edwin."

"Hadn't. Not haven't?" Henrietta began to laugh. "Of all the men in all of England, for you to have a tryst with, you chose quite possibly the most dangerous criminal—or worse, the employer of the most dangerous *criminals*—as your partner?"

Honoria rose. "I don't wish to discuss this any further. Had I known you were simply going to tease me—"

Henrietta grasped her wrist. "No. Don't get angry. I'm not teasing. . . well, I am just a bit. But not meanly. You must admit it is a bit unusual to go from a man who was as deadly-dull and boring as Edwin to a man who operates a criminal empire through a gaming hell in Mayfair. That, sister, is quite a leap."

"What should I do? I . . . I feel so different with him. But what if it's awful? What if Edwin was right when he said I could never please a man?"

Henrietta took her hand, squeezing it gently, even as she said, "Don't be, as Sally Dawson would say, a fecking eedjit."

A laugh escaped Honoria and she quickly covered her mouth lest the rousing servants overhear their quite inappropriate conversation. "I'm serious, Hettie."

"So am I! Edwin said things based solely on his desire to be cruel without any factual basis behind most of it. And not that I'm the voice of experience, but I've certainly heard from many of my friends that it's a man's responsibility to bring a woman pleasure . . . especially in the beginning. That's rather the price of having a virgin bride, isn't it?"

There was no refuting that logic. Edwin had never made any attempt to please her. Her wedding night had been painful, humiliating, and traumatizing.

"Is it awful that I'm even considering it?" Honoria asked. There was no need to define what *it* was.

"Not awful. Human. Very, very human. You're entitled to something of your own, Honoria. Between the misery Edwin inflicted on you and the endless amount of good you do for others, shouldn't you have something for yourself?"

Temptation at every turn. Honoria was more confused than ever.

Chapter Eleven

NELL'S PRIVATE QUARTERS were too ostentatious to be luxurious. They were, in fact, an assault on the senses. Gilt mirrors, pink velvet, crystal chandeliers. Everything was done in shades of deep pink, magenta, and canary yellow. It was rather like walking into a nightmare. The sheer number of crystals and the abundance of luxurious fabrics would seem the height of fashion to someone like Nell, to someone who had grown up with nothing. *Like him.* There was one very important distinction. He wanted to have wealth because wealth meant power. Nell wanted to appear wealthy because the trappings of it appealed to her vanity.

A glance at the clock on the mantel showed it to be after five in the morning. Like gaming hells, bawdy houses and brothels kept the curtains tightly drawn. Time was to have no meaning while one was indulging their every vice. Pesky reminders of obligation and responsibility, like darkness and dawn, were not permitted to interfere.

He'd been waiting for some time, reason enough for his foul mood. Though to be fair, he'd been in a mood to start and that could be laid squarely at the undoubtedly lovely feet of Honoria Blaylock. When the door opened at long last and Nell stepped inside, Vincent eyed her critically. She wasn't so young anymore. Age and the life she had led were beginning to show the toll they had taken. All the powder and paint in the world could not camouflage the lines that crossed her forehead or the deep grooves at the corners of her mouth giving her a perpetually sour expression. Her love of the pipe had resulted in permanent puckering of her mouth, and the broken veins on her cheeks and nose hinted at her love of gin. In short, Nell looked like a woman who had lived a very hard life. Silk gowns and jewels would not change that.

"You normally send one of your men to collect. Or are you here to raise my rates?" she asked sharply.

"I may have to offer you a discount if your girls keep getting murdered." It was a calculated maneuver, shocking her by being direct. And it worked. He saw her eyes flash with knowing and then quickly the mask fell back into place.

"I don't know what you mean."

"Mary Collins, Sally Dawson, Esther James, and Lottie Endicott," for each name he'd uttered, he'd raised one finger. "Four in all, though Sally yet lives. Why are your girls taking side work, Nell?"

She crossed the room, pulled a blue bottle from a cupboard and turned it up, drinking her gin straight from it. When she was done, she wiped her mouth, smearing the small bit of paint that remained on her lips. "Don't know, do I? If they were smart they wouldn't have wound up here in the first place, now would they?"

Vincent's eyes narrowed. "Nell, the girls pay you and you pay me. I protect your business, but I protect them, just the same. Why are they taking side work? I won't ask again."

"Rent's gone up," she said with a shrug. "I been taking a bigger cut from the girls and maybe they're feeling the pinch just a bit."

"It stops. And who do you rent from?"

"As if you don't know the answer!"

"I have the answer, Nell. Tucked away in a ledger in my office. Having it doesn't necessarily mean I know it. Give me a bloody name!"

"Trenton Devore."

"Bloody slum lord. How the hell did he get his hands on the deed to the property?"

Nell shrugged. "Dice. Sherwood lost it to him in the alley just out back. You know how that is. Don't you? Man makes his living on the poor bets of others, he ought not be surprised at how the world works."

Ignoring the jab, Vincent pointed at her and bit out his command, "You go back to the percentage you were taking before, and if you need to make up the difference, start charging more for brandy and . . . other things. I'll have a word with Devore."

"They won't pay it!"

Vincent smirked. "For a woman who has spent her life seeing to the pleasures of men, you don't seem to understand them at all. They'll pay, Nell. And if they won't, there's others that will . . . And you tell your girls to stay off the street. It's not safe."

"Now who doesn't know how to do their job?"

"Watch yourself, Nell. You have this place on my good graces. Or do you not remember the loan I gave you to get it started?"

Contrition wasn't something that came naturally to Nell, but she gave it a good go. Ducking her head, she nodded. "I remember, Hound. And I'm grateful. I'll let the girls know, but I don't lock 'em in. That's not how I work and you know why!"

He did know. It was the primary reason he was willing to tolerate a bit of her insolence. "Just tell them. Hopefully they will be smart enough to listen." He considered her for a long moment. "Do you know anything, Nell? Anything that would help me find this man?"

"Joan saw him," she answered. "She was coming back from her sister's. Why she takes that wretched cow food when she wouldn't turn her hand to help Joan, I'll never know. Takes more than blood to make sisters, in my book!"

"The man, Nell."

"Right," she said, reining in her temper. "He was young.

Dressed like a gentleman. Wasn't no street rat. And he was wearing a hat, she said. Decked out. Not just expensive but flashy. She never saw his face . . . said he was tall and thin."

It wasn't much, but it was a start. He would need Ettinger. Now retired from Bow Street after the terrible injuries he'd sustained while helping to protect the Duchess of Clarenden, formerly Miss Euphemia Darrow, the investigator had much time on his hands. It would be good for him to do something other than feel sorry for himself.

Leaving Nell's, he walked outside to his waiting carriage. He made the ride back to his own establishment with the window of the carriage open to the very last vestiges of the night. London wasn't exactly renowned for its fresh air, but after being inside with the cloying scent of a dozen or more perfumes, brandy, smoke, and other much earthier aromas, it was good to breathe in anything else. But it wasn't what he longed for. The soft scent of lemongrass and a bit of lavender—familiar, clean, and very tidy, rather like the woman who often wore it. That was what he wanted.

It was for that reason—that she'd been so heavily on his mind—that he didn't first realize the scent was actually present in his rooms when he finally returned home and not merely a phantom scent created by an overburdened mind. But then the reality of it penetrated the haze of exhaustion. It was real. She was real. And she was right there in his rooms. Again.

"What is this about?" He asked, turning toward the same chair she had occupied upon his arrival the night before. "Has Stavers given you a key that you may come and go as you please?"

"No," she replied from the darkness. "I told him I had something urgent to discuss with you and, as we are all aware, I could hardly wait for you in a public area."

He shook his head even as he stripped off his coat and cravat. It would likely make her uncomfortable for him to be in such a state of undress, but that wasn't really his problem. After all, she was the one who kept turning up in his private quarters.

"What is it now?" He asked. "Are there kittens that need rescuing? Should I fund a new orphanage or—better yet—toss out the Faro tables and put cots in downstairs so they can all live here?"

She rose as if to take her leave. "You are in a foul mood. I shouldn't have come."

"Not without telling me what brought you here," he snapped. If she was going to disturb his peace and torment his senses, he'd damned well know why. "What sort of catastrophe has happened now?"

"There is no catastrophe," she said softly, her voice halting and low in the darkness. "That isn't why I came here."

"Then why did you?"

Dawn had broken fully just before his carriage had halted outside and now there was just enough light spilling between the curtains that he could see her silhouette. When she dropped her arms to her side, her shawl sliding down to dangle on the carpets, she murmured, "You are not the only one who was curious, Mr. Carrow."

The breath seized in his lungs. Surely there was no god benevolent enough for her to have meant that as he hoped. "What, Mrs. Blaylock, has piqued your curiosity so?"

"You have. I had hoped that if I came here . . . that you might kiss me again."

"And why would I do that?"

She threw his own words back at him then. "To see if it is as I remember . . . earth shattering."

Chapter Twelve

SHE HAD ALMOST turned back. Half a dozen times between her home and his, she had been tempted to tell the driver simply to take her back. After all, who was she to be bursting into a man's home uninvited at this hour of the morning? There were a dozen different scenarios that could have proved too humiliating to survive. She could have been denied entrance. She could have been allowed entrance and then rejected. Or she might have come there and found his bed already occupied by someone else.

Yet, here they were. His trusted servant had admitted her, offered her refreshment, and made himself scarce while she waited for—what? What precisely did she want to happen? In truth she had no idea.

Silence stretched taut between them, no sound in the room but that of their breathing. And then the clock struck. Six times. The chimes acted like a spark to tinder. He stepped forward, closing the distance between them in two long strides. He caught her wrists in his hands, lifting them so that her hands were trapped between their bodies. Then he let go of them, his arms sliding around her. Had he thought she meant to reject him? Had he expected that she would suddenly change her mind and not allow him to do the very things she had come there to have him do?

His mouth was on hers, his lips moving in that heavenly way.

Every caress, every nip of his teeth and sweep of his tongue, had her all but melting against him. From the first kiss to the second, six months had passed. Six months where she could forget, where she could convince herself that it hadn't been exquisitely perfect. But with only the span of a day between their second kiss and now their third, there'd been no such opportunity. Thus, she was doubly intoxicated by the memories of the previous kiss and its lingering effects while held in sway by the sensations of the current one.

His hands roamed over her, skating over her ribs and the indentation of her spine, down to the curve of her waist and the flare of her hips. Immediately, she felt terribly self-conscious. How often had Edwin told her she was fat? Or sturdy? Built like a farmhand, he'd once said, like she ought to be able to squat in a field and birth a child—and still they were childless because she was a failure at everything, including being a woman.

"Stop it," he murmured, his lips having left hers to trace the line of her jaw.

"Stop what?"

"Thinking of whatever it is that pulled you away from me," he insisted. "There is no room, Honoria Blaylock, for anyone in this room but us. And you didn't come here just for a kiss, did you?"

"No," she admitted. "I didn't."

"Then leave everything else behind and let me give you what you want."

"What if I do not know what I want?"

"Then let me show you," he offered.

Honoria wasn't even certain how it happened. Pins were removed from her hair. Buttons were undone. Clothing was rearranged or removed entirely, and through all of it, he kissed her. He touched her with his lips, with his teeth, his tongue . . . with deliciously callused roving hands that left her breathless.

Knowing the mechanics of a thing did not make one an expert. She knew to dip a brush in paint and apply it to a canvas to create a work of art, but that hardly made her an artist. Her late husband had understood the mechanics, but the rest of it—that had eluded him entirely. Meanwhile, Vincent Carrow appeared to be a master of the carnal arts, a man who could make her body erupt in flames with nothing more than a glance. When not limited to a glance—dear heavens. She was simply lost.

"Tell me to stop," he said. "Before it is too late."

"I do not think I can," she said. "This . . . for a year and a half, it's been building to this, hasn't it?"

LONGER THAN THAT. The awareness of one another had occurred then, but the truth was far more terrifying. He felt as if he'd been born to want the woman before him, as if desiring her was simply his destiny.

He'd certainly never say such a thing aloud. Not to her. Not to anyone. That was the sort of vulnerability that left a man open to destruction, and he was not about to give her any more power over him than she already possessed.

His bed was too far away. But there was a chaise longue before the fire, a ridiculous piece of furniture left by the previous owner—an idle lord who had fancied himself an artist and had used those rooms as a studio. More than likely it had simply been a ruse to get scantily clad women into his rooms. Regardless, it was the sort of piece that called for a half-naked woman to lounge on it. And not a day had gone by that he had not imagined her there in just such a fashion. Pale, alabaster skin glowing in the firelight while her dark hair spread over the velvet upholstery, wearing a come-hither smile and nothing else—but he was tired of imagining. He wanted to see her. Even if it was only once, he wanted to know every inch of her and commit them all to memory.

He raised one hand, undoing the buttons at the front of her

dress until the garment simply slipped from her shoulders. If he'd had any qualms about her willingness to move forward, they would have been eliminated by the decisive way in which she shrugged out of the garment, letting it fall to the floor. Next, the underdress—it laced up the back and he expertly untied it. Slowly, layer by layer, the sheer perfection of her was revealed.

When he felt the first tentative touch of her hands at the buttons of his waistcoat, he held his breath. The last thing he wanted to do was frighten her. Everything felt tenuous. As if the sensual spell cast about them was as fragile as the most delicate of glass—the slightest wrong movement could shatter it.

Guiding her backward, step by step, until the backs of her knees had bumped against the edge of the chaise longue, Vincent eased her down. And when she lay back, wearing only her chemise and stays, he did not follow her down immediately. Instead he stayed where he was, slipping off his waistcoat, then his shirt. His boots followed. And the entire time, his eyes never left her. They roamed from head to toe, taking in every lush curve.

And when she moved to shield herself from his roving gaze, drawing in on herself in a rare display of vulnerability from a woman who would face down anything and anyone, he murmured, "Do not. Do not hide yourself from me."

"It's . . . habit, I suppose. My husband did not find me particularly appealing. Physically or otherwise."

He met her gaze, saw the uncertainty in her eyes, but more than that, he saw the fear. She was afraid of what he would say to her, what he would say about her. "I think we've established that your late husband was a goddamned fool. Don't let him in here, Honoria. Don't let ugly memories and the doubts he created in you to soothe his own fragile vanity spoil what we have right now."

"Then touch me . . . touch me so that I do not think, so that all my senses are consumed by you."

It was an invitation he could not refuse.

Chapter Thirteen

Honoria felt the weight of him on her as he settled onto the chaise longue with her. His long limbs lay over hers, his chest pressed against hers. But she did not feel trapped by him. Rather, she felt anchored. He held her not where he wanted her, but precisely where she wanted to be.

He kissed her again, more deeply and urgently than before. She responded in kind, clinging to him, wrapping herself about him in such a wanton display that she ought to have been mortified. But as she felt the firm ridge of his arousal against her thigh, mortification was the furthest thing from her mind. A hot, aching feeling stirred inside her—an emptiness that she knew he could fill. Desire—elusive and unfamiliar, but not unrecognized. She had longed to have such feelings, to know real desire and passion, but she'd never found them within her marriage, and she'd always been too frightened to seek them elsewhere. Frightened of what her husband would have done, yes, but also terrified that what he'd told her—that she was somehow broken—was true. At least in not knowing, there had been hope. But now, with this supposedly wicked man touching her, there was a fire in her blood and a maelstrom of sensations that she simply could not categorize.

As his mouth left hers, his lips trailing over her neck and down to the swells of her breasts rising above the embroidered edge of her chemise, she closed her eyes. It wasn't a conscious thing, to arch her back and offer herself to him, but she did it just the same. And when his lips pressed fervently to that soft flesh, followed by the slight sting of his teeth grazing over her, only for that sting to be soothed away by his wicked tongue, the world spun away along with all the worries that might have curbed her wanton behavior. As the remaining layers of her garments were stripped from her, her only concern was to get closer to him still, to feel the heat of his skin against hers.

His lips closed over the bud of her nipple and Honoria couldn't halt the desperate gasp that escaped her. And then he became relentless. His hands and mouth moved over her like he was starved for her. And soon she felt as if she was starving for him. The ache inside her had grown to the point of being unbearable. She chanted a soft plea, over and over again.

"Please what?" he demanded, levering himself up so that they were face to face. His lips were just inches from hers as his hips settled between her parted thighs.

She could not say it—not because she did not want to but because she simply lacked the words to ask for what she wanted. "I don't know what to ask for."

"Ask for pleasure," he murmured, his voice thick and deep. "Ask to be worshipped."

"Can you give that to me?"

She felt him smile against her skin. "Oh, most definitely."

Before she could say another word, his hand had slipped between their bodies, sliding over her thigh and then touching her intimately. There was no embarrassment, no reticence. He stroked one finger along the seam of her sex, and she tensed with anticipation of what was to come next.

When he parted her flesh, his fingers stroking her gently, and with undeniable skill, she cried out softly. But his lips were on hers once more, swallowing that sound and every one that followed.

Honoria trembled, clinging to him as her muscles drew taut,

her body tight as a bow string. But she was not prepared for the rush of feeling when that tension broke, when wave after wave of pleasure crashed through her, leaving her shivering against him.

HE'D THOUGHT HER exquisite from the first moment he'd seen her. But in the full flower of passion, her cheeks flushed, lips parted and eyes sparkling, she was beyond perfection. Nothing in his most erotic imaginings of her could compare to the reality. And she was his, at least for the moment.

When her breathing began to slow, easing into a normal rhythm, she smiled up at him. Her kiss-swollen lips, still flushed from her pleasure, were an intoxicating sight. But it was the gentle touch of her hands, her fingers moving less than nimbly over the buttons at the fall of his breeches, that reminded him of his own painful state.

"I may not know many things about carnal matters, but I know we are not quite finished yet," she observed softly.

"No. We are not," he agreed. In truth, they would never be finished. Because that one small taste of the passion they could have together had been simultaneously too much and never enough. He would crave her the remainder of his days, but for one night . . . for one night he would have his fill.

When the last button had been undone and she had freed him from the constraints of clothing, he moved with deliberate gentleness. Easing into her, savoring each second, he watched her face, watching her expression shift and alter as she climbed toward the glory of release once more.

For as long as he could maintain his own tenuous control, he kept that same slow rhythm, one that allowed the anticipation and tension to build. But his own needs were too strong, too insistent, and soon he was compelled to do more, take more—and give more.

And when she found her pleasure a second time, he followed with her.

Lying there with her afterward, their limbs entwined and sweat cooling on their skin, the silence of the room enveloped them. Neither of them spoke. Words would have spoiled the moment. So he simply wrapped her in his arms, winding her hair about his hand and held her close for the very limited time he would be permitted to do so.

Chapter Fourteen

SHE HADN'T INTENDED to sleep. But then she hadn't imagined just how tiring such activities could be either. He had made love to her a second time. She knew that wasn't the right term for it. After all, love had little to do with what was between them. Attraction, maybe—lust. Some indefinable thing that drew them together against all odds. But they didn't get along—most of the time. The few times they'd been in one another's presence, they'd been quite disagreeable to one another. She couldn't even lay that entirely at his door. The guilt was shared because he could make her, with a single glance, bristling mad and ready to fight. Where had that passion been when she'd been a married woman? She'd never dared fight with Edwin. Her supposedly upstanding husband would have been vicious in his retaliation. But she was certainly bold with her opinions with Vincent Carrow, a man most would be terrified of.

There had been many times as a newly married woman when other married ladies had spoken of the insatiability of their husbands or speculated on hers, given their newly wedded state. Indeed, they had alluded to hours of lovemaking that would rival the most decadent scenes in scandalous novels. And during those conversations, she had remained quiet. Others had interpreted it as shyness or even disapproval, thinking her standoffish or puffed up. No one had ever considered that she had nothing to add to those conversations because all she'd experienced had been her husband's blessedly brief if somewhat painful fumbling in the dark.

But now she understood. *Now, she knew.* And it had changed her. It had altered something inside her irrevocably. She would not term it a mistake. Nothing so perfect, so beautiful could ever be called that. But it would be a lie if she said she'd understood how it would shift the dynamic between them before she'd embarked on that particular course of action.

"Not yet."

The whispered words startled her. She hadn't made a sound or attempted to get up, but he'd known she was awake. "Not yet what?"

"The world intrudes soon enough, Honoria. For just a moment or two longer, let's hold it at bay."

Oh, how she wanted to do that. How she wanted to pretend nothing else existed outside that room! But that was a luxury she did not possess. The longer she lay there in the circle of his arms, the longer she would want to stay. He had the ability to make her forget herself, and that was something she would never do again. "I cannot. I am expected at the charity hospital this morning and I must go home first."

There was silence then, tense and not especially comfortable. Finally, he asked, "Will you return?"

They might have both kept their secrets, but they'd never actually lied to one another. She wished to continue in that vein. So in the interest of honesty, she answered, "It would be unwise to do so."

"That isn't an answer."

Sitting up, she grasped the blanket that he'd thrown over her at some point and drew it about her shoulders. It was more for modesty than warmth. Still, she shivered—and that coldness was inside herself. Without his arms around her, she feared she might never be warm again. "Then I can only say that I do not know the answer. This . . . it's dangerous."

"Because you fear for your reputation?"

Honoria reached for her chemise, needing the armor of at least some article of clothing to shield her nakedness. "No. My reputation is not even a factor. I find that I care less and less about that the more time goes by. It's dangerous because—I was faithful to Edwin. Even when I was miserably unhappy and would have done almost anything to be free of him, still I remained faithful. Because marriage wasn't about my promise to my husband but about my promise to God. You may think such things are naïve and foolish, but I'm not cut out to be a man's mistress. There will be a point where one of us will want more and the other one will want less. I must guard my heart and my pride." She hadn't even understood that truth until she uttered it.

"I am not husband material, Honoria. I never have been."

"No," she agreed, "You are not. And I'm not even certain that I would ever wish to be a wife again. But what one thinks and what one feels are very often not the same at all. And that is why I should not return. Because there is no outcome to this that will see us both happy."

"We could be happy enough for now," he offered in a low voice that made her waver.

"I cannot only think of now. I must think of tomorrow. That is the burden of all women . . . that we must forever look ahead in order to protect ourselves from the consequences of this sort of happiness. Once was a risk. Repetition would be foolish and well you know it."

He rolled away, sitting up on the other side of the chaise longue and reaching for his discarded breeches. He rose, pulling them on with an economy of motion that defied the anger she felt emanating from him.

"Get dressed," he said. "I will see you home. There's no need to disturb Stavers at this hour."

"I've offended you," she said. "And that was not my intent. I do not want us to part badly."

HE WASN'T ANGRY at her. How could he be when she had only spoken the truth? While he certainly was not eager to call a halt to whatever it was they had embarked upon—calling it an affair seemed wrong somehow, but it wasn't love and it was, much to his dismay, more than just sex—he could not refute anything she had said. He'd made it to his rather mature age without, to his knowledge, siring a single bastard, and he would continue that. She wasn't the sort of woman who would know how to prevent such things and she certainly wasn't the sort who would ever take drastic measures should those consequences materialize.

"I'm angry at the situation, Honoria, not at you. You have a right to protect yourself. I'd never hurt you intentionally, but intentions, as we both know, aren't worth a damn."

"And what situation is that?" she asked. "Your life of crime or my life of respectability?"

He was angry at the situation that saw him raised in the gutter when he was the son of a duke. He was angry at the situation that allowed another man to be recognized by law as the duke's son when there was no relation between them at all. And he was angry that there was no way in which he could ever redeem himself enough in the eyes of society to be worthy of her. He was naught but a criminal, after all. It didn't matter that his clothes were made by tailors on Savile Row, that his boots were made by Hoby, that he could buy and sell half the gentleman in Mayfair. The only thing that kept those gentlemen from living in the streets was that most of them resided in entailed properties that no one could touch. By countenance alone, he was indistinguishable from gentlemen of the *ton*. And not a damn bit of it made a difference. "Both, Honoria, I am angry at both. And too angry to be poked and prodded at about it right now."

He pulled his Hoby boots on, then donned his shirt and coat. The cravat and waistcoat were left where they lay discarded. He certainly knew what that felt like—being discarded.

Frustrated by the morose and melancholy nature of his own thoughts, he ran his hands through his hair in a gesture that fully expressed his irritation. Feeling sorry for himself would change nothing and he had little patience for self-pity in others, so indulging in it himself was the worst sort of hypocrisy. The whole of it made no sense. He'd gotten what he wanted, hadn't he? Honoria Blaylock in his bed. The crux of his disappointment centered solely on his inability to keep her there and that was not a problem that would be solved easily. Or at all.

Chapter Fifteen

HONORIA HAD BEEN in a foul mood—a series of sleepless nights would do that to a person. Since she'd gone to him three days past, the night she'd broken every rule that any gently bred woman was indoctrinated with from birth, she hadn't slept more than an hour without interruption. Because he haunted her dreams. Because when she closed her eyes, she could only remember the way his hands had felt on her skin. His mouth on hers. It all came back to her in stark relief.

But it wasn't just her nights that were tormented by the memory of him. Her days were filled with such instances, as well. Obsessively thinking about a man who could be nothing but trouble for her was exhausting. It didn't help that she was also concerned for her sister. She had not seen Henrietta either in those three days—not since her sister had turned up on her doorstep with a bruised face.

In his disdain for her, Lord Ernsdale had long ago refused her any admittance into his home and forbade Henrietta from accepting her letters. Thus, all their communication had to be initiated by her sister. And they never went so long without speaking. Honoria feared what might have happened.

To keep herself occupied, she'd spent the day doing ridiculously menial tasks. The globes to every lamp in the house had been washed and dried until they sparkled. The decorative crystals hanging from the fixtures had been polished to an almost blinding shine. It was a task out of rotation, but it offered some reprieve from her own worried thoughts.

Had it not been cold and raining, she'd have taken the carpets to the back garden and beaten them until some of the tension finally left her body. No doubt the servants were glad of the weather for it kept them from doing anything too terribly strenuous beyond their regular duties. But if Honoria had hoped to still her worried mind, she had been sorely disappointed.

As if her thoughts had summoned it, the soft knock at the door had her whipping her head around. Was it Henrietta? *Was it, against all odds and reason, him?*

With her heart in her throat, she watched the doorway with bated breath. And when her sister walked in, she was not at all disappointed to see her, but she was very disappointed not to see him. It made no sense. He was staying away—just as she'd asked. And that only made her angry at him.

"You look awful," Henrietta observed. "If I didn't know better, I would think you were ill. But as every speck of dust in this home has fled in fear of its existence, I know that you are not sick but troubled."

Her sister sounded strange, her speech much less clear and crisp than it normally would be. Peering at her, Honoria realized that Henrietta's lip was swollen. "He struck you again."

"Of course he did. He's a bully, Honoria. That is what they do," Henrietta answered breezily. "But that is why I am here. We need to review our plan once more."

Honoria patted the sofa beside her. "Come and sit. Tell me what has happened."

Henrietta shook her head. "It is the same thing that always happens. He is in his cups and takes offense to something I said, did, or am. That is all. But what of you? Something is different, I know it. Tell me."

Honoria could feel herself blushing, but she shook her head. "That doesn't matter now."

Henrietta took one of Honoria's hands, clasping it between hers. "Oh, I think it does, sister. What have you done?"

Honoria closed her eyes. "I . . . may have been imprudent."

Henrietta, knowing her sister better than anyone, instantly understood the depth of what she had just confessed. "With *him*? The Hound of Whitehall?"

Honoria nodded. "Yes. Several days past. . . I went to him. And, of course, we both know why I went to him."

"What was it like?" Henrietta posed the question almost wistfully, almost reverently.

Honoria realized then that her sister was as she had been until she'd gone to him—ignorant of the pleasures that could be had between a man and a woman. "I should not . . . this is not a conversation we should have. It is something that you should discover for yourself with a man who makes your blood sing."

Henrietta smiled sadly. "That man does not exist, sister. And after what I have endured at the hands of my husband—the pain, the degradation, the humiliation—I do not think I could ever truly give myself to a man. Not now. So in this instance, as in so many others, I will sit here in awe of your bravery and live vicariously."

"My bravery?" Honoria scoffed. "You could not be more wrong. I am terrified of him . . . of what I feel when I am in his presence. He has invaded my thoughts and dreams for the past year. Longer, really. From the night we first met, his presence has hovered there constantly. It wasn't bravery that prompted me to go to him. It was simply that I could not imagine living out my days with never knowing his touch . . . bravery would have been staying afterward, letting whatever lies between us to run its course. But—no, sister, I am not brave. I left him that same night and we have not spoken since."

They lapsed into silence, both of them lost in thoughts of what might have been had they been permitted to determine their own fate.

THE SOUND OF flesh striking flesh echoed in the room, along with grunts and smell of sweat—it was a veritable cacophony for the senses.

With his knuckles stinging and his head aching, partly from the brandy he'd consumed and partly from the sheer number of blows his opponents had landed, Vincent sat at the edge of the large ring that had been constructed. His wrists rested on his knees, his battered hands hanging between them, bloodied and swollen.

It was time. Time to acknowledge that all the bloody bare-knuckle fights in London and every cask of brandy that passed through the city's docks was not enough to wipe her from his mind.

"Hound, there's a man here for you."

Vincent looked up at the wiry little man who ran the makeshift boxing arena. "No more fights, Georgie. I'm done for."

The little man grinned. "I'd say you are, sir. That's not what I mean. It's your Bow Street lad. He's over by the door."

Cursing, Vincent reached for his shirt. It was sweat stained and bloodied, but it was the only one he had with him. Pulling it over his head, wincing at bruised ribs and aching muscles, he rose and walked the short distance to the door. Ettinger had been dodging him and had finally run out of excuses.

"About bloody time you showed up," Vincent all but growled.

"What's climbed up your arse? I'm the one you've been hunting down. Can't walk into a single establishment in the entire city without someone telling me that you wish to speak to me!" Ettinger groused. "And you look like hell. Did you even win a bout?"

"I won the fourth one. I lost the fifth. The first three I was too drunk to remember."

Ettinger's mouth dropped open. "How many did you fight?"

"This last one was number six."

"Win, lose or draw?"

Vincent sighed. "He knocked me on my ass."

"Did it help?"

"Not especially, no. But what I really want to know is what you've discovered." Vincent began unwrapping the bindings on his hands as they walked toward his waiting carriage.

"There's more than three dead. And more than one beaten within an inch of her life. This has been going on for the past two years. But dead prostitutes do not garner a lot of sympathy or attention, sadly." Ettinger opened the carriage door, holding it wide so that Vincent might climb in.

It was lowering to realize that his legs were shaking as he did so. Never, in the entirety of his life, had he fought six matches in a single night. It had been a foolhardy attempt to erase her image from his mind. And, quite obviously, it had failed.

"How many?"

"Ten," Ettinger answered, biting off the word. "Ten in all. Two still live. Sally Dawson and Rosie Higgins. Sally's not up for talking to me just yet. But I'll go see Rosie later today and find out what I can. But I do not work for you. This is a simple favor that I am doing because I know the parties involved. That is all."

Vincent didn't smile. One, it would have hurt to do so. Terribly. Two, he knew that Ettinger was hooked. The case had sparked his interest whether he wanted to admit it or not. The man loved a riddle or a mystery. He was like a dog with a bone, now, and would work it to the bitter end.

"You'll keep me updated on anything you get from Rosie."

"I will," Ettinger agreed. "What is this really about? You have a temper to be sure and a fight now and again is the perfect cure for that. But this kind of abuse—it's not like you. You don't do a damn thing unless you're getting something out of it. What does letting a queue of pugilists beat you beyond recognition do for you?"

It's a distraction. It's the only thing that offers momentary relief from thoughts of her. "Leave it alone, Joss. I do not poke at your scars. You do not poke at mine."

Ettinger settled back against the seat, clearly wanting to say more. But after a moment, nodded. They remained silent as the carriage wound its way through the dirty, narrow lanes and alleys of the city and back to the more pristinely kept cobbled streets of Mayfair.

"You can take the boy out of the gutter, Ettinger," he mused, "But you sure as hell cannot keep him out of it."

Chapter Sixteen

HER SISTER HAD departed hours earlier, hoping that her husband would have already left for his club for the day. It was a sound strategy on Henrietta's part—to avoid contact with him as much as possible. Through the remainder of the day, Honoria had brooded about their visit. She'd brooded about other things, as well.

Knowing how deeply unhappy Henrietta was, she could not help but compare it to the misery she had felt during her own marriage. She had felt trapped. No, she had been trapped. It wasn't simply what she had perceived but actual fact. The law did not allow women to simply leave their husbands, regardless of how terrible those husbands were. The burden of proof for women to justify such a measure was exhaustive—likely on purpose. No doubt the laws had been written to discourage such behavior. But soon that would not matter.

Prior to Henrietta's departure this morning, they had reviewed their plan. All was set and in motion. Her sister would have her freedom, no matter what the cost. She would leave for the Continent and Honoria would use the terribly scandalous things she'd learned about Lord Daventry, an acquaintance of Lord Ernsdale whose feelings toward him had soured, to persuade him to act as her sister's representative and challenge the legitimacy of the marriage.

Blackmail was an ugly word, but under the circumstances, there was no other option. If there was one benefit to having spent so much time with the soiled doves who worked the streets in Soho and St. Giles, it was that she'd learned a great deal about the men who frequented them for services—men in very high positions who would not want their darker proclivities to be known.

Until she'd discovered the truth of just how horrific Henrietta's marriage was, it had never occurred to her to use that knowledge for her own benefit. But she would now. Whatever it took, she would see her sister freed from him.

You know someone who could make that happen . . . if you asked him.

That little voice whispering in her mind spoke more frequently than she would like. Since he'd escorted her home that night—*after*—she'd been plagued by such thoughts. Wayward and terribly tempting, they had come upon her time and again. As had vivid memories of what had already passed between them . . . and what might still if she only had the courage.

From the first night she'd met him on that dirty street, this outcome had been inevitable. He'd been an irresistible force. But such an event should not have altered her life so dramatically. It defied reason that he should have then crossed her mind almost daily. *But he did.* More than once per day if she were honest. And now she feared that would always be the case.

Every man she encountered compared unfavorably to him. Thinking of poor Mr. Walpole, the young man had not stood a chance. He was too young. His hair was too light. His features were too delicate. His hands were too soft. His voice lacked the rich timbre that she could feel as much as hear. And he had most decidedly lacked that edge of danger and excitement that tormented her so.

Perhaps she truly was a perverse sort of creature. For the very things that made him unsuitable were the same things that made her long to be near him. Nothing had ever affected her as much as that first kiss had. Not until the second, at any rate. It had not been an aberration, as both of them had clearly hoped. And giving in to the temptation that had dogged her constantly, to share such previously unimaginable intimacies—well, she would simply never be free of him. He was a part of her now and always would be. She'd been right to be hesitant, to be cautious. Though in the end it hadn't mattered. Like a boulder rolling downhill—it might be slowed but it would not be stopped.

He'd said much the same that night when he'd demanded a kiss as payment. Curiosity had spurred him on, had made him issue that ridiculous challenge. And in the aftermath of their most intimate encounter, they'd both had to face the undeniable truth that something existed between them—something that could only lead to disaster.

"Mrs. Blaylock? Ma'am?"

Honoria, grateful for the distraction from her own thoughts, looked up to see a maid entering the small drawing room that had been receiving her domestic attentions. But it was not one of her maids. No, the woman who stood so timidly in the doorway was Henrietta's lady's maid, a shy and hesitant young woman who had a way with hair dressing and was quite skilled with her needle and thread. Immediately, alarm raced through Honoria. For Foster to be there, something had occurred. Something terrible.

"What is it? What is wrong, Foster?" Honoria asked.

"Lady Ernsdale, ma'am . . . she's gone."

Honoria's heart thudded in her chest and then seemed to stop. Everything felt tight, squeezed in the vice of panic. "Gone? What does that mean, Foster?"

"She never came home, ma'am. I know she left to pay a call here this morning, but she had planned to return immediately after as she intended to spend the day preparing for the Scarsdens' ball tonight. I was given very specific instructions on what to prepare for her to wear. She'd had a new gown made for it in the loveliest shade of green . . . I just know she'd not have missed out on the chance to wear it for any reason."

Honoria felt the breath rush out of her. When Foster had said that Henrietta was gone, her first thought was that her sister was dead. After all, her husband had proven himself to be a cruel man. With the deaths of his first two wives remaining shrouded in mystery and scandal there was precedent for drawing such conclusions.

Honoria knew only too well just what sort of damage a man could inflict when the law was on his side. Not to mention the fact that there was a coldness in Lord Ernsdale that had worried her from the start. He'd buried two wives already. A third would surprise no one. "Has Lord Ernsdale sent anyone out to search for her?"

Foster, teary eyed, shook her head. "No, ma'am. But a letter came, and I heard him say he'd not pay a dime for her, then he threw it in the fire. But I rescued what I could of it, and I brought it with me. I can't read, so I don't know what it says."

Honoria accepted the proffered letter, her stomach tight with fear. Nothing good could come from any of this, she was certain.

There were two pieces of the missive. Apparently, Lord Ernsdale had torn it in half before tossing it, with thankfully abysmal aim, into the fire. Holding the scorched document carefully, she pieced it together as best as possible. A word was missing, others were difficult to decipher. But not impossible. After studying it for a few moments, it was still perfectly legible given context and content. But it took her several passes of reading it for it to make sense. Not because of the words written, but because of the unimaginable reality they represented.

As she scanned the contents for possibly the fifth time, the realization of just what had happened finally settled in. The hot fear which had gripped her suddenly went cold. It congealed inside her, even her blood seeming to slow to a sluggish pace as it moved through her veins. The entire world slowed down, becoming indistinct as the letter before her became the sharp and ugly reality.

If you want to see —— again, it will cost you £5,000.

One sentence scrawled across that page. One line of sweeping script that told a terrible tale. The single word in the middle, missing with the edges blackened, could have said *your wife*. It could have said *her*. It could have even been her sister's name. Regardless, they all meant the same thing. Someone had taken Henrietta and was demanding an impossible ransom for her return. Five hundred pounds, she could have managed. One thousand pounds, if she'd robbed Peter to pay Paul, would have been possible. But five thousand? The jointure provided for her by her husband's will paid for household expenses, wages for servants and one hundred pounds per month. It was, by the standards of most, incredibly generous. It also hadn't been his choice. Her father had negotiated those amounts in the marriage contracts. But generous or not, it would not be enough. Not in the face of such demands. Even with the amount she had scrimped and saved by cutting corners in order to provide for Henrietta's escape, she could not hope to pay it—certainly not in the time allotted.

"What does it say, ma'am?" Foster asked, clenching and unclenching her hands in fear.

Pulled back from the brink of complete despair by that question, Honoria's mind began to work again. The haze of fear that had frozen her to the spot was not lifted precisely, but no longer held her completely in its sway. "She's been kidnapped. Abducted for ransom," Honoria stated, as if somehow saying the words aloud would make the reality of it easier to fathom. Her mind was spinning, a dozen thoughts popping in and then just as quickly dismissed. In a matter of seconds, her entire world had shifted into some nightmare realm.

The maid gasped and then began to sob. "Oh, no! He'll never pay a ransom for her. He'll let her die sure as anything, ma'am! What will you do?"

Honoria nodded firmly. He would let her die. "I know, Foster. I know what he is. So, I must ask for help from another quarter, from someone who cannot be cowed by him."

"Who is that, ma'am?"

Glancing up at the wide-eyed maid, there were some secrets that should not be shared. They would be too damning for all of them. Also, she wasn't entirely certain of his assistance. He had made no attempt to contact her, just as she had not tried to contact him. She had made the very deliberate choice not to see him ever again. After all, he posed too great a threat to her hard-won peace of mind. He posed a threat to every part of her—body and mind, as well as heart and soul. But he was the only man in all of London to whom she could turn in the face of what she had just learned.

Dread filled her. His aid was not a foregone conclusion. He could just as easily tell her to go to the devil. After she had walked away from him, would it be any great surprise if he refused her now?

Honoria shook her head. "Someone who would not wish to be named."

"I know she's my employer... but she's also my friend. I don't know what I'd do if something happened to her," Foster sobbed.

That sentiment echoed Honoria's own feelings on the matter. Sister. Confidante. Friend. The only family she had. What would she do without her? And that gave her the resolve she needed to face him. "You will not have to find out, Foster. Henrietta will come home. I will not entertain any other possibility. Whatever it takes, she will come home."

Chapter Seventeen

EVENING WAS APPROACHING and Vincent, who'd indulged in copious amounts of brandy in order to dull some of the pain from the beating he'd taken, had finally slept. It was not a peaceful or restful sleep. Even battered, bruised, and half drunk, she invaded his dreams.

It was almost a relief when he was awakened by the pounding, not in his head, but at his door. Rolling onto his back, he stared at the gilded bed crown and the rich, crimson bed curtains that hung from it. His head ached, but not so terribly that he couldn't function. Just enough, he thought, to give him the devil's own mood. His ribs were another matter entirely. Bruised but not broken, they still hurt like the devil.

Getting to his feet, he grabbed his discarded trousers and put them on, moving as quickly as his battered body would allow. Generally speaking, people pounding at one's door wanted something. Being caught in such a situation would leave him at a disadvantage. He'd learned long ago to keep the upper hand. Always.

Striding from the bedroom and through the sitting room, he yanked the door open with such suddenness and force that the person pounding upon it stumbled forward. Honoria Blaylock, garbed once more in head to toe black, fell against him. He caught her, his hands grasping her upper arms and her body pressed to his naked chest.

A curse escaped him—bitter and beleaguered.

It should have been a moment that he enjoyed, that he savored. He'd certainly imagined it often enough. The now familiar feel of her against him was enough to stir the embers of desire. And at any other time, he likely would have prolonged that contact. But her obvious distress took any pleasure he might have experienced from such nearness and dissolved it entirely. Her eyes were dry, but they were still red from crying. Whatever had caused her tears, she would not weep before him. Not before him nor anyone else, he was certain.

"What has happened?" he demanded, as he set her back on her feet.

"She was taken," Honoria answered breathlessly.

Perhaps it was the fact that he'd just been awakened, or it might have been the previous night's inebriation, or possibly even the numerous punches he'd taken, but the statement left him puzzled. "Sally?"

"No, my sister. Henrietta, Lady Ernsdale. She's been taken."

"Taken by whom?"

"I do not know," she answered, reaching into her pocket and producing the charred remnants of a letter. "That is the ransom demand that was sent to her husband . . . and that he has refused to pay."

Handling the badly singed foolscap with care, he turned it over in his hands and examined it front and back. Certain things were instantly apparent. The person who had written it was well educated—their penmanship was precise and well practiced. The stationery, despite its current damaged state, had been of good quality. There was also the amount of ransom demanded. People in the lower classes could likely not even conceive of such an amount. It was more money than most would see in their lifetime. Five thousand pounds to someone in a rookery was an astronomical sum. Even to those in society, it was no small amount, but it was an amount that most people of a certain station, would be able to raise.

"I cannot pay them. It's impossible. The trustees of my late husband's estate would never permit it," she said. "One thousand pounds I could possibly raise. But five? Never."

His brows flew upward as he stared at her in shock. "Are you asking for a loan?" The very idea of it rankled.

If she needed something, he would provide it.

That thought shocked him more than a little. He was not her husband. He had no desire to be anyone's husband. She was not his wife that he should attend to her needs in such a manner. And yet, it was gut deep. He wanted to take care of her, and that was absolutely terrifying. It was a weakness—a vulnerability to be exploited.

"I'll repay it. Whatever they are asking for, I will—I must—give it to them. I would give them anything they require that is within my power and perhaps even things that are not—I just need to know who they are in order to do so. And nothing of this sort happens in London without your knowledge and approval."

Vincent shook his head. "This is not an action that was undertaken with my awareness. Had I been consulted, I would have refused."

"Why?"

That single word was uttered so softly that at first he wasn't certain he had heard it or simply that he wished to have. Regardless, he answered, "You know why . . . I do not know your sister, but I certainly know who she is. And for better or worse, the protection I granted to you extends to her. No one who works for me or ever wishes to do so would raise a hand against either of you."

Her eyes widened in surprise and her startled gaze locked with his steely one. Silence stretched between them for a moment—silence as she digested that bit of information, as the significance of what he had said truly sank in. For the past year and a half, she had moved freely and unmolested through the worst hellholes in London, not because of the favors they exchanged but *because he had deemed it so*. His feelings for her had been his only motivation and he could see the recognition of that fact reflected in her expression.

After a moment, she lowered her eyes, not so much in deference or shyness but perhaps to hide things she did not wish him to see. "If you didn't approve this act . . . they could be anyone. Heaven only knows what she will endure at their hands."

"Sadly, you are in a better position than most to understand that. There is some safety, or at least the illusion of it, in naïveté."

"You must help me! Please?" There were tears in her eyes when she looked up at him again. She did not shed them. Clinging to her lashes, they were like diamonds—sparkling in the light, of great cost and greater rarity.

Shaking his head, he began to pace back and forth on the carpet. His mind was racing as he considered the possibilities. "These are independent operators. People who come up from the country and do not know how this city operates, or people from corners of this city that are beyond even my reach. But there is more to this than meets the eye. Of that, I am certain."

"I thought no one was beyond your reach," she protested.

He shrugged. "No man is omnipotent, not even me. There are always those who are desperate enough to work outside what I allow—hedging their bets that I will not find out, though they are rarely so lucky. And if this is someone in the Liberties, then they are not only protected from the law but from me. But that," he gestured toward the ransom demand which now rested on the top of an inlaid table, "that is the hand of an educated person. If they were in my employ, I would have recognized the writing."

"You cannot help me." The whispered words were low and soft. They also revealed just how broken she was in that moment.

"I didn't say that," he insisted. He hated the sound of fear in her voice. He despised the pain he could feel emanating from her. There was nothing he would not give to spare her that. "I may not know who they are at this moment, but I have ways of finding out. The ransom letter tells me quite a bit about them already. But, Honoria, you must understand, my ability to provide assistance is limited. I cannot simply snap my fingers and produce your sister, but I will look into it."

"What does that mean, precisely? Look into it?"

He sighed, shoving his bruised hands into the pockets of his trousers. "It means that I will find out who is responsible, though it could take some time. And the amount of time we have is in the hands of those who have taken her. When it comes to her safety, I will not lie to you—that cannot be guaranteed."

She turned to him. "I will give you whatever you want if you will only help me. My sister—she is everything to me. She is all that I have. Our father made this match for her against every bit of advice and all her protests, and now she is paying the ultimate price for it! I know you—"

"You do not!" The protest came out sharply, the words harsh and the volume thundering. He had not meant to be rough with her, but she did not know him, and it was wiser now not to let her believe that she did. In all likelihood, she never would. "You do not know me, Honoria Blaylock. Fate had our paths cross. We are not friends. At best, we are allies. And whatever else may have occurred between us, you do not know me."

"I know some things. I know that, despite what others say, you are not a man without a code of honor!" she protested vehemently.

Vincent wished, for just a moment, that he was what she believed him to be. But they were not living in some fairy story and he was not some petty thief with a heart of gold. Extortion. Assault. And some things that were better left unsaid. He was guilty of them all and, most days, felt not a pang of regret. Even now, his regret was not for the actions but for the insurmountable gap they had created between him and this woman. "I interceded on your behalf in the past. First in the rookery, then with your arrest. In the interim we have done mutual favors for one another if they did not require too much trouble on either of our parts. And together, we made one colossal mistake. That is all. You know nothing of me. Do not presume altruism on my part. Everything I do comes at a price."

She clasped her hands tightly in front of her. When she began to speak again, her tone was calmer, more measured, and impossibly cool. "Our mistakes and faults aside, my sister is innocent. She has been a pawn in the games of men for too long. We both have been. And whatever may be said of you, *Mr. Carrow*, I know you have always gone out of your way to protect innocent young women. You've also been a champion for those who are far from innocent. The ladies whom I assist have only ever had kind words to say about you and, given their usual experiences with men, that speaks to the nature of your character, sir."

He waved a hand dismissively. "Or it could be that I simply associate with prostitutes on a regular basis, *Mrs. Blaylock*," he emphasized the formal address just as she had. He knew he was being an ass, but he was fairly certain that, in the long run, that would be for the best. "A kind word or a bit of coin they do not have to earn makes me appear a saint in their eyes. On these streets, alliances are purchased. They are never given. As to innocence, most of the people I know are far, far from innocent. Do not paint me in a heroic light when I am anything but."

Honoria shook her head in denial. "I do not believe that. What motivates you to do so, I cannot guess, but I cannot believe it is something so simple or so base. Women talk. Whether they are highborn ladies or the lowest of common prostitutes. *We talk*. And I know you do not take advantage of their services. You may keep a mistress or have lovers, but it is not women you pay for the privilege."

"And that matters?" he asked. The very idea that she was discussing him with others, that she was risking having others know of their connection without thought to what it would do to her, infuriated him. "Why? If a man pays a woman for sex, does that instantly make him less trustworthy? You don't get to have an interest in who I'm fucking, Honoria! That is, unless you plan to occupy my bed again?"

He'd said it to shock her, to make her realize just how far outside her own sheltered life she had come. But she didn't shrink from him or appear scandalized at the vulgarity of his language. Instead, she simply stared at him in that direct and challenging manner that withered some men and excited others. For his sins, he was one of the latter.

"I don't wish to argue or hurl barbs at one another. I came here because I need your help. Shall I beg?" she asked softly. "I can. I can fall to my knees and plead with you as my pride has never allowed me to beg for anything else, please help me. She is all I have, and I will do anything!"

Vincent looked at her, his gaze raking over her. He would help her, but she would pay for the privilege. Her terribly optimistic view of his character would be obliterated—as it should. He hadn't gotten to where he was by being kind or by having a code. He'd done it through a keen sense of observation and a lack of scruples about using others' secrets to secure their cooperation in his endeavors. He wanted her. As he'd never wanted another woman, he wanted her. And he was not above using this horrible situation to his advantage. That was, after all, how he'd climbed up out of the gutters. *By using every advantage.*

She looked back at him steadily, her hands clasped together imploringly. "Please."

If he felt a pang of conscience, he squelched it immediately. She was not so innocent that she did not know what she offered, after all. No one who spent as much time as she did in the rookeries could retain that degree of naïveté. "Anything? Be careful when making deals with the devil, Mrs. Blaylock . . . you may find that the reward is not worth the cost."

"If I can save my sister, nothing else matters." From her expression, it was quite clear that, even as she uttered those words, she understood the fatefulness of that moment.

He stared intently at her for a moment, then he spoke very precisely, each word slowly and perfectly enunciated. "Then my price is quite simple . . . and nonnegotiable. You, Mrs. Blaylock, in my bed. And you do not run away this time."

She said nothing. Instead, she simply stared at him with those curious eyes and a look of quiet resolve about her.

He didn't want quiet resolve. He wanted passion and fire from her. He wanted her to be the woman who'd faced down six men with a sword. He wanted the woman who had been so sweetly passionate in his bed once before. "You will be mine until my interest has waned. That may be either before or after your sister is recovered. You will have my aid until that task is done, regardless. You have until I open the door to decide."

"What happens when you open the door?" There was hesitation in her voice—provoked by fear rather than pride.

He didn't smile. His expression remained hard and inscrutable. "You will be escorted through it and will never darken it again."

He took three deliberate strides. His hand was poised only a hair's breadth from the intricately wrought doorknob when she spoke. She spoke a single word, uttered so faintly he wasn't certain he'd heard her.

Then he turned back, meeting her gaze over the broad expanse of his shoulder. "Did you have something to say, Mrs. Blaylock?"

"Yes."

"Yes, you have something to say or yes—"

"I agree to your terms, Mr. Carrow. I would sell my soul to save her. Selling my body is a small enough price, all things given."

"How very practical, Mrs. Blaylock," he said with amusement. "That is only one of the many things I admire about you."

"Yet we are not acquainted. We are not friends. *We do not know one another.*" There was a bite to her tone as she threw his words back at him. "You said so yourself. How could you admire me then?"

"I know all I need to about you. A man has only to look at

you to want you—to the point of both madness and violence. Surely you are aware of it." It was a deliberately hurtful thing to say. Yes, she was beautiful. Some accident of nature had resulted in her striking coloring and the pleasing symmetry of her features. But that was not the source of her beauty. It came from within her. That he recognized that—believed it with every fiber of his being—terrified him.

HONORIA SHIFTED, UNCOMFORTABLE beneath his gaze. Their eyes met, the moment charged, and she looked away. It was an unfortunate reminder of the night they had met. She'd been in a place that was not fit for ladies, surrounded by men who were angry at all the injustices heaped upon them by life. And she'd been the opportune target for their revenge—for them to take back a little of what they felt they deserved, what they thought the world and society had denied them.

She understood those men. She didn't like them, nor did she condone their behavior. But she certainly understood it. How many times had she heard of families falling apart and husbands abandoning their wives and children because they felt less than a man? The humiliation of constant poverty and strife, the feeling of complete emasculation watching those you love suffer without having any ability to aid them—it shaped and formed people. Including the man before her. After all, he had not started out in an elegant house in Mayfair.

And through all of it, one question plagued her. It shamed her, as well. Was it some point of pride for him to seduce a "respectable" woman? Did he want her, or did he simply want the conquest? The former she could live with. The latter would destroy her pride even when her late husband had failed in his every attempt.

"Tomorrow night, Mrs. Blaylock. At midnight. You will be

here," he said.

"As you wish, Mr. Carrow. I am clearly yours to command." As the words escaped her lips, they resonated with a truth that was undeniable and inescapable. She had just made a deal with her very own devil. It should have made her angry. It should have frightened her. And while those things were certainly part of the strange mix of emotions roiling within her, there was also excitement, curiosity... anticipation. She might have been backed into a corner, but it was precisely where she wanted to be.

Chapter Eighteen

"How much was the marriage settlement Ernsdale received when he wed your sister?" The question was uttered softly, so softly that Honoria almost didn't hear it over the rumbling of carriage wheels.

He was seeing her home in an unmarked carriage, escorting her personally in an effort to see her retain at least some respectability. She'd been secreted out of the club with all the subterfuge of a master spy slipping behind enemy lines.

Realizing that she'd been quiet for far too long, Honoria answered, "Ten thousand pounds."

He frowned, his dark brows drawing together in thought. "I find it suspect that the ransom demanded falls conveniently within the limits of what Ernsdale received. Don't you?"

She blinked in surprise. "I hadn't considered it honestly. This is your area. Despite my forays into the rookeries, I remain woefully ignorant of how crimes such as these would be carried out. Have you any experience with this sort of thing?"

He shook his head. "Not this. There are certain things I would never sanction and the abduction and ransom of a lady is one of them. Anyone engaging in these sorts of crimes would be smart enough to conceal those activities from me."

Honoria seized on that immediately. "There! That is a perfect example of the conundrum you present. Are you or are you not an honorable man?"

"It's practicality, love. Honor's got nothing to do with it. Your sister is off limits not least because she's the wife of a peer. The penalties for committing a crime against someone like you—a mere missus—versus the penalties for committing one against a peer of the realm, and by extension, his wife, would be far too great."

"Oh. That's all it is to you then? Simply a way to mitigate potential consequences?" She couldn't keep the disappointment from her voice.

"Do you really think that? You—and occasionally your sister—have worked, unmolested, in the worst rookeries in London for the past year without incident. You know the reason why."

She didn't know it, had no idea of his true motivation for extending her protection this last year. She was beginning to think she knew nothing at all. Everything in her life was unpredictable at that moment, and she was like a piece of flotsam, buffeted by crashing waves until she didn't even know the direction of the shore. "It would be better if you had sanctioned her abduction. I thought—if you knew then you could simply tell them to return her. But now . . . I truly have no idea where my sister is. I do not know if she's hurt, if she's being mistreated! I thought her marriage to Ernsdale was the worst thing that could ever happen to her and now I must reconsider that."

"I told you I cannot make promises regarding your sister's safety, but there is one promise that I absolutely can make: whoever these men are, they will be caught, and they will pay."

His voice was cold and the words blunt. She had never anticipated that false reassurances were something he would dole out simply to ease her worries. He was, if nothing else, treating her as an equal and being transparent. For the first time in her life, though, she rather wished to be treated as the "little woman," some intellectually inferior creature who required protection from the real world at all costs. But no, he'd rather treat her like the prostitutes she'd devoted herself to helping—as a woman who understood the ways of the world.

"And in trade for your services," she said somewhat bitterly, "I will provide my own."

"It is a fairly simple exchange," he agreed, as he leaned across the seat and parted the velvet curtains. Sunshine did not necessarily pour in. It was London, after all. The haze of coal smoke was nearly impenetrable, but the interior of the coach did lighten to some degree. "I will provide the ransom while also actively looking for your sister, and in exchange, you will come to my bed."

Honoria, even in the haze of fear and worry for her sister, was not entirely immune to him. *How she wished she were!* It would make the whole matter easier to bear. From the moment of their first meeting, he'd been ever present in her thoughts. Even when she had no wish to admit it, his image hovered on the periphery of her mind. Every gentleman she had encountered since their first meeting was compared to him and found wanting. Not that she'd been actively seeking the company of any man, gentleman or otherwise. It was part of human nature, certainly part of being a woman, to size up every man based on his virility, his ability to provide and protect. He was uniquely capable on both counts and the former was undeniable. She felt drawn to him in ways she could not explain and had never planned to explore.

Now is your chance. You can have what you want free of guilt . . . because you're doing it to save your sister.

That niggling voice in her head, the very same one that often led to having a second piece of cake or overindulging in some other treat, now prodded her in his direction. Perverse as she was, she resented it. She resented the pull of attraction she felt.

Her gaze traveled over the broad expanse of his chest. He hadn't bothered with a cravat or stock. He wore only a waistcoat and white linen beneath it. The linen parted enough to reveal a bit of crisp, dark hair and smooth, bronzed skin. But she'd already seen far more than that. And yet there was a curiosity within her—to see all of him.

The only other man she had ever seen in such a state of undress was her late husband and they could not have been more different. Where Edwin had appeared soft and pale, Vincent Carrow appeared powerfully masculine with firm and well-defined musculature. He looked more like the sculptures of ancient warriors from the Classical Era than like a modern Englishman.

"Once?" she asked. They were both perfectly aware of her meaning.

He stared at her for a moment, cocking his head to one side as if to gauge her seriousness in the matter. Then one corner of his mouth lifted in a slightly bemused half-smile. "No, Honoria. I have spent the last year and a half wanting you. And if the other night proved anything, it is that once will definitely not be enough. It will require more than once to assuage my desire for you."

"How many times?"

He shrugged. "Once, twice. Ten times. A hundred. Does it matter?"

Thinking of the misery of her husband's visits to her chamber and how she'd grown to hate him more with each one, yes it did. It would be worse with Vincent, because he could make her burn for him. Even when giving him her body in trade, he would take far more from her than just that. "It might."

His eyes locked on her in the dim carriage. And in a surprisingly gentle tone, he offered, "You can still change your mind. Now. Before I begin any investigation, but the moment you step out of this carriage that chance is gone. So make up your mind and do so quickly. Every second counts. We have just turned onto your street."

There was simply no other option. Her sister was depending on her, even if Hettie did not know it. So, just as she'd agreed in his apartment above the club, she would agree again now. Ultimately, it did not matter. She would have bedded the devil himself to save her sister. This man certainly looked the part. And heaven knew he was temptation personified.

"Very well," she agreed. "Do we require a contract, or will a handshake suffice to seal the deal?"

"No. That is not how any bargains between us going forward shall be sealed. A kiss will do."

Uncertain of how to proceed, Honoria was considering the mechanics of how she would kiss him in a moving carriage. Whether it was because he'd sensed her uncertainty or simply because he wanted to remove any obstacles to securing her agreement, he reached over and grasped her wrist. In one fluid motion, he pulled her across the expanse of the carriage until she was on the seat beside him. Except that she wasn't only on the seat. Her legs were on the seat, her hips were perched on his impossibly firm thigh and her upper body was draped over him, pressed against the hard wall of his chest. Their mouths were scant inches apart. She could feel his breath fanning over her skin. Her body responded instantly—to his present nearness, to memories of their past encounters. Would her blood ever not heat in his presence? Circumstances be damned, she thought.

More boldly than she would have anticipated, Honoria placed her hand firmly against his chest and rose up slightly to reach his mouth. She had kissed him before, hadn't she? She'd felt his body pressed firmly against hers, felt him moving within her. But this wasn't simply a kiss. This was the final seal on a bargain struck that would change her life forever. It was positively Faustian.

Their lips touched and, for at least that moment, everything else vanished. Her worries and fear, her uncertainty about the course she had just embarked upon—all of that simply fell away and the world consisted of nothing but the two of them, of the brushing of their lips and the heat of his flesh beneath the layers of cloth separating them.

The feel of his arms closing around of her, of warmth and strength, was beyond seductive. It called to something primitive inside her—something she hadn't known existed until she'd met the man before her. It terrified her. That instinctive desire to submit to him, to let him take care of things for her was so foreign to her that she could barely put it into words.

Then his lips moved from hers, pressing softly to her cheek, then her jawline. His whiskered cheek rubbed against hers. His breath fanned over her ear, making her shiver. His lips caressed her neck, just below her ear. Lower they coasted, down to her collar bone, only slightly bared by the modest cut of her dress. When she felt his tongue painting a delicate pattern over the skin there, the breath left her body entirely. She swayed, dizzy from it, and his arms closed about her more tightly.

Forcing herself to think, to retain some degree of composure, she said "You said a kiss, Mr. Carrow." The slight quavering of her voice was humiliating. Could she be seduced so easily?

"So, I did, Mrs. Blaylock," he agreed, and yet he continued those silken strokes of his tongue over her skin between words. "But I never said where or of what nature, did I?"

He shifted slightly, his mouth once again moving over her neck. His teeth scraped against her skin, a delicious sting that had her pulse beating a wicked tattoo. The heat of it spread through her body like warm honey. It suffused her. The decadent sensation of reveling in his slow, languid exploration overwhelmed her senses and her conscience. Her thoughts to resist him, to hold herself somehow apart from him while letting him simply use her body seemed laughable in that moment. He was not Edwin. She was not the woman she had been with Edwin. *And apparently she could be seduced that easily.*

And then the carriage stopped. From the box, the driver called out, "Sir, we've arrived at the address."

He lifted his head, placing a bit of distance between them, but did not let her go. "I will send word when we are to meet and will arrange a discreet carriage to cart you to and fro. You should not come during daylight hours, Honoria. I want you, and I mean to have you, but not at that cost."

She didn't answer immediately. It was impossible. The ability to speak had simply been taken from her. Or perhaps she had willingly forfeited it.

"Mrs. Blaylock?"

Honoria blinked and then met his gaze. Finally, she nodded. "I understand."

The moment he released her, his arms falling to his sides, his hands clenched into tight fists as if he might reach for her once more. She felt bereft at the loss. When he'd been holding her, kissing her, touching her—she'd felt warm then, and now the cold was seeping in once more.

There was no dignified way to remove oneself from a man's lap, but she tried. When she had managed it, rather gracelessly, she pulled her cloak about herself once more and lifted the hood to shroud her face. Covered from head to toe, she opened the carriage door and one of the footmen helped her down. She walked away from the carriage—*from him*—but she knew she'd left a very important part of herself behind.

Chapter Nineteen

Pitch black—not even a sliver of light. No voices.
Lying on the hard floor, she remained perfectly still even as wakefulness slowly crept through her. It was not merely the fogginess of sleep. *Drugged.* She had been drugged.

Henrietta Dalgleish, Lady Ernsdale, tried, in spite of her addled state, to take note of even the smallest detail. Sight was useless, but smell . . . the scent of the river permeated the space around her. Though she could see nothing, that space seemed small and close, infused also with the scents of tar, oil, and wood. Dank and a little dirty, it was unmistakable.

Even if she hadn't smelled it, the slight swaying would have given it away—she was on a ship. Likely below deck, given the darkness. She was also very much alone, save for the rats. Their infernal squeaking sparked terror within her and brought a kind of clarity about her current situation and just how dire it was.

How long had she been there? With no light, the passage of time was impossible to gauge. Moving carefully, she tested her wrists. They were bound in front of her, but much more loosely than they had been when she'd wakened before—in a different place.

The memories of that were less distinct, blurred. *Laudanum.* The few times in her life when she'd been forced to take the drug had resulted in distorted recollections after the fact. It jumbled her mind and all the events just before and after it.

Her last clear memory was leaving Honoria's house just after dawn. She'd hailed a hack but could not recall getting in it. That was confirmation, to her mind, of when she'd been taken. But who could have done so? Who could have known to capture her there when there had been no plan in place to go to Honoria's? *Unless it was her husband.* But even then, Ernsdale would have had to plan everything well in advance, orchestrate an argument with her and be able to direct the plan after he'd consumed his belladonna-infused brandy. It made no sense.

Unless she had not been the intended target. Swathed in a heavy, dark cloak, she'd been leaving Honoria's house. Perhaps they had not intended to take her at all but had been after her sister. Struggling to piece it all together, she was grasping at the fragments of memory.

It came to her slowly... she hadn't hailed a hack at all. There'd been no chance to do so. A carriage had stopped before the steps of the house next door. She hadn't immediately been worried because it was not uncommon for people to attend parties and balls that kept them out until dawn. It also wasn't uncommon for people to return at such a time from late night trysts. But rather than climbing the steps to the neighboring house, they'd rushed at her.

Even as she'd opened her mouth to scream for help, one of them had forced a dirty cloth into her mouth. Another of her attackers had used her own cloak to bind her, wrapping it about her tightly before shoving her into the carriage. They'd first taken her to a tavern, a tumble-down place she had not recognized. After carting her in over someone's shoulder, they'd dumped her in a filthy room. The dirty cloth in her mouth had been removed and a foul-tasting liquid had been forced upon her then. The single candle in the room had been doused, the door locked, and she'd been left bound in the dark to sink into oblivion.

My God! How long has it been? That thought raised a panic inside her. Hours? Days? She didn't know. Why had they taken her? Had it been because they mistook her for her sister? Was it for ransom? Would her husband even consider paying her captors?

Pressing her hands flat against the floor, Henrietta pushed herself up to a sitting position. Her gown and stays were gone, along with the fashionable spencer and well-fitting kid boots she'd worn beneath her cloak. Her corset and petticoat were gone, as well. She was dressed now in coarse fabric—a simple dress that was rough against her skin. Her long hair had been braided and tucked into a woolen cap, the silver hairpins stolen along with her dress and underpinnings. A memory stirred in her mind of a woman covetously caressing the fabric of her gown.

The boards creaked beneath her, and her heart stopped. But there were no sounds of rushing feet. No one was coming running to investigate the cause. Her breath rushed out, but she remained perfectly still.

After a moment, feeling a bit bolder, now that she knew no one was listening for her slightest sound, she tried to climb to her feet. Instead, she swayed unsteadily and had to lean against the wall to keep from falling. The wooden boards were rough and cold beneath her feet, her shoes and stockings having been taken as well.

When she was able, she began to move. Carefully, one step at a time, with her hands against the wall for support and for orientation, she began mapping out the room in her mind. It was small. Terribly so. If her hands had been free, she could have stretched them out wall to wall. Raising them up, she found the ceiling just scant inches above her head. Shuffling from one corner to the next, she noted the rough wooden texture of the walls. When she turned the next corner, her hands touched on something protruding from the wall. Running them over the object, she realized it was the rung of a ladder. Further exploration uncovered the next one just above it. *A way out.*

She needed her hands free to be able to climb them. The distance from rung to rung was too great even with her slack bindings. Plopping down on the floor once again, she began to frantically work at the bonds of her wrists. If she could just get them free, she could climb up, possibly free herself, and . . . what? She was on a ship. And if that ship was not docked, she could not swim to shore. She could barely tread water and even that was a skill that had not been tested in more than a decade. An incident in childhood, when she had nearly drowned, had left her with a terrible fear of deep water.

"Honoria," she whispered, "How I wish you were here to make me brave!"

VINCENT ENTERED THE rabbit warren of the opium den just as night was falling. If he'd gone straight home, he'd have just sat about brooding over her for hours. Second-guessing himself and castigating himself for being precisely what others believed him to be would serve no purpose. Instead, he elected to get to work.

He was not there to partake of the all-too-popular drug, and that fact was well known by the proprietor. But Fish didn't only deal in opium. He dealt in information, as well, and information was precisely what Vincent required.

Slipping through the ramshackle corridors created by swaths of curtains, he thought—and not for the first time—that it was a death trap. Between the opium's lethality, the fact that anyone there would cut a man's throat for his portion, and the poppy-fueled haze as people smoked pipes in a veritable tinderbox; the place was terrifying. If Ettinger had been in a different frame of mind, he'd have sent the former inspector. But Ettinger wasn't himself and had not been for some time. *If wishes were horses, as the saying went.*

Ettinger's recovery from his injuries had been complicated, to put it mildly. In truth, he would never be the same and that fact weighed on them both. But it wasn't the injury that haunted the man now. It was the laudanum that had been doled out to him during his convalescence. Some people could keep that demon at bay, no matter how often they flirted with it. Ettinger had not been so lucky. It had taken hold of him, body and soul. Shaking that curse had nearly been the end of him. Sending him to such a place, to walk headlong into temptation, he might as well ask the man to put his head in the lion's mouth.

When at last he'd made his way through the maze, he found Fish sitting on a silk cushion, surrounded by rich, sweeping fabrics hanging all about him. Draped in silk robes, Fish could have been sixty years old. He could just as easily have been thirty. It was impossible to tell, and Vincent thought the man rather liked it that way. Being enigmatic was simply part of Fish's character. At present, he was like a raja ruling over his own little kingdom.

"You are out of your element," the little man observed. "That is not your way. Your business and my business coexist, but never mingle. Why has the Hound entered the dragon's den?"

"A woman was abducted. A lady. I need to know who did it." He didn't mince words. It wasn't precisely respect they had for one another, but a wary appreciation of the strength of one's opponent. Fish has his own little army, and the man was more than ruthless.

Fish smiled enigmatically, his little black mustache twitching from the movement. "Such activities are under your command, are they not?"

Vincent refused to sit on the cushions on the floor. That would leave him vulnerable to attack and he trusted no one. "No one came to me. I would have declined to sanction such an action even if it had been brought to me."

Fish smiled in that enigmatic way he had and replied, "Ah, yes. Your rule about harming women. What a curious code for a man who owns brothels."

No one knew exactly where Fish was from. It could have been somewhere in Asia or Eastern Europe. Or he might simply be a very good actor from Yorkshire. Just one more thing about him that was impossible to guess and most likely intentionally so.

No one would ever know how much of Fish's appearance and manner were natural and how much was simply a clever disguise and affectation.

"I do not own brothels," Vincent corrected. "I employ certain men who provide security to brothels at a price. And those brothels abide by the parameters I have set to ensure no one is being exploited unduly. There is a difference. Regardless of my rule, I would not have permitted this particular action. The abduction of the young bride of a peer attracts more attention than anyone from our world can afford."

Fish's smile faded instantly, and his eyes lost the slightly faraway look that he wore to appear mystical and otherworldly. Suddenly he was quite shrewd in appearance. "That is more trouble than any of us need. I have heard nothing yet, but I will consult with the others and send word on what I learn."

The others. Fish owned an entire network of such hellholes as they one they currently conversed in. Opium dens had sprung up all over London. "You do that. In the meantime, Ettinger will be looking into things. If you see him, you can tell him what you know."

Fish nodded his head.

There were no goodbyes, just as there had been no hellos. They were not friends, after all. Fish held dominion over the opium dens. Vincent wanted no part of that trade, but they had an agreement. He and Fish respected one another's territory and one another's claims. And when necessary, they did favors for one another. But when it was done, he always felt a bit dirtier for it.

Pausing before he exited, Vincent didn't bother to look back as he spoke. "And Fish?"

"Yes?"

Vincent spoke softly, not wanting to be overheard by anyone who might be listening, "No opium for Ettinger. Even if he asks." With that, Vincent did turn his head to meet the other man's gaze. "Let's call it a professional courtesy, all right?"

Fish nodded in agreement. "So it is, Hound. So it is."

Satisfied, Vincent exited through the maze of curtains, doing his damnedest to block out all the sights, sounds, and smells. Back on the street, he hailed a hack. It was time to put Ettinger back to work, even if the man didn't know it yet.

Chapter Twenty

It was too early in the morning to be yelled at. Vincent was rarely out of bed before the early afternoon. But since he rarely found his bed until after dawn, that worked well. Now, being thrust into the middle of a singularly troubling abduction and investigation into the murders of several women, sleep was becoming a much-desired commodity.

Being haunted by dreams of Honoria Blaylock's naked form spread out before him to ravage as he pleased certainly did not help matters at all. Cursing under his breath, he considered whether or not he was capable of knocking Ettinger on his ass. Given the other man's Titan-like stature, that was debatable. Regardless, he was too tired to attempt it at the moment.

Settling back in his chair, Vincent let him rant. He'd sent a messenger to the man just as he was closing down the club, which would have made it roughly four in the morning. No doubt he'd woken Ettinger with it and now he was here to take his due. There'd be time enough to sway him to his way of thinking after his temper had been spent.

"I'm not your bloody errand boy to be summoned at your whim. I have a business now—a legitimate one—of my own. I am not beholden to you for the scraps you toss at my feet!"

Vincent stared at Ettinger, his expression pointedly blank as the former inspector railed. He'd expected refusal, of course.

Ettinger had been threatening to quit working for him since the day he had begun working for him. And yet, more than a decade later, here they were.

"Furthermore, you are to blame for my change in careers! If not for you and your inability to refuse any request to embroil yourself in other people's dramas and disasters, I'd still be happily working for Bow Street. Instead, I'm now a clientless private inquiry agent with only one good arm, and I've pissed in chamber pots bigger than my current office!"

When Ettinger had finished, Vincent considered the idea that Ettinger might blame him for the career change. It wasn't untrue, but it also wasn't as dire as the man made it sound. "You are right. It is my fault. I dragged you into the mess with Highcliff and Bechard. If I hadn't, you'd still be working for Bow Street. But *not* happily. You hated it, if I recall. You kept that position as long as you did because it was useful in our other endeavors and profitable. *Because I made it profitable for you.*"

Ettinger's expression darkened, his black brows sinking low over his eyes as he all but growled, "Bugger yourself."

"I have a proposition for you now... a profitable one. It would dramatically improve your reputation and might even earn you more than one paying client for your new endeavor as a private inquiry agent. And it would certainly help you to afford an office larger than a piss pot," Vincent continued, ignoring Ettinger's foul mood. For several months the man had languished in an opium den, consuming enough essence of the poppy to kill him and several others besides. That was one of the many reasons that Ettinger's clothes were hanging off his thinner but still impressive frame.

Vincent had intervened six weeks prior, sending Stavers and several other able-bodied men to drag the man out of it and put him to rights. Had he not done so, he knew that Ettinger would not have been standing before him now. Since then, the investigator had been in a foul temper. "I had initially asked you to look into the murders of the prostitutes in Soho."

"And I told you I'm done with that. I got the information you asked for by talking to contacts at Bow Street. I have nothing else to offer!"

Vincent continued as if Ettinger hadn't spoken. "Most of them were Nell's girls. The last few had taken to servicing their clients on the side to keep more of their earnings."

"Well, there you have it," Ettinger said, throwing his hands up in exasperation. "Nell did them in. Case closed."

On the verge of losing his patience, Vincent insisted, "It wasn't Nell. I spoke with her."

"And abbesses are known for their honesty?" the former Runner asked derisively.

A muscle ticking in his jaw as he tried to hold his temper, Vincent explained, "Nell demanded a bigger cut of the girls' income. That's why they were on the street. And Sally Dawson doesn't work for Nell at all. You remember Sally, don't you? And her four children?"

Ettinger's lips firmed and a muscle worked in his jaw. "I remember Sally. I remember all of them. Get to your point."

"Her oldest boy had been working with a lamplighter. He heard his mother calling for help and went to see. The attacker ran away."

Ettinger stopped pacing. It was a sign that he was finally ready to listen. "How did you find that out?"

Vincent shrugged. "I went straight to the source. I spoke with Sally's son. I didn't want to bother her under the circumstances."

"That's not what I meant and you know it. Who brought this to your attention?"

"Stavers," Vincent hedged.

Ettinger merely lifted one dark brow. It was a look he typically reserved for suspects that he was questioning... or threatening.

"I found out about Sally from Honoria Blaylock. And it's her sister who has been abducted."

Ettinger was back to pacing. "Of course it was her. Who else could cause this much trouble? She's the reason you were at Georgie's letting all comers take a shot at beating the piss out of you."

Vincent slammed his hand down on the desk, the sharp crack rending the air. "Ten women, Joss. Ten. I can't look into that and try to find Lady Ernsdale. So you choose which of those mysteries you wish to solve."

"Lady Ernsdale . . . the missing do-gooder sister or the doxies she pities? All at the behest of another do-gooder woman who stirs up more trouble and discord for you than a damned cyclone," Ettinger mused.

Vincent bristled. It was one thing for *him* to take exception to Honoria Blaylock's activities. It was quite another for someone else to criticize her. "Yes . . . but that is an unfair characterization of them. My understanding is that they both are thought very highly of by the women they help, and their actions are not motivated by any desire for recognition." He realized precisely how priggish he sounded the very second he'd finished speaking.

Ettinger shook his head. "It's been a year and she's still in your head."

"Yes, she is. But I've offered my assistance and I mean to give her answers. So take your pick . . . and no, that isn't a request. I may owe you, Joss, but you owe me too. It's time to collect."

Ettinger cocked his head to the side for a moment, considering. Then he said, quite simply, "No."

"No?" Vincent's voice thundered with anger. Incredulously, he demanded, "You are refusing to take a paid case? Contrary to what you'd have me believe, I know you have had a dearth of clients."

"I'm not refusing," Ettinger said with an exasperated shake of his head. "They are not separate cases."

His temper was still riding high, but Vincent didn't immediately discount the theory. "Why aren't they?"

"Four women attacked in the last month. Three dead, one near death. Six others in the months before that. And now a woman who routinely interacts with all those women—benevolently, I might add—is missing. How could they not be connected?"

"And the ransom demand?"

"I don't have all the answers . . . yet. But I cannot imagine, given your moratorium on any attacks on women in the areas you govern, that there would be two individuals defying your edicts. Especially those governing the safety of Mrs. Blaylock and all her compatriots. Different motives perhaps, but very likely it is the same perpetrator . . . or perpetrators. No guarantee that it's only one, after all," Ettinger proposed.

It made as much sense as anything did to him at that point in time. And he'd learned to trust Ettinger's instincts. The man understood crime and criminals perhaps better than he did. "You'll let me know if you find anything?"

"You'll do the same."

Vincent nodded. "Since you're a bit missish about actually breaking the law, you should probably go. I'm about to violate several. If it's fruitful, I'll send word."

Chapter Twenty-One

ONLY AN HOUR after Ettinger's departure, Lord Ernsdale sprawled on the floor of Vincent's study. The peer's soft hands were visibly scuffed from the rough nap of the carpet. He'd been shoved there by two burly men in rough clothing—the same men who had bent sent to pluck him from the street outside his club. Thankfully, he hadn't put up too much of a fight or caused a ruckus as the men each brandished a weapon. Though given their burliness, such armaments were hardly necessary. He likely would not have resisted. But they had done their job: retrieve him, speak as little as possible, and bring him to the club. Yes, they had fulfilled their assigned duties admirably.

It was Vincent's experience that allowing the mark to build everything up in their own mind before any confrontation occurred would skew the encounter in his favor. Off balance and nervous, they would give away far more than they would have in a civil conversation during regular social hours.

"What is the meaning of this?" Ernsdale shouted.

"Mind your tongue and your tone," Vincent snapped. He let a bit of the street into his accent, just enough that Ernsdale would fear him but also hold him in disdain. "You're in my 'ouse, Ernsdale. I will ask the questions."

"As I am only in your house because you dragged me here, I hardly think it matters," the man complained petulantly.

At his grousing, the two men who had brought him there hoisted him up again and placed him, none too gently, in the chair that faced Vincent's desk.

There was silence for the longest time. Vincent scribbled notes in his ledger, paying no attention to the man at all. It took approximately a minute for Ernsdale to begin fidgeting. They hadn't even reached the two-minute mark when the older man began to shout.

"What is the meaning of this? I demand to know why I've been dragged here like some sort of common criminal!"

Placing his pen in the receptacle on the ink stand, Vincent leveled a cold stare at the peer. And then, with complete conviction and no small amount of menace, he uttered two words. "I know."

"Whatever you think you know, you are wrong," Ernsdale said with a sniff of displeasure.

"I know you got a ransom note for your wife," Vincent said, his tone low and warning as he tapped the hilt of a dagger-like letter opener on his desk.

Ernsdale's florid face paled suddenly. "My wife is not missing. She simply failed to come home. I think her having absconded is a more likely explanation. She most certainly has not been abducted," he insisted with a dismissive sneer that appeared somewhat overdone. Worthy of Drury Lane, even. "I received a *ruse* of a ransom demand. She requires a great deal of attention, my young wife, and will go to any lengths to get it!"

The man was an absolute prick, Vincent thought, as he crossed his arms and leaned back in his chair. With a speculative look, he continued his questioning. "Doesn't sound like you like her much, this young, pretty wife of yours."

"She's a woman," Ernsdale said dismissively. "All women are prone to such antics. They lack the ability to reason as a man does. One must simply treat them as one would treat a child and go on. But I do not dislike her. She serves her purpose."

"Treat them like a child . . . and don't spare the rod?"

Ernsdale shrugged. "The law is perfectly clear and reasonable about my rights in regard to striking my wife, sir. When it is required, I do so... but I am a generous and understanding husband."

"So you and Lady Ernsdale are on good terms?"

"As good as any married couple can be," Ernsdale snapped defensively.

"Then you and your lovely young wife weren't screaming at each other like fishmongers a few nights back? And she wasn't using powder and paint to cover up bruises on her face from your fair and reasonable treatment of her? Or did someone lie to me 'bout that?" He let the cockney creep in just a bit more. It was best, after all, if Ernsdale thought he was smarter than Vincent. He'd be more inclined to give something away. So Vincent let the question hover between them. Ernsdale was the first to look away.

After a long and uncomfortable silence, Ernsdale grumbled, "What happens between my wife and me is not your concern."

"It is when she goes missing. And when I've been asked by a concerned family member to help locate the missing wife of a lord. You might be exempt from the law, Ernsdale, but you're not exempt from me. If I find that you've caused any harm to your lovely wife, I'll see you pay for it with flesh, blood, and bone. Understood?"

"I understand," Ernsdale snapped.

"Then you tell me what I want to know. Did she have a lover?"

"Possibly. Likely, in fact," Ernsdale replied. "No doubt that's who she has run off with. Now I am left behind to look like a fool."

"Is that your only worry? How it makes you look? Seems to me, Ernsdale, that you'd be worried about your bride. And you owe money. A lot of money and to a lot of people—I'm one of them. But you didn't know her wealth was all tied up in trusts, did you? That you'd only be able to get hold of it a piece at a time... unless she died, of course. Then it'd come to you in one fat payment, wouldn't it?"

"I have not murdered my wife!"

"No, but you will not be overcome with grief if someone does it for you," Vincent observed. Dropping all semblance of his cockney accent, he went on. "The kidnapping is genuine—not a ruse at all. Neither was it perpetrated by you or her ladyship. She has been abducted by persons unknown and you are perfectly willing to let them murder her because it solves all of your problems. All of the restrictions on her fortune will be lifted and you'll have the lot of it—all at once."

Ernsdale blinked in surprise, digesting the information that had just been hurled at him like a volley of shot. Rather than address the accusations about himself, he seized on one slightly less pertinent point. "Why do you suddenly sound like a gentleman?"

Vincent smiled, "I'll sound how I want when I want. It served my purpose to be underestimated by you initially. It's the way of your class, after all . . . to look down on those from the streets."

"What would you know of men of my class?" Ernsdale sneered. "You're nothing but a filthy guttersnipe who managed to amass enough coin to put on airs!"

Vincent didn't disagree with him. He simply smiled—but it was not a warm expression. Indeed, Ernsdale would have to be a fool to miss the threat in it. "I will let you go for now, but if I discover through the course of my investigation that you have lied to me, that you are in any way involved in her ladyship's abduction, I will make you regret it. That is a promise And unlike you, sir, I keep my promises."

"How do I know that you are not her lover? That this isn't some sort of confidence game?" Ernsdale challenged.

"You don't. But I can tell you, as lovely as she is, your wife holds no interest for me beyond seeing her safely returned to her life. Further, I will say that women as beautiful and as sought after as your young wife do not kidnap themselves for attention," Vincent insisted. Stranger things had happened, but he bloody well knew that wasn't what was occurring this time. He hadn't dragged Ernsdale here without cause, after all. "I know a dozen men right now who would happily give her all the attention she desires. I am simply not one of them."

Ernsdale's face twisted into a bitter mask. "How dare you speak to me that way about my own wife! And whatever you may be alluding to—it's vile."

The man's outrage rang false, but that interpretation might have been the result of Vincent's own suspicions. Long before he'd agreed to be party to the investigation into the events surrounding the disappearance of Lady Ernsdale, he'd had his eye on Lord Ernsdale. The amount of information he had gathered about the man thus far had given him an inkling of what some of the issues in the Ernsdale's marriage were.

Vincent warned, "I dare what I like, *my lord*. You are in my domain, and there is no place I cannot reach you. If you think your title protects you, you are mistaken."

Ernsdale sneered at him. "You may speak like a gentleman, but you still act like a cockney street tough!"

"I am a cockney street tough . . . and a gentleman. I am whatever the situation calls for, Ernsdale. Remember that and remember it well. Now I want you to tell me what happened the last time you saw your wife."

Ernsdale tensed. "That is none of your concern."

"Were you arguing over love, lust, or money? Those are the only things which would typically incite such passionate disagreement."

"We—I was foxed. I can't say what we argued about. I passed out and have little memory of it. When I awoke, she was out paying her morning calls. Likely to that termagant sister of hers. I left for my club before she was expected to return home. Later that afternoon, the ridiculous ransom demand was delivered."

Vincent had already verified the facts as Ernsdale presented them. Stavers had paid one of the neighboring maids to find out through the effective and efficient grapevine of servants' gossip precisely what had been going on in between the couple. They had argued bitterly over her charitable works the night before. Not because of the money. Not even because of the danger in going to such questionable neighborhoods. Ernsdale wanted to control her because he was afraid. The only question was what did he fear so? But as he'd said, he'd lost consciousness at some point, simply collapsing to the floor and snoring loudly enough to rattle the windows. Then the following morning, as per usual, his wife was gone before he'd even stirred.

"If you receive any further communications from her abductors, you will send them to me."

"I would not dare step foot in this establishment ever again."

Vincent smiled. "You do not have to. You have simply to walk outside and snap your fingers. One of the many people I have watching you at present will come and retrieve it."

Ernsdale's face purpled with rage. "I will see you ruined for this."

"You are welcome to try," Vincent stated simply. "Others have and failed." With that, Vincent waved his hand and the same men who had dumped Ernsdale unceremoniously on the carpet then grabbed him by the arms to haul him out once more.

Honoria would know, he thought. She would know what the source of contention and conflict between her sister and Ernsdale truly was. If there was one thing he knew about women, it was that they confided to one another very intimately. Sisters were even more inclined to share such secrets.

"Stavers!" Even as he bellowed the man's name, Vincent was dashing off a note.

The butler appeared in the doorway. "Yes?"

"Have this note delivered to Mrs. Blaylock by the usual method."

Stavers hesitated. "Is this wise?"

"What?" Stavers hadn't questioned any decision he'd made from the age of fifteen on.

"Mrs. Blaylock is a point of consternation for you—a distraction that you do not need."

It was debatable, Vincent thought, whether he needed her or not. He certainly felt as though he did. She seemed as necessary to him now as air and water. That alone should have prompted caution. But it was too late for that.

"Secure a room at Mivart's for this evening. The usual sort of arrangements. Will you need someone else to help you with the club tonight?"

"No. I can handle it. There's no swaying you from this course, is there?"

"What course is that? She's hardly the first woman I've bedded," Vincent stated dismissively. Even to his own ears it rang false.

"You can lie to others, boy. You can even lie to me. But don't lie to yourself."

It was murmured gently—not as colleagues, but as mentor and protege. Father and son. Stavers was the closest thing he'd ever had to a father, at any rate. He'd taken him in and taught him to survive. As their position in the strata of London's classes altered, Stavers had taken on the guise of servant, but they both knew it was far from the truth. The club, the veneer of sophistication—that had been Stavers' idea all along. Vincent, in his youth, had simply been pretty enough to pull it off—to move amongst the upper classes without anyone questioning whether or not he belonged there. Stavers had always been—would always be—more mentor than servant. Some might even go so far as to call him the mastermind of their operation.

"No, Stavers. There is nothing you can do to sway me from this course. I'm like a boulder rolling down a hill at this point. Is that honest enough for you?"

"You're in over your head with her," the older man observed, his worry evident. "You have been from the first night you met her. I knew it then. I knew it every time I had a note delivered to her house. This—whatever it is—has been building for the past year and a half. I suppose there's nothing to do but let it run its course."

"Yes. Indeed. Run its course." Ease the fire in his blood and the obsessive thoughts of her that had driven him half mad.

The older man nodded. "All right then. I'll make the arrangements."

Chapter Twenty-Two

It was afternoon, not quite teatime and hours still until dinner. Honoria was attempting to act as though her life hadn't been turned entirely upside down. Keeping herself busy held the worst of her fears for Henrietta at bay, so she sat in the morning room, answering correspondence and planning the itinerary for the next meeting of the reform society. It was a slow and tedious process as she had to read everything at least four times to make sense of it.

Thus far, every single letter she had sent out to various doctors had gone unanswered or had resulted in outright rejection. Some of those rejections had even resulted in the doctors informing her that she was bound for Hell due to her wickedness.

Providing adequate medical training to the ladies who volunteered at the charity hospitals on how to treat the poor, ill women who came in from the streets without contracting those illnesses themselves—that was the sin which would see her in Hell. They should hardly have taken such exception to it as anything that aided them in preventing the spread of diseases amongst working girls would ultimately protect gentlemen such as themselves from contracting them.

Perhaps she was taking the wrong tactic. While an actual physician would have been ideal as an instructor, there were many times when she had found midwives to be far more knowledgeable and certainly more compassionate.

The front door of the house banged open. She heard the footmen stammering but it was clear that whoever had forced their way into the house was someone to whom they felt a distinct subservience. Who could possibly have the gall to simply burst into her house in that way? Within seconds, her question was answered.

The pocket doors to the morning room slammed open, rattling the walls so forcefully that a painting fell to the floor. Her brother-in-law, Lord Ernsdale, stood there, breathing heavily and on the cusp of full temper. "What have you done?"

He was a cruel man. Honoria knew that without question. Her sister had told her often enough about it. But his cruelty was not only of a physical nature. He also chose to attack the spirit with hateful, hurtful words in an unending stream. It was that, more so than even his heavy hands and ready fists, which was crushing her sister's spirits. The light and joy that her sister had always exuded had diminished day by day since her marriage to him.

Raising one eyebrow, she queried, "I presume you mean my decision to treat my sister's abduction as an actual crime and ask for intervention?"

"You know damned well that is why I am here. I will not tolerate interference in this matter!" There was something in his voice, a hesitancy that revealed far more than he might have realized. Lord Ernsdale was afraid, and it wasn't his wife's kidnappers that inspired his fear. It was the man currently investigating it.

Honoria's expression remained neutral as she suggested, "Think about the source of that intervention, Lord Ernsdale. Do you really want me telling him that you came here today and made threats?"

"I've made no threats," he denied instantly.

"But isn't that why you are here? To threaten me into submission? To make me leave the matter alone and wait for

Henrietta's body to be discovered? That's your plan, isn't it—allowing someone else to do the work you yourself lack the courage to do? Typical," Honoria sneered. She knew better than to show any fear to a man like him.

"You consort with that baseborn bastard. Have you no shame?" Ernsdale all but spat the words at her in accusation.

Whether it was true or not, it was no concern of his. Honoria no longer answered to a man—to any man, baseborn bastard or otherwise. "I am a widow of independent means, Lord Ernsdale. I consort when, where, and with whom I please. You have no say in the matter. And your opinions matter to me not at all. Now, I'd very much like for you to leave. The very sight of you, knowing how cruelly you have treated my sister and that you are cowardly enough to simply wait for others to end her life rather than intercede, makes me ill."

"I'll not be ordered around by the likes of you, Honoria Blaylock!"

Honoria rose to her feet and walked to the still open door. Peering into the hall, she offered a reassuring nod to the footman who was staring worriedly at the morning room and the raised voices that had been coming from within. She would not show fear. Not to anyone. "Wallace, fetch James and then the two of you will escort Lord Ernsdale from the premises. He is not to be admitted again under any circumstances."

"Yes, ma'am." The young man immediately turned to do as she had asked.

"You wouldn't dare! I am a lord," Ernsdale insisted. "My title goes back to the time of Henry VIII. You and your sister are nothing but middle class upstarts! I should never have agreed to marry her."

"We may be middle class upstarts, but we had something you, with your illustrious family history, did not. We had money. You were rewarded very handsomely for marrying my sister, as my own husband was rewarded for marrying me. You need not act as if you are the wronged party. With a beautiful, young wife and a hefty fortune at your disposal, you've come out of this rather well."

At that moment, Wallace and James entered the room. The two footmen were both very mild mannered but they were still significantly larger, younger, and much more physically capable than Ernsdale could ever hope to be.

"Do not touch me," he warned them. "I will leave of my own accord, but be assured, Mrs. Blaylock, that I will not tolerate further interference from you in this matter. She may be your sister, but she is my *wife*. The law is on my side."

"Morality is not," Honoria snapped. "And I believe that justice—that goodness—in this instance will prevail. If that is so, my lord, then you have no chance. I will do as I please and you may also. But be prepared to explain yourself to all of society when it is learned that your wife was abducted and you did nothing to bring her home."

Ernsdale tossed one final menacing glower in her direction before walking past the footmen and exiting the house.

"We would have thrown him out, ma'am."

Honoria smiled. "I know that, Wallace. But I am grateful it did not require a physical altercation. He is a lord, after all. And as much as it pains me to admit when he is right, the law *is* on his side, even when he is trespassing in my home."

"What shall we do if he returns?"

Honoria's jaw firmed and her chin came up stubbornly. "He will not. I will make certain of it." Even if it required putting herself in a position of greater obligation to the Hound of Whitehall.

James the other footman added, "He won't get in again, ma'am. A note arrived for you while he was here. I was hesitant to interrupt."

"Bring it in. And thank you both."

The young men left, and a moment later, James returned carrying the missive on a silver salver. Taking it cautiously from the tray, almost as if it would bite, Honoria did her best to still the trembling of her hand. Just because she hadn't shown her fear to Ernsdale didn't mean she hadn't felt it.

Looking down at the very expensive parchment, neatly folded and sealed, she knew instantly that it was from *him*. Her direction had been written in a scrawling hand that was very familiar to her. She had seen it often enough during the past twelve months. Honoria dared not hope that Henrietta had already been found, but it wasn't unreasonable to presume that he might have discovered something of note.

Breaking the wax seal, she scanned the contents.

Change of plans. Mivart's at seven o'clock. I'll send a carriage.
V.

A glance at the clock on the mantel showed that it was just past two. In truth, she was glad that the appointed time of their assignation had changed. It lessened the span of time she had to endure the agony of anxiety about what was to come.

Her anxiety was twofold. The intimacies they had shared before remained permanently at the forefront of her mind. How could they not? But fear was there, as well. Fear that her ability to actually enjoy lovemaking had been some sort of fluke. That she'd built it up in her mind so much that the reality of it had been obscured entirely.

There were other fears, as well. Fear that it would be as perfect and wonderful as it had been before. Because that left her vulnerable to him in a way that struck terror in her heart.

THE SHIP WAS not as silent as she had first imagined. If she laid perfectly still in the darkness and listened intently, Henrietta could hear movement. Footfalls. The low hum of conversation in passing. The hatch obviously opened into a corridor of some sort. While she couldn't be entirely certain and her familiarity with ships was somewhat limited, she thought she was in some sort of hold. That meant she was below deck. She could hear water lapping at the wall to her left which meant she was just at or below the water line—hence the lack of windows. That also meant it should be relatively quick to reach the upper deck and escape.

So what was above her? The deck? Or perhaps it was the captain's cabin? It would make sense if that were the case. If not everyone aboard ship knew of her presence, then keeping her directly below the cabin of one of the responsible parties—for surely the captain would be aware of all that happened on his ship—would help them to further conceal her imprisonment there. If that were the case, it would complicate her escape.

She could not make an attempt to escape during hours when people were moving freely about the ship. But if she waited until everything was entirely silent and they were all likely abed, then the space directly above her might be occupied and her efforts could be overheard.

"I will not die in this dark, dirty little place," she whispered to the empty room. "I have not endured the misery of marriage to Arthur Dalgleish, *Lord Ernsdale*, only to have my life end this way."

Speaking had been a mistake. It made her aware of just how thirsty she was, how dry and cracked her lips felt. She wondered how long it had been since she'd had water or food. Bruised and battered from the abduction itself and now she had hours, possibly, to lie in the dark and fight off the fear that threatened to paralyze her.

A thump above her followed by a muffled curse. *One. Two. Three. Four. Five.* Another sound, a sharp order called out at such a distance that she would not have heard it had she not been listening for such things. Then she began to count again. She was searching for the pattern, figuring out what was happening above her to know when she might be able to begin moving again and make her escape. *If she could make her escape.* She had not finished her exploration of the small space in favor of staying quiet. Perhaps she might find a weapon yet or some other means which might allow her to escape. Could she climb that ladder with her hands bound? Possibly, but what would become of her once she reached the top? She needed her hands freed before she did anything else.

Chapter Twenty-Three

HONORIA'S WARDROBE WAS limited. She had nothing in it that was not black. Fresh from her bath, she selected the one gown that she thought might be most suited to her plans for the evening.

She had never worn it. It had been hanging in her wardrobe for more than a year with her intent to have the somewhat scandalous neckline altered. After all, it was difficult to give the appearance of determined widowhood when one displayed nearly their entire bosom. It was perfect for the evening ahead of her.

It was a bit redundant to dress for seduction when the course of the evening was essentially set, but it was less about seduction than about giving herself every advantage. The balance of power was not in her favor, and she desperately needed to change that.

With the gown chosen, she sat down at her dressing table and surveyed her hair. Pulling the pins from the tight and severe chignon that she favored, it fell gently around her shoulders. The unexpected benefit of the tightly coiled coiffure was that it had left her hair nicely curled. Carefully, she began to loop coils of it, pinning them in place until she had achieved the illusion of a precariously contained curls, with a few tendrils left to frame her face and draw attention to the slenderness of her neck—and the expanse of flesh below.

It was the style she had worn when she was younger, before

her father had forced her to marry Edwin. Before every bit of joy and hope inside her had been squashed beneath her husband's oppressive thumb. For ten years, she'd borne the weight of his constant criticism, and on more than one occasion, the back of his hand. She'd been consumed by the overwhelming dread that came from living in constant fear of him.

Over time during the course of their marriage, she'd stopped worrying about whether or not she looked pretty, whether her gowns were flattering—because any efforts she made were met with derision or jealousy. He would call her a fat cow or a dowdy mouse of a woman, and in the next breath shout at her for flirting with someone or accuse her of all manner of wickedness. Being accused of infidelity when she rarely left the house outside her husband's company or being told she looked frumpy or portly or like a trollop—that had been her daily existence, just as it was now Henrietta's.

Her heart stuttered once more. It had been Henrietta's. *Had been*. She didn't know if her sister would live to endure even another day of Ernsdale's miserable company, and that thought, along with the memories of her husband, darkened her mood considerably.

Determinedly shaking off the gloom such thoughts induced, Honoria then selected her jewelry. She did not have many pieces. Edwin's mother had kept most of her things and passed them to his sister. But she did have a lovely pearl choker with a carved onyx cameo.

It dawned on her that she was getting ready to meet *him*, Vincent Carrow, in much the same way she had readied herself for her wedding night.

Honoria's hands, still gripping the necklace she'd intended to put on, fell to her lap. She sat there in the silence of her room, contemplating what she had agreed to and what it would cost her in the end. She wasn't afraid of him. She wasn't even afraid of the act that was to come, though she certainly had never been given cause to enjoy it. What she feared more than anything was losing herself. Could she give him her body and keep her deeper feelings somehow sheltered from him? She didn't know. He left her... unsettled. It was a poor description but the only one she could seize upon. There was something about Vincent Carrow that left her strangely defenseless, and that was utterly terrifying.

Guilt hovered on the periphery of her thoughts, as well. She shouldn't even be thinking about her own pleasure or her own happiness when her sister's fate remained so terrifyingly unknown. Was she a horrid person for that?

With those uncomfortable doubts still weighing heavily on her mind, she finished her toilette and made her way downstairs to await the carriage.

VINCENT HAD MADE arrangements with one of the hotel's very discreet employees to bring Honoria to his room both immediately and quietly. When the door to the suite of rooms opened, courtesy of that same employee, Vincent did not even bother to look up. He didn't have to. Out of habit, he'd positioned himself so that he could have a full view of the room, and conveniently placed mirror offered him a view of the door.

She was swathed in a heavy black cloak, the hood pulled up to conceal her face. But he'd know it was her regardless. He could smell the soft, subtle scent that she favored—lemongrass and a hint of lavender.

The door closed behind her and then she pushed back the hood of her cloak. She looked different. Softer. Younger. But confident in a way that only came from a woman understanding her own beauty and the power she wielded with it. Her confidence had been hard won, he knew. The not so dearly departed Mr. Blaylock had certainly done everything in his power to strip her of it and somehow, despite everything, she had prevailed.

Getting up from the chair he'd occupied, Vincent then moved

to the small settee before the fireplace. The table that had been placed there was draped in fine linens. Another of Fortnum & Mason's exquisite hampers had been procured. Undoubtedly the work of Stavers who, despite his appearance, was something of a romantic. One need only ask his ladylove from the Darrow School, the normally churlish Mrs. Wheaton who all but glowed in the man's presence.

"Come in. Sit down. I will not bite," he said. *Not yet... but soon.*

She did step inside then, hesitating for just a moment before she moved away from the closed door. She paused only long enough to turn and remove her cloak draping it over a small chair positioned near the room's entrance. Then she turned and faced him.

Her confidence was well deserved.

From the moment he'd first seen her, he'd thought her beautiful. But what he understood now, seeing her in her current state, was that beauty was a weapon she wielded as effectively as the small sword she'd had the night of their initial encounter. The gown she wore was black, like everything else in her wardrobe. But it showed much more of her than he was accustomed to seeing. The cross front of the gown was deep and wide, the upper swells of her breasts rising above the delicately embroidered trim. At her throat she wore a pearl and onyx necklace. It was unnecessary to his mind. She did not need such ornamentation to draw his eye. In truth, he couldn't look away from her.

And she knew it—that was evident in the way she strode decisively toward the settee. Her commitment to their current course of action was quite obvious. Once she made her decisions, she did not shy away from them.

When she reached the settee, she perched on the edge of the deceptively delicate looking piece of furniture. The parallel there did not escape him, nor did the very pretty picture she made.

He was half convinced women only sat that way because it somehow made the sweep of their skirts on the floor more flattering. It also allowed him to look down at the lush display provided by the décolleté of her dress. Did they practice such techniques under the critical eye of a governess?

The black pooled around her feet. In the dimness of the rooms with only the firelight and a few lamps burning around the perimeter, the stark contrast of her pale skin against the inky blackness of her widows' weeds was both startling and beautiful. He'd seen a sketch of Da Vinci's once. A half completed drawing, it showed a woman's face in three quarter profile and the barest hint of a gown. But the face and the hands had been complete and what a story they had told. She reminded him of that sketch... delicate, feminine hands and a face so beautiful that it defied belief. And yet, like that image, she had the ability to hold men entirely in sway.

"I had a visitor today," she said.

It took a moment for him to process what she had said, so utterly transfixed was he by her appearance. It didn't take a great deal of intelligence to know that had been her plan all along. As strategies went, he had to give credit where it was due. Her methods were infallible. He closed the distance between them, moving nearer to the settee, close enough that he could see the slightest alteration in her expression. She would have been an excellent card player if she had been inclined, he thought. Her ability to reveal only what she wished to was enviable.

"Who was your visitor?"

"Lord Ernsdale," she said, the crispness of her speech an indication of just how fractious the petulant lord had been.

"Of course, he did. I expected nothing less of him."

Chapter Twenty-Four

For the longest moment, Honoria remained silent. Perhaps she was considering the wisdom in giving him even more reason to despise the lord. But at last, she answered, "He was quite perturbed at your high-handedness. He . . . well, he came to threaten, intimidate, and bully me. I gathered it was retaliation for your attempts to threaten, intimidate, and bully him."

When he glanced at her, he could see the fear she had almost succeeded in hiding from him. Most would have missed it entirely, but he was in the business of reading people, after all. His responding flash of anger was surprising only in its ferocity. But the surge of protectiveness he felt—that was shocking. He wanted to find the spoiled, entitled, and utterly useless lord and beat him with his bare hands until he begged for mercy. Sadly, Vincent knew that would take very little effort on his part and would not prove a satisfactory outlet for his temper.

"It will not happen again," he vowed. "He will be dealt with. But I do have to say that, for what it's worth, I do not think Ernsdale had her taken."

She blinked in surprise. "You think he's innocent?"

"Never that. From what he said, I think he did not plan this particular crime, but he is perfectly willing to take advantage of it. This situation solves a problem for him—namely that he doesn't really wish to be married to her."

A puzzled and strangely pleased smile curved her lips. "You went to Ernsdale House and questioned him?"

Vincent crossed his arms over his chest and planted his feet firmly, despite his desire to pace the room. He'd had an instinctual reaction to her question at first, borne of a lifetime of slights, to her startled tone, as if she could not imagine him ever being admitted to the home of a gentleman. But she wore an earnest expression, one that did not hint of mockery. And it was not her way to hold anyone's origins against them. So he shook his head very slightly to clear it and to keep the chip on his shoulder from ruining an evening that he had been looking forward to from the moment it first entered his mind.

"No," he replied softly. "I would never question a man in his own home. It would give him an advantage. I had him brought to the club." He nearly laughed at the thought of Lord Ernsdale letting him step a single foot inside his rarified domain. The man would sooner have taken a pistol ball than to be seen publicly associating with the likes of him. The fact that she did not see it was either a testament to the true goodness of her nature or to her lack of intelligence. And he did not think her unintelligent. It prompted an uncomfortable stirring of conscience.

"Oh . . . did he tell you about the ransom demand? About why he has refused to pay it."

"Only that he'd received one," he replied. "And that his refusal is based entirely on his belief that it is a ruse. He hinted that your sister had a lover with whom she might be conspiring."

Vincent poured her a glass of wine and placed it in her hand. It was a strategic move on his part to let their fingers brush against one another, to see how she responded to that touch. Her quickly indrawn breath was answer enough. "I am sorry that he came to you. It will not happen again. I have information on Lord Ernsdale—information that is entirely separate from anything related to your sister's abduction. I will remind him of his past foibles. That should curb his behavior."

"Thank you for that." She sipped her wine, her eyes widening a bit.

He took a sip of his own and was startled himself. It was potent. Watching her closely, he saw that after a few sips, the rigid set of her shoulders began to soften.

After a moment, she asked, "Do you even care what he said to me?" As she waited for him to answer, she leaned back, lounging on the settee like a painting of an odalisque come to life.

His gaze roamed over her, mapping every line as the black fabric draped over her, the curve of her hip and indentation of her waist clearly defined. "No. Because he doesn't know anything. That was apparent to me this morning when I spoke with him. I do have some questions for you, however."

"You are perfectly welcome to ask your questions, but I cannot guarantee that I will answer." Even slightly giddy from the wine, she sounded sharp.

"It is quite clear that they despise one another. Why did they marry?"

Honoria frowned thoughtfully. "It wasn't her choice. It wasn't his either, I suppose. My father selected our husbands for us, and we were not given the option of refusal. Lord Ernsdale owed him a great deal of money."

"Lord Ernsdale owes everyone a great deal of money," he remarked, to which she nodded in agreement. He watched, fascinated, by the play of lamplight on her shiny, raven hair. Whatever this style was, it looked as if he could remove one single pin and the mass of it would simply fall.

"In exchange for the forgiveness of his debt to my father and a substantial settlement, Ernsdale would marry Henrietta and give my father the thing he craved most—connections amongst the *ton*. Of course, the settlement is long since gone and all that remains is Hettie's marriage portion, which he can touch only in very limited circumstances."

"And he despises her because he sees her as beneath him and is embarrassed by her. Hence why he is so relieved at the thought of her abductors eliminating his humiliation."

"No. I mean, certainly he does despise her and see her as beneath him—but that's not his motivation, at least not entirely. Now that my father is dead and cannot simply reclaim the settlement, he fears that Henrietta will seek an annulment. And he's right to do so because she has every intention of taking that particular course."

Vincent moved to sit down on the other end of the settee beside her. "There are very limited reasons a woman can seek an annulment."

"Their marriage has never been consummated," she sat up, peering into her wine glass in puzzlement. "His refusal of the demand for a ransom . . . well, I think he wants them to kill her because he suspects her plan—our plan—or perhaps because he's already run through her fortune and wishes to find himself another wealthy bride."

It might have been the slight tremor in her voice when she spoke of her sister's potential demise, but for the first time since finding her in his private quarters two nights past, he saw a real crack in her armor. She was not as steely as most believed her to be. Still waters did indeed run deep.

"That's a serious allegation. If that is true . . ." He trailed off, just short of making an accusation that was, as yet, unfounded. He couldn't help but wonder if he was wrong about Lord Ernsdale, if perhaps the man was simply a very good liar. In light of the new information she had just shared with him, it became a legitimate possibility.

Could it be that the young Lady Ernsdale's husband had arranged it all to salvage his reputation and spare himself the indignity of having his manhood brought into question? And the greater indignity of losing out on his young bride's fortune? He knew precisely how large the settlement was that Ernsdale had received upon their marriage. Even the most profligate gambler could not exhaust such a sum in so short a time.

"If he is responsible, I will find out and I will make him pay. Of that you can be certain," Vincent promised.

"Because of our bargain?"

"Because of you," he answered. It was a far more vulnerable answer than he had expected from himself. A glance down at the wine glass in his hand and he wondered what, precisely, Stavers had requested for them. A glance at Honoria's puzzled expression and he knew that it was time to turn the tables a bit. If the wine was making him admit things he wasn't ready to, could it do the same for her? "Why do you continue to wear mourning when I know your husband is not mourned by you at all?"

She looked at him then, her eyebrows lifting and her face a mask of challenge. "I like being a widow. And so long as I look the part, few are inclined to bedevil me by trying to change that status."

"Fair enough," he said. Reaching for the hamper once more, he began to unpack the items inside. Stavers might be a romantic, but he lacked anything remotely resembling subtlety. Strawberries with cream, oysters, figs, pomegranates, chocolates, fresh bread with rich honey and butter—based on the reported aphrodisiacal properties of the foods included, they could have raised a cockstand on a corpse.

"What an unusual assortment," she remarked.

"You have no idea," Vincent replied ruefully. "You have absolutely no idea."

"Why did you save me that night? You didn't have to intervene and yet you did. Why?"

At that softly murmured question, Vincent glanced over at her. She was sitting so primly now, hands folded neatly in her lap, the pale oval of her face so delicately lovely that it was impossible not to be moved but it. Still, he was surprised by what she'd asked. *And why she might have asked it.* It had to be the effects of the wine.

"I liked the way you looked," he answered honestly. "Fierce and beautiful—taking on six grown men with a sword. I suppose I admired you for it."

"But not enough to help me save my sister without a price—a

rather hefty one. Yet you are capable of kindness and generosity. I've seen it—for the past year, I've seen it."

A sigh escaped him. He was exasperated by it all, frustrated, even. He refused to admit to feeling saddened by it. Still that sigh conveyed so many things. "Do not paint me a misunderstood hero, Honoria. That is not who I am. You can be certain that every person I have aided has done something to earn my assistance and protection."

At his answer, he watched the play of emotions over her face. Shock, disappointment, curiosity—they all flashed rapidly before settling once more into a deceptively still mask.

Why did she keep insisting that he was not a villain? Maybe it was because he had not been the only one haunted by that first kiss they had shared, or by the things that had transpired between them in his apartment. In fact, he would have bet money on it.

Perhaps that certainty was why he was willing to take a significant risk now. To be entirely honest and to do something... unexpected. "I saved you that night because it amused me to do so. I did not have to. And while my generosity has its limits, I am inclined to extend it further."

"I don't understand."

"Then I shall endeavor to explain it . . . poorly in all likelihood as I do not truly understand it myself."

Chapter Twenty-Five

HENRIETTA HEARD FOOTFALLS. Heavy booted feet trod directly overhead. In a panic, she rose and scurried back around the room to the spot where she had originally been placed, or as close to it as she could approximate. It was to her benefit for them to think she was still unconscious or to think she was so cowed by them she would not attempt to escape.

Despite her earlier moment of despair, she had not lost all hope. She had just managed to get herself onto the floor. Lying on her side with her hair covering her face, she focused on slowing her breathing. Deep and even, each inhale and exhale was measured.

Above her a hatch opened. The dim glow of a lantern appeared in that opening. A moment later, booted feet appeared on the ladder.

Peering through her hair, watching their steady progress as they lowered themselves into that horrible space with her, she forced herself to remain relaxed. If they were to believe she was still unconscious, it was imperative that she appear limp and still.

If there was one thing she had learned during the course of her marriage, it was the value in allowing men to underestimate her.

"How much did you give her?"

The question was a surprise—not because of its content but

because of the refined speech of the querent. This was not someone from the gutters or rookeries. Whoever he was, he had been raised a gentleman—well educated, well spoken, and likely known to her.

"I don't know," the second man answered. His voice was quite different. There was more than a hint of Yorkshire in his speech. "I didn't exactly measure it, did I? Poured enough down her gullet to keep her quiet 'til we could get her here. Now, even when she wakes, we'll have no trouble with her at all. Not like she can go anywhere."

"No. As I understand it from her husband, she has a terrible fear of water. Keeping her on a ship was the best possible option to prevent escape. You sent the ransom note?"

"I did," the second man replied. "What do we do now?"

"We let him stew for a bit."

The second man laughed nervously. "He's not worried for her. Ernsdale will not condescend to pay for her. Said as much. Couldn't be bothered with it, could he?"

That voice was terrifyingly familiar. One of the footmen from her husband's home, Henrietta realized. But he'd been turned off without a reference several weeks earlier. So how would he know what her husband had said? Because others inside the house were still confiding in him.

"If he doesn't, we'll kill the bitch."

The former footman squeaked in protest. "That's what he wants us to do!"

"Yes, but he doesn't want her body displayed in front of Bow Street Magistrates' Court with a note pinned to her saying that he had her murdered. Not even his lofty title can save him from that."

She could feel him leaning over her. It took every last shred of self-control not to react to his presence.

"Are you certain we didn't give her too much?" The worried footman asked.

The other man, the truly vile one laughed. "I hope not. It's not that I am opposed to killing her, but he may yet demand proof she lives, which would be decidedly inconvenient if she were already dead."

At that point, a booted foot connected with her thigh. The jolt sent her rolling to her back. Knowing that something was expected of her, Henrietta let out a soft groan—mumbled softly as if she were still asleep—and then she settled once more.

"She'll come round," the second man sounded more confident now, his Yorkshire accent thicker and more pronounced the longer he spoke. "Keeping her drugged will keep her cooperative. When she's given food and water in the morning, I'll make sure that it's dosed. That'll keep her quiet until the ship's crew clears out tomorrow. If those mongrels catch wind of a woman on board, she'll wish she were dead. She dies now, we're dead men with her."

"Fine. But not so much next time. Cooperative is one thing. Dead is another. When the money is in hand, then it won't matter either way."

The remainder of their conversation drifted away as they once more climbed the ladder and went through the hatch above. Only when she could hear their receding steps did she get to her feet once more. It was time to finish her examination of the room. Rather than go in the same direction she had at first, she moved the other way, following the perimeter with her hands placed against the rough wooded planks for guidance.

When her hip bumped against the corner of either a crate or a table, she stopped instantly. Running her hands along the edge of it, when she encountered the latch, she knew it was a trunk. Carefully, she opened it and felt about.

It was mostly empty, but in the very bottom, hidden beneath a pile of clothing, was a small knife in a sheath. But she didn't crow with victory. Not yet. Armed did not mean free. She immediately sat down and started sawing at her already loosening bonds. She would have only one chance to escape. Patience was the key. If she squandered it unwisely, her fate would be sealed. All she had to do was wait until the ship had grown silent for the night, then she would make a break for it.

Chapter Twenty-Six

VINCENT STARED AT Honoria for a long moment, poised on the brink of something he would not have expected and had no hope of understanding. What he was about to do went against every instinct he possessed—instincts which urged him to simply take, to seize what he wanted and damn the consequences. But he'd realized that he didn't want to have her because of an obligation. She was too important for that. With her, he wanted to know that she was in his bed because she wanted to be. Not for trinkets or wealth, not for the power he wielded or the protection he could offer. In short, he wanted her to want him—to want him badly enough that not even his low birth and questionable dealings would make a difference.

When she'd walked away from him after—what? Making love was too tame a description for the fiery passion that had burned between them. He wouldn't sully it by just calling it fucking, either. It had involved much more than just their bodies. Regardless of what he cared to term it, having her walk away had been one of the most difficult things he'd ever endured. He'd wanted to keep her with him, to hold onto the peace she'd offered him. With her, he'd felt such a sense of . . . completeness. In a way that he'd never felt such contentment before, he had felt complete that night. The restlessness that was so much a part of everything he had done and everything he had become in his life, it eased in her presence.

He wanted that again. But he didn't want it as a form of payment, wasn't even sure it would come to him at all that way. Surrender to settle a debt would not be nearly as sweet as having her surrender to him because she was overwhelmed with desire of her own, because she wanted him too much to do the right thing, *the wise thing*. There was a bit of pride in it, as well. He didn't want her viewing what happened between them as some sort of *transaction*, even though that's how he'd presented it to her initially. No, he wanted her to *want* him to make love to her, and he would be ruthless in stoking her desire. There would be no denying afterward that she had been not just a willing participant, but an eager one.

"I summoned you because I wanted your company . . . and to discuss what I have learned so far and to set some rules or parameters for our *arrangement*." Broaching that subject, he waited to see what her response was.

"Parameters? I think it's rather simple. You beckon and I rush to your side."

"You're hardly a trained spaniel," he observed drolly.

"No. I am not," she replied sharply. Still, she maintained her seat, back rigid and hands folded neatly in her lap. "But I am on a short leash at present. My options are limited, as well you know. You are, after all, the one who limited them."

He shrugged. It was true. There was no point denying it. Leaning back so that he could see her clearly, he settled against the tufted back of the settee. "It need not be such a chore."

If he hadn't been watching her, he might not have caught the slight in-drawn breath, the way her lashes lowered and the sudden increase of the color in her cheeks.

Without ever raising her gaze to meet his, she asked, "By *it*, I can only presume you mean . . . carnal relations?"

It was uttered so primly that it was all he could not to laugh. After all, he'd seen just how carnal she could be. And in that moment, with that sinful black gown draping her body, she was lush and enticing. Her face, colored from both the wine and a bit of embarrassment, brought to mind another time when he'd seen her cheeks so pink. Laid out before him, her cheeks flushed with passion, her lips red and swollen from his kissed and so sweetly dazed from pleasure—she'd been exquisite.

Biting the inside of his cheek, he nodded. "Indeed, Mrs. Blaylock. That is precisely what I speak of. *Carnal relations*. You enjoyed yourself the other night, did you not?"

Her blush deepened and she looked away. "Must we have this conversation?"

"Oh, yes. We must. Tell me you did not enjoy all that passed between us. I dare you."

Her head cocked to one side, those dark curls sliding over the silken skin of her shoulder. "I told you that I had never found it to be anything but a chore. Certainly not with my late husband. I didn't know—I had no idea that it could feel like . . . that I was capable of feeling what I did with you."

"And yet you have no desire to repeat it."

She shook her head. "That's not . . . it isn't about what I want. Men's desires and women's needs rarely coincide. Women mistake such attentions for affection when, in point of fact, affection and attraction have no relation to one another. I cannot afford to let my judgment be clouded by passion. I will give no man the power to hurt me. Never again."

Vincent had known that her husband could be cold. And it had been hinted that he had been cruel. He would not ask questions that she was not prepared to answer. Not on that subject at least. That particular tale of woe would be saved for another day.

She drank deeply from the glass of wine. Knowing for himself how potent it was, he offered, "Let me get you something to eat."

"I don't want anything, thank you."

Vincent placed choice bits of the various dishes onto a plate for her anyway. That wine would not do well on an empty stomach, and he doubted that she had eaten that day. "As to your earlier point, you can certainly have affection without attraction and vice versa . . . but when you have affection and attraction together, that is something rather magical."

"I wouldn't know." Her tone was completely flat.

He knew that Honoria was a passionate woman if a man took the time to engage both her mind and her body. But ten years of her husband taking his own pleasure while never seeing to hers had clearly done more than just sour her on love. It had made her feel less, somehow. And there was little doubt that Edwin Blaylock had done more than just make her feel small. "Your husband was a bastard, Mrs. Blaylock. If not by his birth, then certainly by his character. I don't imagine that you do know, and I have a very good idea as to why."

"We have finally found a point of agreement, Mr. Carrow."

Vincent leaned back, idly swirling the wine in his glass as he surveyed her. "About my proposition, for you is . . . an alteration, if you will, to our agreement."

<hr />

Honoria could feel her heart racing as it always did in his presence, and memories of his touch assailed her. They heated her skin and quickened her pulse and resulted in a now familiar warmth in certain areas of her body that—well, she had no wish to think of what that signified. Of all the men to have such an effect on her, it had to be him! Could he honestly incite her passions without even touching her? *Yes. Yes, he could.*

"What sort of alteration?" The change in her speech was rather shocking. Not slurred, but certainly slower. And infinitely more flirtatious than she could have ever imagined.

"You are not required to come to my bed . . . but you are required to provide opportunities that I might persuade you there."

To say it was unexpected was beyond an understatement.

After all, he had been the one to establish the terms of their bargain. She had simply agreed to them. Had she not shown up that very night dressed like a woman bent on seducing him or being seduced by him? "I beg your pardon?"

An awful thought occurred to her then. What if he didn't want her? What if, after having time to reflect on the matter, after having already been with her, he found her not as desirable as he once had?

As if he'd read her mind, he stated, "I still want you in my bed, Honoria Blaylock." His voice was pitched low, the words rumbling in a deep baritone that elicited a slight tremor from her. He continued, "But I want you there of your own free will. There will be no question that you are there because you want to be."

She ought to have been relieved to have the transactional condition removed. And yet there was a part of her that resented him for doing so. She had vowed to herself on the death of her husband to never allow any man to bed her of her own free will—because that required a level of vulnerability she would never permit. And she had already broken that vow with him once. The bargain they had struck, even it if wounded her dignity, would still have given her what she wanted while allowing her to hang onto that prideful promise.

Now, it was entirely her decision. If she broke her vow again, it would only be because she wanted to and not because she had to. She would have to be a willing participant. Nay, an eager one. And it had already been proven just how much he affected her, how much he muddled her senses. "To what sort of opportunities are you referring? Please be precise in your answer."

"Nights like this . . . alone, enjoying a meal together, conversation . . . a bit of kissing."

Kissing. With Edwin she had detested it. Not that her late husband had indulged in the practice very frequently. He'd called it distasteful and common. Wet, sloppy, invasive. Those were the words he'd used to describe the practice. And in truth, when he had kissed her, it had been precisely those things. But that hadn't been the case when *the Hound of Whitehall* had kissed her. Nearly every time they had been alone together, they had shared a kiss. And each time she had welcomed it. She was the one who had gone to him, offered herself to him. He made her forget herself. Or perhaps he made her remember who she would have been if Edwin Blaylock hadn't chipped away at her on a daily basis.

But it wasn't just the fact that her willpower failed her entirely near him. It wasn't just falling into his arms—and his bed. Whenever things were difficult or she needed assistance of any kind, he was her first thought, running to him whenever she was in need.

It shamed her that she had allowed such dependence to form, that she had begun to think of him, not as her white knight, but as her own leashed dragon in the shadows. Now she understood that no woman would ever leash him, just as no man would control her. It was foolish to imagine otherwise. Was there any way to get out of it all with both her pride and her heart intact? Would he keep his word if she gave in to her own cowardly impulses and ran away? And if not, could she keep her wits about her and not become some pathetic, lovesick idiot? She had seen debutantes her first year out mooning about after so-called dangerous men: rakes and ne'er-do-wells that were, in truth, nothing more than spoiled little boys. But the Hound of Whitehall, Vincent Carrow, was truly a man. A complicated one who could be both a hero and a villain in the same breath. He was the type of man who inspired more women to utter the phrase "should have known better" than perhaps anyone else ever would.

Ultimately, there was only one way to have those questions answered. Jump into the fray, so to speak. She would have to permit him to kiss her again. To tempt her. And very likely, to best her. Because they both knew she did not have the ability to resist him.

Perhaps it was unwise, but she needed the courage. Honoria lifted her wine glass to her lips once more and drained the contents.

Chapter Twenty-Seven

"I SUPPOSE THAT is a fair compromise," she finally managed to mutter. And it was fair. Logically she could admit that, even if it infuriated her. "Before we begin with that portion of our evening, perhaps we could discuss what you've learned about my sister."

"Very little at present. I did engage the services of a . . . we'll call him a friend. He used to work for Bow Street but has since started his own business as a private inquiry agent. He feels, and perhaps rightly so, that the attacks on the other women and the abduction of your sister might all be connected."

Even through the warm haze created by the wine, the very thought of it made her heart stutter. Those words caused no small amount of panic. "Oh. Oh, dear. Do you think . . ."

"I do believe she is alive. It's not a certainty, obviously. But it is difficult to imagine that they would be so bold or foolish as to attempt a ransom if she were already dead. But at this point, we must simply wait for them to contact Ernsdale again. In the meantime, Mr. Ettinger will be doing what he does best—finding out all the things people wish to keep hidden."

Those words offered her more relief than she'd had since first finding out that Henrietta had been taken. Having worked for Bow Street, Mr. Ettinger would know how the darker elements of London functioned, and if he thought she lived—well, there was no one more qualified to offer an opinion.

He stood to refill her wine glass and then his own before stepping back. He seemed to want to keep some space between them. "I visited another friend today, as well. Someone who certainly knows and hears all in this city. Even he is puzzled about your sister's disappearance. He had no notion of who might be responsible for her abduction. That leads me to wonder if perhaps we are not taking a wrong turn. Perhaps the perpetrators of this crime are not from my world, or even yours. Perhaps they are from your sister's."

Honoria blinked in surprise. It certainly had not occurred to her, though in retrospect, it should have. Ernsdale's enemies posed the greatest threat to her sister, and they were members of the *ton*, after all.

"I am quite ashamed to say that I had not thought it," Honoria confessed.

"Because you think those of your class would never commit such acts?"

The censure in his voice was as unmistakable as it was misplaced. "No. Because I initially only thought of opportunity and not motive. Like myself, Henrietta volunteers in places where she regularly encounters those who engage in criminal activities. But if she was taken in a calculated manner, not simply because she was convenient, then it would likely be someone in the upper classes. And that would make her a pawn and Ernsdale the ultimate mark. Little do they know he cares for her not at all."

"Did the pair of you make a pact to find the worst possible husbands?"

Honoria laughed at that. "Most certainly not. Neither of us had any choice in the matter. Our father made my match. He had money but he had limited connections in society. And that was what he wanted—position. Edwin was his entrée. Ernsdale was his ultimate goal, though—a title. Refusal on our part was not an option, and I've always wondered if it might well have been the same for them." She paused before asking, "How did you determine that she was not taken by someone from the rookeries?"

"No one has any knowledge of her, of the scheme, or who might have perpetrated it. Someone would know something if the kidnapper came from among them. Living on top of one another as people in the rookeries do, there is no privacy and secrets are never truly secret. And I've spoken to everyone I can. Everyone who has any degree of influence in the criminal world," he explained. Even as he did so, he leaned forward and refilled her glass once more. This time, he did not step back. Instead, he settled himself on the settee beside her. It was a curved piece, one that had them facing the fireplace but also still looking at one another. "As that has proffered little success, I am taking a different course now. Ettinger, my associate, will dig into every aspect of your sister's life. He will know who she has spoken to, where she has been. Anyone who has crossed her path will be in his sights. If she can be found, he will be the one to do so."

He'd mentioned the investigator, the former Bow Street Runner, earlier. But now, Honoria seized on one fact in all of that. One fact that would give her the out she so desperately desired. No, not desired. In truth she didn't want an out—she needed one. Desiring him, wanting him, was nothing more than guaranteed catastrophe. "Oh . . . so, then our bargain is at an end. You are not locating my sister. This other gentleman is."

"Our bargain was not for my success but for my assistance," he pointed out, neatly sidestepping her. "It has been provided. This man works for me, and it is at my request he takes on this task."

Honoria wanted to be angry, but the wine had left her feeling impossibly warm. It was difficult to maintain that kind of rigid fury when one's muscles refused to hold any tension at all. "Would you forbid him from working for me?"

"I wouldn't have to. He doesn't work for me because he wants to, Honoria."

The use of her first name wasn't new. But the way he said it had changed. And she liked this new way of saying it, the way his lips caressed each syllable. It was a horrid name. Ugly and terribly out of fashion. How she and Henrietta had both lamented their names as girls! Oh, to be a Caroline or a Juliette. Even something as simple as Sarah or Jane would have been nice. But no. Their father had given them names he thought befitted those who would hold positions of power and influence in society.

Suspicion flared in her mind. "Am I foxed?"

"Perhaps a little," he answered with a smile.

"Did you do that on purpose?"

"No. It is an unexpected advantage, I admit . . . but I will not take liberties. Not even a kiss if it is not freely given. I thought we needed to speak honestly with one another and that it would be much easier for you to do so if you were relaxed. What do you think?"

Honoria looked at her wine glass, half empty for the second time. Abruptly and without hesitation, she raised it and downed the remainder. After the last swallow, she looked at him. With far more reckless boldness than she might have imagined herself capable of, she asked, "Why are you doing this?"

"One kiss . . . a year and a half ago," he said. He leaned in. "I'd like to blame it on our encounter the other night, but my obsession started much earlier. One kiss. That was all it took. Now you occupy my thoughts on a daily basis. You are my demon, Honoria Blaylock, and come what may, I will exorcise you from my blood . . . from my soul."

Of all the answers he might have given, that was the one least expected. It was also the most seductive. What woman, after all, did not want to be the torment of such a formidable man? It gave one a sense of power, and in her world, power was something women were rarely allowed to wield. That sense of it was as intoxicating as the wine.

"You said you would not take advantage. Not even a kiss?" she asked.

"That is what I said," he agreed.

"And if I kiss you?"

His lips curved upward, but only on one side, twisting into a now familiar smirk. "You answer to no man, Honoria. What you do is entirely your choice."

It was a mistake. Without question, it was a terrible mistake. It was also inevitable. Like falling. There was a point, when you had gone so far, where there was no way to stop, only to cushion the impact.

She moved across the expanse of the small sofa. It was less than an arm's length between them, and yet as she closed that distance, it might have been miles. When she was near enough, she rose up onto her knees, so that her face was above his. Then she hesitated.

Looking down, she could see his face far more clearly than she had the previous night. There were faint lines at the corners of his eyes. A few strands of silver glinted in the firelight as they wove through his dark hair. Rough whiskers shadowed his jaw. And she could see that his eyes were not brown or even black as she had imagined, but such a deep blue that the only color she could latch upon was indigo. But that was impossible. No one truly had indigo eyes. And yet the proof was before her.

"My face cannot be that interesting." He offered the comment casually, as if he truly had no notion of how fascinating he was.

From the small scar beneath his left eye, resting high on the crest of his cheekbone, to those vividly colored eyes, she had never seen a man more handsome, even with the fading bruises from his latest pugilistic endeavors. But it wasn't simply that. It was the vitality in him—the intelligence that was so evident in his gaze, and yes, even the ruthlessness. "Then you should look again, Mr. Carrow."

"Vincent," he corrected. "My name is Vincent."

She didn't utter it. Instead, she collected it, tucking it away into her mind like a child's treasure of pretty rocks or pressed leaves. And then she did something she would never have expected of herself. She placed one hand on each side of that very arresting face and boldly pressed her lips to his.

It was more than simply a kiss and she knew it. It was surrender and triumph all it once. She would fall under his spell and give far more of herself to him than she could afford, and she would enjoy every moment of it. Even seeing the disaster that loomed before them, she wouldn't have altered it. It might lead to rack and ruin, but whatever lay between them was undeniable. Unstoppable. Powerful. Honoria realized something—something she might not have admitted, even to herself, without the potency of the wine they had shared. *She wanted to be swept away.* She wanted to, at least once in her life, be a woman who ruled with and was ruled by her passion.

When his arms closed around her, pulling her down onto his lap, the kiss deepened. It shifted into something more than just curiosity, more than just a single gesture. They were on a path now, and that kiss had sparked the journey.

Chapter Twenty-Eight

Honoria awoke with an aching head. Too much wine, she thought. *Or perhaps wine that had been entirely too potent.* An ugly suspicion rose in her mind, but she quashed it quickly. He'd said he would not take advantage of her, and he'd been true to his word. She had kissed him. In truth, she had behaved rather shamelessly. And he, despite an upbringing some would call questionable, had behaved more like a gentleman than any man of her acquaintance who was in possession of a title.

With one hand to her head and another pressed against her stomach which was in very real danger of betraying her entirely, she carefully rose from the bed. Swaying on her feet for just a moment, she leaned against the bedpost for support. Once she felt a bit steadier, she struggled to recall exactly what had transpired. She could recall that he refilled her glass again. And again once more. She'd kissed him again. And, heaven help her, he had kissed her in return. The way she had pressed herself against him in blatant invitation—it galled her to admit that she would gladly have gone to his bed. But he had turned her away.

After that last searing kiss they had shared, he escorted her down the backstairs, bundled her into her cloak, tucked her into a carriage and sent her on her way . . . alone.

One of the maids bustled in then, carrying a tray that bore some foul-smelling concoction. "Mrs. Ivers said to bring this up, ma'am. She said it's the only cure for a night of exce—for a sleepless night."

"Thank you, Molly. Leave it on the table and go. I'll be down shortly."

"Will you be wanting breakfast, ma'am?"

Honoria's stomach rolled treacherously at the mere mention of it. "No. No, I do not think I will. A bath, I think—that will be the place to start."

"I'll see to it," the girl said and then hurried away.

Crossing to the table, Honoria examined the cup and its malodorous contents. The sore head and nausea were a smaller price to pay than ingesting whatever Mrs. Ivers had cooked up. Easing back from the repulsive mixture, she began stripping off the clothes she'd worn the night before. The same clothes she'd climbed into bed wearing that were now rumpled beyond repair.

When she was stripped down to her chemise, she donned a wrapper and waited. She could hear the maids and footmen pouring heated water into the heavy copper tub that was in the bathing room next door. After a moment, once that room had grown silent, she opened the connecting door. The tub of steaming water looked heavenly.

Once she removed her remaining garments and slipped into the scented water, a sigh escaped her. Oh, yes—a bath was exactly what she had needed. The aches and pains began to seep away. But as they receded, memories became clearer. Memories of the questions Vincent Carrow had asked her, of the confessions he had teased out of her regarding the way she and Henrietta had been raised, of how their marriages had been arranged by their father. She'd revealed terrible, shameful secrets from her marriage to him. In short, she'd made herself far more vulnerable to him than she would have by simply giving him her body.

Suddenly, the bath was no longer relaxing. The knowledge that she had been taken advantage of in such a way, that confidences had been teased out of her while he plied her with wine—it infuriated her.

Climbing from the tub, Honoria dried herself briskly. Hurrying through her morning toilette, she completed her ablutions as quickly as possible before donning one of her customary black dresses. It was a round gown, with simple ties at the neck and the waist. Those were typical for her as they allowed her to dress without having to call for a maid. The long, fitted sleeves were slightly puffed at the shoulder and jet buttons closed the sleeves at her wrist. Along with the embroidery at the hem, they were the only ornamentation on her clothing.

Grabbing the same hooded cloak she had worn the night before, she made her way down the stairs and out into the street beyond. She didn't bother with a hack. Instead, she walked, or rather marched, toward the notorious house that served as the Hound's lair. He'd sparked her temper and he would pay the consequences.

HE WAS NURSING an aching head and a stomach that was intent upon reminding him that he was further from his youth than his grave. Stavers had left his foul curative on the desk and Vincent was steadfastly refusing to drink it, just as he always did. There were worse things than the natural consequences of a night of excess.

Leaning back in his chair, he closed his eyes. But only for a moment. A commotion in the corridor had him sitting up, ready for whatever might come.

Suddenly, the door crashed inward, and a wraith of black-draped feminine fury entered the room. "How dare you!"

God, she was magnificent. Even green and suffering from the copious amount of wine they had both consumed last night, she was still exquisite. "This is an unexpected and very loud pleasure, Mrs. Blaylock. What is it that I have done to incite your anger?"

"*What is it?* You know perfectly well what you did! What

precisely was in that wine you gave me?" she demanded.

"Grapes, madame," Vincent replied, his own temper rising at such a vile accusation.

"You intentionally gave me very potent wine last night knowing that I never take strong spirits. And you did so for the sole purpose of taking advantage of my inebriated state," she accused.

"I served you wine . . . the same wine I was drinking myself. And yes, it was potent. More so than I had anticipated. But that is not my doing. I've a bit of a sore head myself this morning as that was rather unexpected. To that end, I shall forgive your insinuation that I behaved in any way that was less than—well, we can't say honorable, can we? I'm not a gentleman and therefore honor is not my purview. Ethical. That's a solid word, isn't it? Even the lower classes can lay claim to that," he said with a sneer.

"Do not twist this to make it appear this is an issue of my snobbery rather than your underhandedness!"

"It was not intentional, Honoria! If I'd wanted you in my bed, I already had your agreement, did I not? Instead, I elected to behave as the gentleman you think me incapable of being—"

"Not just you! There are few men of my acquaintance who actually deserved to be termed such."

Vincent nodded in concession to that point. He could certainly understand why she felt that way given her experiences.

"Very well. But I had you where I wanted you, Honoria, and I gave you a reprieve, a choice," he pointed out. "I would not use spirits to take that away. I want your full consent and your full surrender, with no excuses or rationalizations."

She laughed bitterly. "Is that what you think this is about?"

"What else could it be?"

A shake of her head sent her dark hair bouncing. It was not pinned up as tightly as it normally would have been. Even in their current heated conversation, he could not help but hope it simply fell. Pins skittering across the floor and that mass of dark hair tumbling over her shoulders. He was not unaware of just how pathetic that made him.

"I'm not talking about seduction! I would give you my body before I would ever give you my secrets," she snapped.

"What secrets? I had them already." Getting up from his desk, he moved to the shelves that held the many leatherbound journals and ledgers. He pulled two from the shelves and carried them to her. "Your husband and your father are both on my books, Honoria. There is nothing that they have done that I do not know or could not find out from other sources!"

"Why?"

"Knowledge is power, Honoria. Do you think I'd have been permitted to purchase a house in Mayfair and make it a de facto gaming hell if I didn't hold sway over someone?" He'd used blackmail, extortion, and outright threats to get what he wanted, to build the empire that he currently ruled. To seize control of the criminal ranks, he'd needed a toehold in the upper echelons, as well. From Bow Street to Parliament, they were all in his pocket. After all, what was the point of paying for protection if it didn't protect one from all sides?

And in all that he had done, there was one truth that had been proven to him again and again. Getting power was easy enough. Keeping it was a matter of skill, strategy, and ruthlessness—all underscored with a decided lack of scruples. He'd devoted his life to it. In his current position, in his club, information was a plentiful commodity.

Chapter Twenty-Nine

Honoria felt the weight of those ledgers in her arms. But the heaviness in her heart, the fear that his comments had prompted, threatened to bring her to her knees. "What information did you have on my father? Yes, I could read it for myself, but I'd rather hear it directly from your lips."

His measuring gaze settled on her, searching her face. Then he answered, far more gently than she could have expected, "Your father created those sham investment opportunities that Mr. Blaylock and then, a few years later, Lord Ernsdale bought into. Those failed investments left both men in such terrible positions financially that they were both forced to seek new fortunes the only way men in their positions can—by getting themselves a wealthy wife. He intentionally beggared them in order to force their hands . . . and yours."

"Henrietta and I were not given the option of refusal," she stated. "No protest would be brooked regardless of any misgivings we might have felt. We were threatened with being disowned, with being penniless and turned out into the street. And you knew all this before I ever married him . . . before I was forced to endure every miserable moment of it. You could have prevented it with a word of warning. To me or my father, you might have at least offered some insight that could have altered the course of . . . well, everything."

"No," he denied, quickly. "I had never looked at Ernsdale at all before he was married to your sister. And your husband... well, as I'd said, he'd borrowed money. But beyond ensuring he paid his debts, I had no interest in him. Besides, I doubt anything would have swayed your father from his course. He knew what your husband was before he made the match. It was certainly not a secret."

"When? When did you start digging into all the sordid details of our lives?" she demanded breathlessly. Honoria felt so exposed, so vulnerable to have all the dirty secrets of their lives jotted down in one of his books. Another thing to be bought and sold by him.

"After I met you," he admitted.

"And do you have a minute-by-minute account of my marriage in here? Did you bribe one of the servants to tell you how many times he struck me? How often he came to my bedchamber? Exactly what is it that you know about the hell that was my marriage, Mr. Carrow?"

"I know that if I'd encountered you in that rookery while your husband yet lived, he would not have done so for long." For such violent words, they were uttered very gently.

It was not the answer Honoria had expected. But it was also not a denial that he had personal details that were beyond humiliating. "And I presume you have documented my husband's many indiscretions in here?"

"Among other things. His frequent cruelty to the soiled doves at certain houses, and his refusal to pay at one time or another, resulted in his being banned from many of them. I hardly need to tell you about that, however. I daresay you know his cruelty and his tightfisted ways very well."

Disgusted, Honoria pushed the books back at him. "Take them. I don't want them. I've no need of the secrets they hold. Neither of them has the power to harm me ever again. But I want the truth from you. Can Mr. Ettinger find my sister?"

"If anyone can, it will be Ettinger. I have trusted him with my life and would do so again. That can only be said of one other person."

"And when she's found, is there enough in those books to make Ernsdale grant the annulment?"

"More than likely. I will be certain that it happens, Honoria. That I can promise you."

She nodded. It was difficult to speak. He had upheld his part of the bargain, and he expected little enough of her in return. Her anger at him was fading enough to realize that he was simply a convenient target. A place for her to heap all the hurt, anxiety, and anger she felt in her current powerless situation.

Guilt and shame were ugly and relentless harpies. They hammered away at her. How could she be drinking and embarking on whatever sort of seduction game was afoot between them when Henrietta was missing? When every person in her life would turn their backs on her for abandoning the morality that she preached to others? But that game was the price for his aid and without it her sister had no hope at all. Perhaps her guilt came not from the fact that she was engaging in it, but that she was enjoying it. And that stung her pride more than a little to admit.

"I should not have stormed in shouting accusations," she murmured softly. It wasn't an apology. Her pride would not let her go so far, but it was an acknowledgement of her poor behavior.

"And I should have cautioned you against drinking so much wine knowing that you are unused to such spirits. We have both made our mistakes," he conceded in a tone that was again curiously gentle. "We will not make them again."

"No, we will not. Ours is a temporary arrangement, after all." If she felt a slight pang at that thought, if she might be coming to enjoy his company and, even more to the point, enjoying the excitement he stirred within her, it was of no consequence. He was not the sort of man to ever be a husband. Even if he were, she had no desire to ever again be any man's wife. And being a mistress for some indefinite length of time, beholden and obligated to a man with no promise of a future—that was not for her either. "I should be going."

"No."

"No?"

He was moving then, inching closer to her. It was an instinctive thing, to back up as he crowded her. That was how she found herself with her back pressed against one of the bookshelves and her breasts crushed against his chest.

"What are you doing?" she demanded.

"Altering the terms of our agreement yet again." The words came out almost as a growl. And then his lips were on hers.

This was not the gentle kisses he'd allowed her the night before. It wasn't even the seductive kiss they'd shared the night their arrangement was first made. This was something else altogether and it left Honoria reeling.

Hunger. Need. Obsession. Desire. Those things swirled about her—in her—until everything else faded into nothingness. It was like drowning. Fighting for air, fighting to surface, but ultimately, sinking into it once more because it was so much more powerful than she could ever hope to be.

The last of her coherent thoughts fled. She was left only with the feeling of his lips moving over hers, of the hard press of his body against hers. It was all heat and yearning. Breathless with it and trembling, she could only cling to him as the kiss rendered her mindless.

His lips pulled away from hers, his breathing harsh and ragged. "Why? What is it about you that brings me to the point of madness?"

"I cannot answer that," she admitted. Her voice did not sound like her own. Husky, breathless—she sounded not like a woman seduced, but one bent on seduction. "Whatever is between us, it defies reason and explanation."

His lips twisted with a hint of amusement. "At least there are some points of agreement between us. But you have to go. There are not many guests here in the afternoons, but occasionally someone will drop by to place a wager on something or simply to drink brandy in a place where wives and mothers cannot harangue them. You could be seen and that would be disastrous."

"For my reputation or yours?" she asked.

"Both," he answered ruefully. "Do not come here in daylight hours again, Honoria. I want you. I also want to help you. But, in all seriousness, this would do more than simply ruin you and we both know it."

She knew he spoke the truth, that if she were seen coming and going from such a scandalous location, the *ton* would seize on that and nothing else she said or did in her life would matter. Nodding in agreement, she couldn't stop the sigh of disappointment that escaped her when he stepped back.

Apparently, he'd heard it too. He looked at her with his eyes darkening and a fierceness in his expression that should've frightened her. It didn't. It excited her. It made her want to throw herself back into his embrace.

"Stavers!" he bellowed.

Instantly, the butler appeared. "Yes, sir?"

"Put Mrs. Blaylock in a hack and send her home. Discretion is required," he said simply. His fists were clenched at his side, almost as if he were resisting the urge to reach for her.

"You will come to my home tonight," she said impulsively.

His eyebrows lifted in surprise. "You do not know what you are saying."

"I do. My servants will be in bed by ten. I will unlock the door for you and be waiting in the study," she said.

He stared at her for just a moment. "I will be there before midnight. And, Honoria, I mean to stay until the dawn."

Honoria nodded. Unable to say anything further, she turned on her heel and followed Stavers toward the back exit. For better or worse, the die had been cast and there was no turning back. Strangely enough, that was almost a relief.

Chapter Thirty

THE SUN HAD long since set and night had fallen over London. The lamplighters had no hope of keeping the darkness and smog at bay. They simply created islands of minimal visibility in a sea of blackness. The first of the evening's guests had begun to trickle in, but the wagering and card games taking place in the main salon had little interest for him. Even those games that would occur later in private parlors, the ones where entire fortunes were won and lost on the turn of a card, seemed inconsequential. His mind was consumed with her—with what midnight would bring.

In his study, Vincent was considering his next move very carefully. He'd made her a promise . . . that he would stay until the dawn. A glance at the clock showed it was not quite nine o'clock. He still had a significant amount of time to kill before he could go to her and that was slowly driving him insane.

The door opened and Stavers appeared. The man looked tired. It was perhaps the first time that Vincent had ever seen him so. Was age getting to him? It occurred to him then that he really had no notion of how old the man actually was. When Vincent had first come into his care, if it could be termed such, the man had been approaching middle years. But when one lived in such a rough way and in such a rough place, gauging one's age based on appearance was an impossibility. Stavers had still been brawling then, making his living in the ring. Even now, when he had to be at least sixty-five, the man had a fist like a hammer. When needed, Stavers could knock someone out with a single blow. But at what cost?

"You should go to bed," Vincent said. "I can have someone else watch the club tonight. Or I can cancel my engagement with Mrs. Blaylock and I'll take care of things down here."

Stavers raised one scarred eyebrow. "I did not think there was anything that could keep you from her."

Vincent shrugged. "It would not be my first choice," he answered blandly.

"I don't think you should do that, in any case. We've had movement. Timothy was watching Ernsdale's house. A messenger came right at the dinner hour and then Ernsdale left the house immediately. Tim followed him as far as the George."

Vincent frowned. Dealing with Ernsdale and his inability to follow simple instructions was enough to drive even the sanest of men straight to Bedlam.

Dissecting the information Stavers had imparted, there were a few troubling implications. The George was a reputable inn, but it sat at a crossroads between London's most disparate factions—law abiding and lawless. Just beyond the George was the Liberty of the Mint.

From the beginning, it had been hovering in his mind as a possibility. After all, most in Seven Dials, Soho, Whitechapel, and every other rookery and slum in London knew who he was and knew his rules. No one would have gotten away with kidnapping a wellborn and titled lady.

But the laws of the city did not apply in the Mint, and the information he had procured over the years only granted him sway with those who governed London. In short, he lacked the means to garner cooperation there to find her if that was where they had stashed Lady Ernsdale. While he'd never aspired to rule more than his own little portion of the city, he realized now that it might put him at a disadvantage.

"You man the club and I'll head for the George."

"That won't be necessary. He didn't stay long, and I sent some lads to fetch him before he got very far on his way home. He's here now. Downstairs," Stavers uttered the last word with devious enjoyment. He disliked Ernsdale on principle. Barring a few stellar exceptions, the aristocracy as a whole was something he held in genuine disdain. But recent interactions with Lord Ernsdale had made the man seem far more than simply distasteful.

Vincent's lips curved in a wicked smile. "You are a cunning old bastard, Stavers. I don't give you nearly enough credit."

Leaving his office, he headed for the stairs that would take him to what could essentially be called a cell. The basement of the house was dark in a way that the artificial light of lamps simply could not alleviate. Well below ground level, the only windows were tiny horizontal slits that let in hardly any light even during the brightest of days. At night, the place was like a pit.

Even with the few lamps usually positioned about the room, it would be impossible to see more than a foot or so beyond the end of one's own nose. The stone walls were rough and there was not a creature comfort to be found. In short, it was hardly the sort of place Ernsdale was accustomed to.

Making his way down the stairs into the dungeon-like space, he found Ernsdale seated in a chair, his hands bound, and the same two men who'd picked him up before flanked him. The moment the man saw him, he began shouting.

"I'll see you hanged for this!"

"Not bloody likely," Vincent retorted. "What were you doing at the George?"

"I will not explain myself to you! I am not some errant servant to be questioned about my activities!"

Vincent, casually and without any overtly threatening gestures, moved closer to Ernsdale. When he was within reach, he slapped the man. It wasn't an overly forceful blow, but he hadn't intended it to be. He wasn't after inflicting injury, but insult. Ernsdale's abundant pride was the intended target.

"You," Vincent said, enunciating the words slowly, "Will do exactly as I say. There will be no further deviations from my orders. Did the note you received this afternoon come from Lady Ernsdale's abductors?"

"No."

Lie. It was obvious in the way Ernsdale's eyes shifted side to side before he uttered the word. "It's a pity."

"What is?"

"That I'm going to have to walk out of this room and leave you to the mercies of these fine men. When they have pulled out your fingernails, perhaps then you'll be willing to give me the truth." With that, Vincent turned and made for the door. He could hear scuffling behind him and Ernsdale's screams which sounded alarmingly like those of a bleating sheep.

"Wait! Wait! They did send it!" The older man cried, almost sobbing. No one had even touched him yet.

Vincent turned back to him and waved a hand, and immediately the two men stepped away from Ernsdale. "Go on."

"They said to be at the George by nine and I'd receive further instruction," he all but sobbed out the words, gasping for breath between as if he'd run a great distance.

Vincent waited, raising one eyebrow when then man remained silent for a second too long.

Hurriedly, Ernsdale went on, "It was just another note. There was nothing more—I swear! I have it in my pocket."

Vincent nodded and one of the men retrieved the note for him. With it in hand, he crossed the far wall where the single lamp was burning. Scanning the contents, he noted that it was the same very neat, precise penmanship. It instructed Ernsdale to deliver the ransom to the sundial at the center of Seven Dials at midnight, alone. If he did so, Lady Ernsdale would be freed. There was no indication in the note of how or when that would occur.

"I do not have those funds readily available," Ernsdale protested. "I cannot do what they ask regardless."

"I have the funds... and you will go there at midnight tonight. But you will not go alone. My men here will take the place of your regular coachman and footman. I'll have other men stationed nearby."

"She isn't worth it... not my wife and not her ice block of a sister." Ernsdale sneered as he uttered the insult.

Vincent wouldn't discuss Honoria in front of anyone else. Nodding to the men who guarded Ernsdale, they simply left the room without saying a word. Ernsdale, still seated with his hands bound, looked at the door as they exited, perhaps realizing he'd made a grave error.

"You have a bad habit, Lord Ernsdale, of saying things you shouldn't about women you have no right to speak of," Vincent stated with icy conviction. "If you dare to speak of either Lady Ernsdale or Mrs. Blaylock in such a way again—if I even suspect you are thinking negatively of them again—I will not simply beat you. I will cut your tongue straight from your head and watch you drown in your own blood... and when it is done, no one will find your body. There are enough fine gentlemen sitting in the house—on both sides—who are in my debt that I can promise you, no one will look very hard for your worthless hide if I tell them not to."

Ernsdale swallowed convulsively, but clearly wasn't intelligent enough to know when to quit. "You're in love with her."

Vincent discounted that immediately. "Love isn't something a man like me is capable of."

"Then you're obsessed with her, which is just as bad, if not worse," Ernsdale said. "I've seen the way men look at her. It is the same way they look at my wife. They are beautiful women but more trouble than they are worth."

"I find Mrs. Blaylock to be worth a great deal of trouble, Ernsdale. I'd urge you to remember that." There was no mistaking the warning tone in his voice. Apparently even

Ernsdale, who had proven to be rather dim, could pick up on it as he, for the moment, remained quiet. "My men will accompany you home and they will stay with you every second until the scheduled meeting. You don't take a piss without one of them present. Is that clear?"

Ernsdale opened his mouth to speak.

"Don't," Vincent said. "Not another word out of you. Just nod."

The older man did just that, his sagging jowls jiggling with the motion. In that moment, Vincent had great sympathy for Lady Ernsdale. What must a young woman have thought when being told she would marry the toad before him? He simply couldn't fathom it.

Turning on his heel, Vincent left the room and climbed the stairs. He found the two men—*Stavers' favorite henchman, he thought*—waiting for him there. "Take him home. Stay with him. He's not to be out of your sight for a second. If he so much as breathes hard, I want to know about it. You'll accompany him tonight in full livery as discussed."

"Yes, sir. Mr. Stavers said to tell you he's finished up with the books."

That bit of news offered more relief than it ought to have. For some reason, he was tired beyond anything he could recall. Perhaps it wasn't just Stavers who was getting old.

Chapter Thirty-One

VINCENT CLIMBED THE stairs to his quarters. If he hurried, he'd have enough time to stop in at Honoria's to at least explain why there was yet another change of plans. The evening was certainly not meeting his own expectations.

Closing the door behind him, he began to immediately strip off what remained of his clothing. The cravat and coat had gone ages ago. The waistcoat and shirt came off, and he tossed them over a chair. He was preparing to do the same with his trousers when a knock sounded on the door.

Cursing under his breath, he closed the buttons once more and yanked the door open. "Stav—" It wasn't Stavers. It wasn't, as some small portion of his mind had fantasized, Honoria. It was Ettinger. And what he saw draped over the other man's arms took him aback.

"Changing your wardrobe?" Vincent asked in a deceptively amused tone. He knew precisely what that gown was.

"Playing coy isn't a good look on a man of your age. This, as you are aware, is the gown Lady Ernsdale was wearing when she was taken. It was in a secondhand shop near Southwark," Ettinger explained.

"How do you know it's hers?"

"One of the street lads saw her being abducted. Snatched up off the street, knocked over the head, hooded and dragged into a hack, no markings ... but the driver had scars on his face—pox most likely. Minutes later, a different woman emerged from that hack carrying this dress. It wasn't a stretch to think she would sell it. The lad's intent was to follow the woman and pick her pocket."

Vincent, despite knowing Ettinger's capabilities, was still astounded by the man's uncanny ability to ferret out the truth in a very small amount of time. "And did he pick her pocket?"

"No. She disappeared into the Mint and he's a smart enough lad not to follow."

The Mint. Again. It kept circling the periphery of all of it. It was a haven for criminals, but also for gentry who were hiding from debt collectors. Considering his previous conversations with Honoria about the origins of the party that might be responsible, that increased the likelihood of it being some disgraced gentleman hiding in the Liberty from the bailiffs.

From the moment he'd heard that the kidnappers had been working out of the George, he'd had a bad feeling about that. The Mint was a place of exile. Fetid and full of naught but disease and despair, profit could be had in such a place, but at a price he was not willing to pay. He'd long ago made the choice to leave that area of London to the scavengers. None of the members of Parliament, Bow Street Runners, or wealthy and influential peers that were in his pocket had any sort of sway in that region. His normal way of doing business was useless there. So he'd have to find another way of doing things. "Would he recognize this woman if he saw her again?"

Ettinger smiled. "Of course he would. He lives on the streets. He can likely tell what I had for breakfast based on the smell of my sweat. You know what it's like when you're on the street ... or have you forgotten?"

He hadn't forgotten anything. "Answer the question."

"Yes, he can, and he's been promised a tidy sum—of your money, I might add—for following her when he feels safe to do so. He won't go into the Mint, but he can stay outside the gates and watch for her to come and go."

"I'll inform Mrs. Blaylock," he said. "This is dire, Joss. Given the state of things in the Mint, and with those who reside there, I fear for Lady Ernsdale's life."

Ettinger looked at him askance. "Oh, it's Lady Ernsdale who is your concern now and not her pretty, widowed sister?"

Why the hell did everyone want to insert themselves into that particular piece of his business? "Leave it alone. I have that under control." He didn't, of course. It was all wildly out of control, but he would hardly admit that.

"Do you? Have you considered that if Lady Ernsdale does die, the beautiful and quite willful Mrs. Blaylock will more than likely refuse to toss up her skirts for you?"

His temper flared, quick and hot. He reached out, slamming Ettinger into the far wall—no mean feat. Rage blinded him for a moment. He hadn't even realized he could be provoked in such a manner until he saw Ettinger's face turning purple as his neckcloth twisted in Vincent's own hand.

Releasing him as abruptly as he'd seized him, Vincent stepped back and Ettinger sagged against the frame of the opposing door.

"So that's the way of it," Ettinger mused. "You're tied up in knots over her and have been from the first. Do you honestly think bedding her will improve the situation? Or will it simply burrow her deeper beneath your skin until she becomes all you can think of?"

"I cannot say," Vincent admitted.

"She is an obsession for you. A demon of your very own."

"You are hardly one to speak to me of obsessions," Vincent fired back. "How long has it been, Joss, since you were sipping from a vial of laudanum?"

Ettinger's expression shuttered, his gaze going strangely blank. "Not long enough. And I'm precisely the person to speak to you of obsession because no one else can or will. No one else knows what it feels like to crave and fear something at the same time. You should stay away from her."

"I cannot," Vincent admitted. "Foolhardy as it may be, I cannot."

"Then I pity you. She will ruin you as opium nearly ruined me."

There were worse vices than a woman to wreck a man, Vincent thought, though there was a hint of bitterness in him. Perhaps that bitterness would not be present if he knew for certain that she was as tormented by this indefinable connection between them as he himself was.

At that moment, Stavers appeared, a small, thin, and bedraggled boy in tow.

"Mr. Ettinger, this child has come in search of you," the butler said, clearly perturbed at having such a young person on the premises. Little did it matter that the child had likely seen more misery in his short years than most people saw in a lifetime. There was no innocence left in those eyes and that was the heartbreaking and very common reality for children in the rookeries.

"Did you see her?" Ettinger asked the boy.

"No. But I saw the man that grabbed the lady off the street," the boy explained. "He came out of the Mint and I followed him . . . all the way here to Mayfair. Delivered a note to a house by the park."

"Ernsdale's," Vincent surmised. That firmly cemented that the kidnappers were hiding out in that lawless region, and that Lady Ernsdale was likely being held somewhere within it. "I'll handle him. You get back to the Mint, Joss, and see if you can intercept this bastard on his way home. If we can find her before the meet tonight, we can end this bloody thing now."

"And Mrs. Blaylock?" Ettinger asked.

"Is not your concern," Vincent snapped.

Chapter Thirty-Two

THE CONFLATION OF worry for Henrietta and of her own terrible fears regarding whatever was happening between herself and Vincent Carrow had created a state of turmoil. The constant elevation of her emotional state, coupled with the excessive amount of wine from the night before, had left her exhausted. And yet, even with her exhaustion, sleep had proved elusive. Her attempts to nap that day had been thwarted at every turn by her own wayward and troubling thoughts. And no small amount of anticipation, if she were honest.

Out of desperation, she'd dismissed the servants for the night. Only one of the maids, the housekeeper, and the cook lived in. The footmen had their own quarters nearby. The truth was that she couldn't think clearly enough to have a conversation with anyone else, and sending them all off for the night had given her a reprieve.

Her thoughts were scattered and chaotic. She had never gone more than two days in her life without speaking to her sister, either in person or via letters and notes. And while she wanted her sister found safely, what she desperately wanted in that moment was her guidance. She might have been the elder sister, but when it came to men, Henrietta was certainly the wiser of them, despite her chaste state. Some women were simply born understanding men and her sister was among their ranks.

For Honoria to say that she was out of her depth with Vincent would have been a vast understatement. After all, she'd been with a grand total of two men in her life. And the second had shown her that the first simply did not count. The experiences could not have been further apart. Painful, humiliating, and blessedly brief—every incident of Edwin exercising his conjugal rights had been pure misery. But one night with Vincent had shown her passion, pleasure, need, and that all if it was so much sweeter when freely undertaken by both parties.

Recalling the horrid things Edwin had said to her—that she was completely frigid, that she was as worthless in bed as she was elsewhere, that bedding her was as pleasurable as bedding a corpse—she was now free of those doubts he had created. It was clear to her, as she had always suspected, that the problem had not truly been with her. But as the less experienced between them, she hadn't the courage to protest or challenge him. Even had she possessed the courage, the repercussions of such an action did not bear imagining.

A knock sounded on the door in the front hall. It was soft—not loud enough to alert the servants belowstairs but clearly loud enough to gain her attention. The room she presently ruminated in had windows that faced the street, so it was easy enough to see that the room was occupied. She'd planned it just so. The fewer people, including her own servants, who saw him arrive for this clandestine and very improper engagement the better. It was still early for Vincent to be arriving, but she hoped it would be him—in part because she was eager for his company and in part because she needed any distraction to stop her from thinking. The more her mind raced the less certain she was of anything.

Getting to her feet, a shawl draped about her to camouflage the plunging neckline of her gown, she braced herself to face him. But when she opened the door, it was not Vincent who greeted her. It was Maurice Walpole. In his hand was a lovely bouquet of flowers: white jasmine for forgiveness, small bindweed for humility, and yellow roses for friendship. A sweet gesture, to be sure, but a more unwelcome sight she could not imagine.

He ducked his head almost sheepishly, staring down at the toes of his tassel bedecked slippers. "Mrs. Blaylock, I have come, most humbly, to beg your pardon."

"Mr. Walpole, this is a very late hour to pay a call," she said as kindly, as possible. "While I thank you, it is most unnecessary."

He smiled at her apologetically. "I am terribly sorry to inconvenience you, Mrs. Blaylock, but after we parted on such a sour note the other day—well, I had to speak with you again. I had considered simply writing, but I felt that, after my behavior, I needed to offer my apologies in person. Please? It will only take a moment."

Honoria would have preferred anything to letting him into her home again, but under the circumstances, there was simply no way to avoid it without creating a scandal. He appeared determined to state his case and having a man lingering on her doorstep at such an hour, regardless of how proper or improper her relationship was with them, could only lead to ruin. "Very well, Mr. Walpole, you may come in. But only for a moment."

He smiled at her and followed her into the house, heading directly for the drawing room without invitation.

Honoria's eyebrows shot up—his gall was astounding. She'd intended to let him into the entry hall only. It would have been the perfect scenario. He would have offered a pretty apology, and then she would have ushered him on his way. But once more, his vanity and conceit led him to taking far more than she wished to give. He strode about her house as if he owned it.

Walking into the drawing room after him, she stated, "I can give you five minutes, Mr. Walpole, and then you must go. It is late and this is quite inappropriate."

He smiled, but it was not the smile he'd worn on her doorstep. This did not look like the smile of a little boy apologizing for a tantrum. It looked, if she had to quantify it, triumphant—and perhaps a bit vicious. There was no contrition in the conceited and arrogant man before her.

"I knew you would not be able to sustain your anger at me. I understand that I must have surprised you with my ardent request to pay court to you," he said. "And for that, Mrs. Blaylock, I am truly sorry. You are a woman of fine character and delicate sensibilities. I should have proceeded more cautiously."

"You should not have proceeded at all, Mr. Walpole. I am not possessed of delicate sensibilities in the least. I am also not interested in being courted by a man who is young enough to be my child!" It came out snappish and she clamped down on the urge to apologize. There were some men in the world whom you simply could not be nice to. Nice wasn't simply seen as a courtesy by them, but an invitation. "Now, I think you should take your flowers and leave."

"Mrs. Blaylock—"

"Mr. Walpole," she reiterated. "I do not wish to have my servants remove you forcefully from my home, but I will." Except that the footmen who were capable of the task were not in the house. *But he did not know that.* To underscore her threat, she walked over to the bell pull.

His lips curled in a sneer. "I have never been so insulted. Mother tried to tell me that you were not good enough for me. I am a gentleman, after all, and you are nothing but the social climbing daughter of a cloth merchant who happened to amass a fortune."

He hadn't happened to amass a fortune. He'd devoted his life and all of his heart to it, leaving no room for her mother, her sister, or herself. To her father, they hadn't been his loved ones but his assets. Possessions. It occurred to her that Mr. Walpole had far more in common with her lowly merchant father than he would ever wish to know. "I was attempting to spare your feelings, Mr. Walpole, as I saw your interest in me as simply youthful infatuation—that of a schoolboy for his governess. I am no longer inclined to be gentle in my rejection of your suit, sir. Get out."

He smirked at her. "I think not. I think I will stay right here. I had thought, *Honoria*, to offer you a respectable arrangement. I had thought to make you my wife, much to mother's dismay. But then I saw you—I saw you running to the Hound. I wanted to give you a chance to deny it. Naively, I assumed it was simply to ask for his aid for one of your pet projects. How wrong I was!"

Honoria's heart began to thunder in her chest. He sounded positively insane. Like a jealous lover, but he had no reason to be so. She'd certainly never given him even the slightest indication that she had any interest in him at all or that she would even consider entertaining a suit from him. "How did you see me go to him?" She demanded the answer without bothering to deny that she had done so. It was too late for that. "Unless you were watching me—which is inappropriate and also quite disturbed, Mr. Walpole—you'd have seen nothing of the sort!"

Walpole reached out, grasping her chin between his thumb and forefinger. It was not gentle. The pinching motion resulted in significant pain. "You think no one knows that you've been given his protection? He has made it quite clear to everyone in those hideous places that you and your fellow reformers are not to be touched."

"Let go of me. I will not ask again," she insisted. It took considerable effort not to show fear, even though she had begun to fear him. He wasn't an overly large man, but he still had the advantage of size and strength. And she was all too familiar with how those advantages could be used against her.

"Tell me, Mrs. Blaylock, what you did to earn the kind regard of such a ruthless man." The ugliness of the insinuation in his tone and expression was impossible to miss.

He looked and sounded as if he already knew the answer, had assumed the answer. Correct or not, it was not his place to judge her behavior. "I do not like what you are implying, Mr. Walpole. But if you presume that the Hound of Whitehall has me under his personal protection, do you not think your current tactics are unwise?"

He continued as if she had not even spoken. "I can only be thankful that I discovered your true character now. I shall be speaking to the other ladies in the society. I've no doubt they will have any number of second thoughts about fraternization with someone whose morals are so lacking." He paused to leer at her. "Unless you wish to make an arrangement with me similar to that you have embarked upon with that criminal. I am not an unreasonable man. What, Mrs. Blaylock, could you possibly have that a man like myself would want? Go on. Tell me precisely what you would be willing to do to entice me to keep your secrets."

"You are not a man," Honoria said with derision, twisting away from him. When he reached for her again, she slapped his hand away more forcefully, as if he were nothing but a pesky and irritating insect. "You are nothing but a little boy in long pants playing a part. I'm astounded, Mr. Walpole, that you could untie yourself from your mother's skirts to go out alone after dark!"

He tossed the bouquet onto the floor at her feet, petals scattering. "You will regret that!"

"I don't think I will. As for your threats, do your worst, sir. You may spread gossip and rumor as you see fit. I'll not be blackmailed by you or anyone else. And I will not tell you again. Leave my house!" She was shouting by then, but she no longer cared. "Leave it and do not return. Neither you nor your mother are welcome here any longer."

She thought he was making for the door and stepped aside to let him pass. But then he grabbed her, shoving her into the doorframe. She could not pivot quickly enough to catch herself, and her shoulder slammed into the wood, even as she kept falling, the floor rushing up to meet her. But she never touched it. A strong arm reached out, grabbed her about her waist and hauled her back to her feet.

A glance over her shoulder confirmed that her worst nightmare had come true. Vincent Carrow stood there in her entryway, *in her house*, glowering at Mr. Walpole. The fury she could see in his expression meant that murder was as likely an outcome as not—and in her entryway, no less. If she'd hoped to avoid scandal, this was not the way to go about it.

"I heard shouting outside," Vincent said, then looked pointedly at Mr. Walpole, "or I would never have pushed my way into a lady's home at night."

"Mr. Walpole was just leaving," Honoria insisted. "And he will not be returning."

Vincent eyed her, his expression inscrutable, then his gaze moved past her to land on the now destroyed flowers that had been thrown at her feet. She turned her head at the same time, noting the direction of his gaze. It was a mistake. The light struck her chin, showing the marks where he had grabbed her, pinching her face.

Without a word, he turned back to Maurice Walpole. He reached out, catching the younger man's face in his grasp—much as Walpole had done to her. It was a demeaning and rather emasculating gesture. Vincent forced him to meet his gaze. "You should learn to control your temper . . . and maybe I should be the one to teach you."

"No! Just let him go," Honoria said. She feared what Vincent would do to him, not for Mr. Walpole's sake, but for his own. He was already so convinced of his own villainy despite all evidence to the contrary. If there was one thing she had learned in her time with the women and children of the rookeries, there were few absolutes, and no one was ever entirely good or entirely wicked. It was human nature to have the capacity of both. If only Vincent could believe that of himself. "He knows that he is not to return. That has been made abundantly clear to him."

Vincent looked at her, a challenge in his gaze, then looked back at the man now cowering in his grasp. "Should I, puppy? Should I just let you go when you've clearly piddled on the rug? I don't think so."

There was no other warning. The crack that rent the air—the explosive sound of the back of Vincent's open hand striking Mr. Walpole's cheek—was deafening. Maurice fell to the tile floor dazed from the blow.

"Get up," Vincent ordered him.

Slowly, the younger man did so, climbing to his feet. "I'll see you tossed in the gaol for that."

He really did not know when to simply stop talking, Honoria thought with exasperation. Vincent held the power, physically and in every other regard. Maurice Walpole could no more have him thrown in the gaol than he could drain the Thames with naught but his bare hands.

<hr />

VINCENT STARED AT the foppish young man with utter disdain. "You're certainly welcome to try. Though you'll have more luck swaying them to your cause if you leave here with your teeth intact." He paused then for effect. "Talking would likely be difficult if I am forced to scatter them across the floor for you."

At that threat, the boy scurried toward the door, pausing only long enough to retrieve his hat and to glare daggers at them before making his less than grand exit. There was something there that disturbed Vincent. Some niggling detail that, once he had time to ruminate on it, would make more sense. There was no time to ruminate on the matter, however. He had to get to the inn and have everything in place before Ernsdale and the others arrived. In the meantime, he would set men to watching Honoria's house. He feared they had not seen the last of Mr. Walpole and that the boy would bring a great deal of misery with him when he returned.

Once they were alone, Vincent turned to Honoria. Her face was pale. There were dark hollows beneath her eyes, and he had no choice but to face the fact that he was at least partially responsible for her current state. Late night rendezvous were not part of her normal routine. Given the amount of distress she was currently enduring for a multitude of reasons, was it any wonder she was beyond exhausted? "Are you hurt?"

That wasn't what he'd wanted to say. There were things he wanted to tell her, things he wanted to set right—but he lacked the words.

"No. I am not hurt. But why are you here so early?"

His expression grim and serious, he replied, "I'm here because there has been another change in plans, unfortunately. And new information has come to light that you need to be made aware of."

"What information?" There was more than a bit of panic in her voice. She was fully aware that something important had happened even if she didn't know what it was yet.

Vincent sighed heavily as he turned to pick up his redingote and the other items he had carried in and dropped to the floor when he'd heard Walpole's nasty accusations. He dreaded the next revelation. The idea of causing her such pain and worry was abhorrent to him, but there was no way to avoid it. Best to get it over with.

Unwrapping the bundle of items, he produced the dress and turned to face her.

Chapter Thirty-Three

HONORIA WAS STILL trying to process all that had transpired—the ugly confrontation with Mr. Walpole, Vincent arriving early for reasons as yet unexplained—then he turned back to her, his redingote over one arm and a familiar swath of saffron silk draped over the other.

Hettie's dress. How many times had she seen her sister in that gown? It was one of her favorites—and she'd been wearing it the last time Honoria had seen her. She glanced at him, noting the expression of concern on his face. He looked at her as if he actually cared for her, but his concern barely even registered. Not anymore.

She'd gone to him for aid in finding her sister. Everything that had passed between them since that agreement had been forged had provided at least some distraction for her, partially masking the harsh realities of what was happening in her life. Thinking of him, of what was transpiring between them, had allowed her to focus on something other than Henrietta's possible fate. Now, faced with the awful possibilities of what might have become of her sister, nothing could distract her from that.

"Oh, God," she muttered. "Oh, God! She's dead." Then her knees buckled. She would have fallen had he not reached for her, caught her against him.

"No," he said instantly, as he swept her up into his arms and carried her through the entry hall to the open door of the study. "We do not know that."

Honoria could hear him, she could hear the calm and soothing tone of his voice. But it did not penetrate the haze of fear and grief that wracked her at the thought of being alone in the world.

He placed her on the same chair she had occupied prior to Mr. Walpole's unexpected visit. As he knelt in front of her, his hands rested on the curved arms of the chair, flanking her, surrounding her. Their faces were only inches apart.

"Look at me, Honoria. Look at me!"

She did. The tone of command in his voice didn't allow for defiance, not when she was so lost in her own thoughts and pain.

When their gazes locked, he explained, "The dress was taken from her at the time she was abducted. She'd been knocked on the head and loaded into a waiting carriage. This was not a crime of opportunity but well-planned. They must have taken it from her inside the carriage because when it stopped, the woman who was with them emerged with the gown."

"Why? Why would they take her dress?" She couldn't even fathom what he was telling her.

"For money, of course. It was sold to a secondhand shop. Ettinger tracked it down that far. Having this is a good thing. It lets us know we're on the right trail. This is solid evidence that Ettinger is getting close to her abductors, and thus, close to your sister."

Somehow, that explanation pierced the veil of panic that had settled over her. Honoria took a deep shuddering breath. Hysterics were not something she indulged in with anything resembling regularity. They were positively exhausting. "Are you certain of that?"

"Yes, I am quite certain. Now it's just a simple matter of tracking the woman who sold it. If anyone can, Honoria, it's Ettinger."

With the worst of the panic fading, she could focus on the particulars. "They sold her dress?" The idea of these unknown people stripping the clothes from her sister's unconscious form left her shaken.

"Yes. It's a very identifiable dress. Especially if they are taking her into less reputable neighborhoods. No one will remember a man carting around a woman in coarse wool or worn cotton. But a man carrying a woman dressed in yellow silk? That would be remarked upon. It would be memorable. And when you're doing something like this, the last thing one would wish to do is risk attracting unwanted attention."

Honoria's hands were shaking. She smoothed them over the fabric of her skirt in an attempt to halt their trembling. "Do you think she is alive? Really? Do not just placate me with what you think I want to hear. If—I'd rather prepare myself for the worst than hope for the best and be disappointed."

He did not utter an immediate denial or agreement. "We have no reason to believe otherwise. And now the primary reason our evening plans must be altered—the kidnappers have sent further instruction to Lord Ernsdale. I have intercepted it. As much as I hate to do so, I have to leave you now. There are plans to be made and executed and I must oversee them."

Honoria lifted her gaze, meeting his. "Could you stay for a while? Just for a little while?"

THAT SIMPLE REQUEST rendered him powerless. Vulnerability was not something she showed to many people. That she had allowed him to see her in such a state, that she had leaned on him and asked for him to offer comfort—how could he possibly deny her? And yet, he knew that he must.

"It would not be wise. I should not be seen here. It would destroy you."

"I don't care."

And she did not. He could see it in her eyes. In that moment, however, other things took precedence.

"I do. I will not be the cause of your ruin."

"I am ruined already. Mr. Walpole followed me... he saw me entering your establishment. And after what happened today, I have no doubt that he will glory in the telling of it. So for the moment, for a little while, just stay with me."

If she hadn't been so upset, if he hadn't seen just how close she was to her breaking point, he would have gone after Walpole and put a stop to his actions. It was hard to spread gossip when one had no tongue to speak with and no fingers with which to hold a pen. That would wait, though. "I can stay for a little while," he agreed.

Taking her hands in his, Vincent pulled her up from the chair and led her the short distance to the well-upholstered sofa. There, he sat down, pulling her with him. He held her close, her body pressed to his and her head resting on his shoulder. The degree of his desire for her had not changed. But his priorities had shifted. It wasn't simply about what he wanted, but about what she needed. Comfort first, and seduction later. He could be a very patient man when it was called for. So he sat there, holding her, offering solace as he never had for anyone else.

Looking down at her, taking in the dark sweep of her dark lashes and the long shadows they cast on her cheeks, it all began to make sense to him. He'd seen her fear for her sister from the outset. But this fear wasn't simply for Lady Ernsdale. It was also fear for herself—fear of grief, pain, and loneliness. Those were things he knew only too well. In that moment, he would have done anything to take her pain away—except the one thing she wanted. *For him to stay.*

However much he hated to do it, he had to go. The cost of staying with her would be too high and she was not truly ready to pay that. But Vincent knew he could not leave her so distraught.

There had been very few women in his life in any capacity that wasn't transitory—and none that he'd ever comforted. But as he held her, it felt not simply natural—it felt right. *Destined.*

Why?

That question plagued him. Why was she so bloody important? Why did he crave her as he had craved no other woman before? Not even Annabel with her voluptuous beauty and auburn hair had moved him so. But a stolen kiss from prim and proper Mrs. Honoria Blaylock had plagued him endlessly, and she consumed his mind. Memories of what had passed between them and fantasies of what could be—they invaded his every hour, sleeping or awake. But why her? What was it about the troublesome woman that compelled him so?

His arms tightened about her and a contented sigh escaped her. Did it matter why? It simply was what it was and there was no fighting it. Only surrender.

She looped her arms about his waist and pulled her feet up onto the sofa to curl up next to him. And that was how they remained—her cradled against him while he watched over her. It wasn't long. Hardly a quarter hour passed until her breathing deepened, growing slower and more even. The tension in her body began to simply seep away.

Looking down at her face—eyes closed, lips parted softly—her beauty was impossible to deny. But the turmoil of the past few days had come at a cost. Worry and strain were already taking their toll on her. The purple shadows beneath her eyes had grown deeper. Even in sleep, a slight furrow remained between her perfectly winged brows. He wanted to take her worries away. And he couldn't do that by staying there with her.

Once he was certain that she was sleeping soundly, he eased away from her. Lowering her head gently onto the sofa, he draped a nearby blanket over and then eased from the room. Closing the door quietly, he turned and found himself face to face with her wide-eyed servants.

No one spoke, and he slipped out once more. He had a battle to wage.

Chapter Thirty-Four

THE DARKNESS WAS as absolute as it had seemed when she had awakened in that hole the first time. But in that dark, dank space, Henrietta had heard enough to know that she was not out on the open sea. She was still very much on the Thames or quite near it. Voices aboard the ship were muffled, but it was the way of the river to carry distant sounds while masking those which were close. The sounds of bells had alerted her—she knew those chimes. If she could reach the shore, if she could get to dry land, she could follow those sounds and make her way home.

The entire day had been spent listening. Cataloguing every sound. From footfalls to jibes and crude jests—the sounds of rough, working men had been audible. But as the hours wore on, those sounds became less and less frequent.

Getting up from the floor again, she crept forward feeling her way along the wall until she once more reached the rungs to the ladder that would take her out of that dark, miserable hole. Tucking the blade into the pocket of her borrowed dress, she tied the skirts up as best she could.

Carefully locating each rung by touch, she began to climb. Days without food or water, and the aftereffects of what was likely laudanum, made it a difficult task. *Morning. Night. Time had no meaning down there in the dark.*

Thinking of the conversation that she'd overheard between

the disgraced footman and whoever his accomplice was, Hettie knew she needed to make her escape soon. They would bring the drugged food and water before long and would likely force it down her throat if she showed any resistance to eating and drinking on her own. She would not give up the advantage of having her wits about her.

She reached for the next rung and her knuckles banged against rough wood overhead. She was at the top. Holding on with one hand, she retrieved the knife from her pocket with the other. Before she did anything, she stretched up as much as possible and tried to peer through any cracks in the floorboards, but there was not enough light coming through to make them visible.

Using the blade of the knife, she began poking at the hatch door where she thought the seams might be. When the blade finally slipped through, her breath caught and held as she waited for someone to raise an alarm. But only silence remained.

When she could breathe again, she continued her work. Sliding the blade carefully along the seams, it finally struck something. The latch. It seemed to be a simple catch, just a thin piece of wood that likely swiveled to lock the hatch. With a little more pressure, it moved but only slightly. The style of the lock wasn't the problem—it was her position. She couldn't get the leverage she needed.

Henrietta would have cried at that moment if it would have done the least bit of good. Frustrated, frightened, and far weaker than she cared to admit, she gave it another go. Angling her body slightly to the left, she pressed the blade against the wood. The latch moved a bit farther that time though still not enough.

"It's like learning the pianoforte or how to embroider," she whispered to herself. "It's all about patience."

And with that bolstering statement, she tried a third time—then a fourth. When at last the latch slid free, she had no idea how many attempts she'd made or even how long it had taken her. What she did know was that she had not been discovered during that time and she was certain that her many attempts, despite her best efforts, had not been silent. That told her she had been correct in her earlier estimation. *The ship was largely unoccupied.*

It was not an easy thing to push the hatch door open and crawl through while maintaining her hold on the knife and making no sound. But somehow she managed, or at least closely enough that no one came running. There were no windows or portholes near her, but at the other end of the corridor was a set of steps leading up to the deck. The silvery blue light that filtered down there told her it was night. Is that why no one seemed to be about? Even with the ship docked and most of the crew at their leisure, some would have remained behind to act as guards. Were all the others on board asleep? Closing the hatch and resetting the latch, she braced herself for what was to come.

With her heart pounding in her chest and sweat beading on her skin, Henrietta made her way toward those stairs. Just as she neared the bottom step, the sound of approaching footsteps halted her in her tracks. Frozen with fear for a split second, she didn't know what to do. Then, it was almost as if she could hear Honoria's voice in her head. *Hide.*

Her options were limited. And she wouldn't go back in that dark hole for anything. Ducking behind the steps, she crouched down and waited.

It was a lone sailor, based on his rolling gait. He descended the steps and then made his way down the corridor without even a backward glance. He was whistling softly as he did so, a jaunty tune that was much too happy for the setting. How could one whistle such sunny melodies in a place where women were held against their will?

The whistling man opened one of the doors midway down the corridor and ducked through it. Silence once more settled around her save for the creaking of wood and the slight sloshing of water.

Afraid he would return, Henrietta removed herself from her

hiding place and climbed the steps quickly. Peering out before she simply popped up above deck, she saw no one around. But there was a full moon above and she could see the outline of St. Paul's dome in the distance, barely visible through the polluted air.

A few steps forward and she was at the railing, but peering over the side made her heart sink. There was a rickety-looking dock. It couldn't even be termed a wharf. But they were far enough away from it that she knew it would require swimming. Even if she were a strong swimmer and not utterly petrified of the water, the moonlight glinting on the filthy water showed how swiftly the current was moving.

If she could get to the back of the ship and lower herself into the water there, she wouldn't have to swim. She'd merely need to tread water well enough not to drown and allow the current to carry her to the wharf. With a little luck, she could then grab onto the pilings and make her way to the shore. If not, she'd drown. *Was that a worse fate than what those men had in store for her?*

Creeping along, concealing herself behind crates and barrels as much as possible, Henrietta was starting to feel almost hopeful. *If hopeful was an emotion anyone could feel in such a desperate situation.* When she could go no farther without stepping fully into the open, she paused. Scanning the area, she saw no one. Moving as quickly as possible, she rushed across the open deck to the railing at the rear.

A shout from above startled her and she turned to look. That was a disaster. Her feet tangled in coiled ropes, and she pitched forward. Her head struck the railing, and the world began swimming around her. But the rush of footfalls prompted her to use the very last bit of strength she possessed. Hoisting herself up until her upper body was hanging over the rail, gravity did the rest.

As the blackness of the river rushed up to meet her, Henrietta's eyes closed. She never felt the jolt as she entered the water. Nor did she know when strong arms grabbed at her beneath the wharf, pulling her toward the shore under the cover of darkness.

The calls from above of the men scrambling aboard the ship as a result of her escape went unheard.

She simply lay still and quiet in a stranger's arms as the water rushed around them.

Chapter Thirty-Five

THE CROWD AT The Cawing Crow was thin to say the least. But then he'd paid for that privilege, hadn't he? A few coins here and there and people had made themselves scarce. A slightly larger payment had been required for the proprietor. In the end, the cooperation of all parties had been secured.

Seated at a table in the corner, Vincent kept a hat pulled low over his face. Giving every appearance of a man passed out cold from over-imbibing, Vincent watched the door. There were a dozen or so men outside, stationed in alleys and doorways. Another half dozen had taken up deceptively nonchalant stances inside the pub. Each and every one of them had a view of the all but sniveling wretch that was Lord Ernsdale.

The aging nobleman, with his soft hands, soft middle, and possibly softer head, paced outside beneath the sundial that marked their current location. Seven Dials—seven roads in and out of the neighborhood, but most only escaped it in death. Vincent could only hope that would be true of their quarry that night. In addition to the men directly outside, there were hired hacks lying in wait along each of those seven thoroughfares, ready for pursuit. If the bastards got away, they'd be hunted throughout the city.

"Ten to midnight," Arliss Batson murmured. He was one of the first men who had come into Vincent's employ and was one of his most trusted.

Vincent nodded slightly. "I know. The seconds are ticking by slowly."

The sound of a birdcall echoed outside, seeming to draw closer. It was the signal. There was movement. Counting the different calls, there were two men heading their way. But no sign of poor Lady Ernsdale.

Every muscle in his body was tense, despite giving every appearance of the contrary. Vincent was ready to spring into action—eager for it, even. And then he could see them, strolling boldly up Monmouth. The streets appeared deceptively normal with the number of men he had in place. After all, even in the dark of night, Seven Dials was not a place that slept. The men and boys who lit lamps through the rest of London resided in such low places, after all. And the prostitutes who were the source of the place's infamy also roamed the streets.

To a person, they were all loyal to him. His suspicion that the person who had arranged the abduction of Lady Ernsdale was from the upper classes had been confirmed by their choice of meeting place. To conduct such ugly business in such public view indicated that the person was not an experienced criminal and that they did not routinely move through his world. Those thoughts did not offer any relief to his worries, however. Inexperience led to panic, and panic could well lead to disaster.

"They're in place, Hound," Arliss said.

"It's time." With that, Vincent rose from his chair and made for the door. He had a pistol in one hand and another in his pocket. Using them was not the goal, but he wouldn't be overly troubled by it if he had to. He just wanted it over. He wanted the threat ended and Lady Ernsdale safely returned to her sister. He wanted a chance to be with Honoria when the world wasn't burning around them.

HONORIA WAS AWAKENED by a soft knock at her door. She had no idea how long she'd been asleep, or even when she'd fallen asleep. But awakening on the sofa in the study, draped in a blanket—an oddly caring gesture from a man who routinely denied he was capable of anything resembling kindness—she struggled to get her wits about her.

Was it Vincent returning? Did he have Henrietta with him?

She rushed to the door, opening it with hope burgeoning inside her. But the sight that greeted her was withering.

"Mrs. Walpole," she acknowledged.

"Mrs. Blaylock," the other woman said coldly. "Step aside and let me enter."

"No," Honoria said instantly. "It's terribly late and this is not a good time."

"It's the perfect time, Mrs. Blaylock, because *he* isn't here—your guard dog," Mrs. Walpole sneered. Then she raised her hand from the folds of her heavy cloak revealing a small muff pistol. "I'd prefer not to shoot you in the doorway."

"I'd prefer you not shoot me at all. And what do you know of my 'guard dog?'" Honoria demanded. Her knees were quaking, but she'd never let the other woman know that.

"Whether or not I shoot you will depend upon you, Mrs. Blaylock. Entirely upon you." The woman drew back the hammer of the small pistol, the loud click echoing in the darkness.

With no other choice, Honoria did step back. She continued to back away from the woman until she bumped into a small console table that stood in the entryway. Concealed in a small dish atop it was ridiculously tiny blade that the footmen used to cut the binding on the news sheets when they were delivered in the morning. It wasn't much of a weapon, but it was the best she could do under the circumstances.

"What is the meaning of this, Mrs. Walpole? Both you and your son seem to have a very loose understanding of what the normal hours are for a social call! Not to mention that most people bring flowers when they pay a call, not weapons."

"Do not speak to me of my son," Mrs. Walpole spat. "I indulged his infatuation for you when he first saw you playing the benevolent angel to a group of common prostitutes. He came home waxing poetic about your beauty and your kindness. Then he insisted on joining your little society. And after he begged and pleaded, I relented—*much to my regret.*"

When had he seen her? Where? And why had he been there? "What was he doing in such a place if he was not already working toward reform?"

Mrs. Walpole lifted one artificially darkened brow imperiously. Swathed in plum velvet, with her silvery blonde hair dressed in the height of fashion, she looked like a patroness at Almack's . . . and she waved a gun about like a madwoman.

"Men have needs, Mrs. Blaylock. Even my son," Mrs. Walpole explained with no small amount of bitterness as she dropped her gaze for a moment. When she lifted her gaze once more, it was haughty disdain that could be seen in her eyes. "You have been a married woman. I'm certain you understand that."

"So your son, who for the last year has been working with the reform society to better the lives of prostitutes, was, until that point, actively utilizing their services?" Honoria asked incredulously.

Mrs. Walpole continued as if Honoria had not even spoken. "Not only that, but you have been consorting with that devil of a man—the Hound of Whitehall. I tried to save Maurice from you. Just as I had to save him from all those other women."

"What other women?" Honoria asked. But she didn't truly require an answer. She knew. With dawning horror, she knew exactly who Mrs. Walpole meant. Both the woman and her son were mad—stark raving mad.

Chapter Thirty-Six

"Do you have it?"
 The question was asked by the kidnapper. The man's face was obscured by shadow, his large hat making it impossible to glimpse any identifying feature. Not that it mattered. Standing in the shadows across the street, Vincent listened to the exchange. He had no intention of letting him get away.

"I do. It's right here," Ernsdale said. Then the aging nobleman did the most foolish and most telling thing he could ever have done: he glanced to his left, unmistakably in Vincent's direction. Only a shouted warning would have been more obvious.

The kidnapper looked around, and for the first time, seemed to note how many men were simply lingering on the street. Seven Dials might never truly sleep, but it was a bit late for such bustling about. By this time of night, most people were in their own beds or someone else's.

"It's a trap," the kidnapper said, seemingly confounded that anyone else could engage in dishonesty. "You were supposed to come alone!"

Ernsdale shrugged. "I hadn't intended to come at all! He made me."

Before the other man could run, in truth before he could even turn, Vincent leapt forward taking him to the ground. He struck him—once, twice. He didn't have to do so a third time.

"I'll tell you everything!"

Not the mastermind, Vincent surmised. Just a lackey come to fetch and carry. Vincent drew the knife he kept tucked handily in his boot. "I will ask only once. If I have to ask again, I'll have your answer in blood. Where is Lady Ernsdale?"

"She's on a ship near the Neckinger River at the St Saviour's Dock," the man burst out, his words all but tripping over one another.

Pressing the blade to the man's neck, just below his chin, he demanded, "And has she been harmed?"

"No. Knocked about a bit when she was snatched off the street but nothing permanent. No one's touched her since. I swear!" The sniveling coward was sweating profusely despite the chill in the air. His fear was a palpable thing.

Vincent had been holding his breath on that score. "Now this is where the conversation will become very interesting... or very violent. And that will depend entirely upon how honest you choose to be with me. Is that understood?"

The man, still lying on the ground, all but curled in on himself like an infant, simply nodded.

"He looks very familiar."

That observation had come from Ernsdale. Vincent spared a glance in the other man's direction. "Now you choose to be helpful? *Now*?"

Ernsdale's eyes widened with recognition. "He worked for me! I turned him off for stealing the silver!"

That would explain how he'd known where to fence Lady Ernsdale's dress. "Is that true?"

The young man, still on the ground, nodded.

"Tell me," Vincent said. "Why did you take her, how, and who else is involved?"

"I was paid to take her. Someone told me to snatch her off the street outside the house on Mount Street... but we got the wrong one. We was supposed to nab the other one and just kill her. But when we realized we'd got her by mistake, the one that was married to a gent, we figured we'd ask for money instead."

Mount Street. Honoria's house. Vincent's blood ran cold at the mere thought of it. "What do you mean you got the wrong one? Who were you supposed to get?"

The man began to weep, sobbing brokenly as he rocked back and forth.

Vincent grabbed him, twisting his cravat in his hand and lifting him up. He still held the blade, but he no longer trusted himself with it. "You answer my goddamn question. Who were you supposed to get and who sent you after her?"

"The sister—we were supposed to grab the sister. The lady—too high in the instep, by far—she sent us. Said she was leaving her house all hours of the day and night and that she always wore a dark cloak. Couldn't tell we had the wrong one 'til we had her in the carriage. That damned yellow dress! Said she'd be all in black."

"Who is this lady?" Vincent was shouting by then, his fist drawn back to hit him again. It wasn't even anger that was driving him. It was fear and desperation.

"Mrs. Walpole. Hester Walpole."

Walpole. Vincent did not believe in coincidence.

"And was it Mrs. Walpole who said to make the exchange tonight?"

"Yes," the coward sobbed. "She sent word to her nephew who then told me. She's been the one calling the shots all along. They said I was to set it all up for tonight so she'd be alone. The other one, that is—the sister . . . Mrs. Blaylock. She wanted her left alone tonight."

Immediately, Vincent dropped him and stepped back. Issuing directions, he shouted, "Have him take you to where Lady Ernsdale is being held. When you've retrieved her, bring her to Mrs. Blaylock's home on Mount Street."

"She's my wife!" Ernsdale shouted.

Vincent had no time to deal with Ernsdale's pompousness.

With a wave of his hand, two of his men came forward and immediately grasped Ernsdale's arms. They hauled him back toward the carriage that had brought him there. His hasty removal was the only thing that saved the bastard's life.

"Do you need one of us with you, Hound?" Arliss asked. "Might be trouble."

Vincent nodded. "Let's go."

His heart was racing, pounding as furiously in his chest as the drums of war. And all he could think was that he might be too late. The very thought of it struck a kind of fear in him that he had never known in all his life. Nothing in his possession—not money, property or even power—held more value to him than she did. *Than the woman he loved.*

And the machinations of the Walpoles could take her from him.

"WHAT OTHER WOMEN?" Honoria repeated.

"Do not think to question me. Not when you consort with that criminal!" Hester Walpole's icy gaze roamed over Honoria's face as her lips curled in a disdainful sneer. "Oh, yes. I know who he is. I made it a point to know. When my son began expressing an interest in you, I had to know all there was to know in order to be certain you were the right choice for him."

Honoria reminded herself that the other woman held a gun. Just because it was small did not mean it was any less deadly than more substantial varieties. Being offended by her high-handedness and the assumption that Honoria had been Maurice's for the taking should be secondary to that. So, she attempted to reason with the woman. "Your son, madame, expressed his interest and was rejected. I never encouraged his interest and I have told him, as plainly as I can, that I have no interest in him."

"And why would you ever reject him? He is perfect! He is

handsome, wealthy, from good family!"

That was certainly debatable. Good families did not typically hold people at gunpoint. "Because he is young, Mrs. Walpole. Your son is a very young man—little more than a boy in truth—and I am not a young woman. There is no common ground for us! While men may seek young brides, the reverse is hardly ever true. It would be scandalous, even if I were interested!"

"Scandal! What matter is scandal in the face of what my dear Maurice wants? You are an experienced woman! If he'd had a widow to marry, someone who understood carnal relations, then he wouldn't have had to—his needs would have been met and he would have been safe!"

She'd have rather had her son marry a woman she detested than to see him continuing his congress with prostitutes—to the point that she was willing to commit all manner of atrocities to see it happen.

A noise sounded from the kitchen below, as if someone had dropped a heavy pot or platter. No one should have been awake. The very few servants who were in residence should long since have been abed. The distraction had been intentionally created. And it worked.

Mrs. Walpole whipped her head in that direction, giving Honoria the opportunity to take two steps back. She stopped when her hip bumped against the console table.

Mrs. Walpole turned back to her and raised the tiny gun, pointing it levelly at Honoria's face. At such a distance, she would not miss. "Who else is in the house?"

As the other woman had asked the question Honoria had angled her body slightly away from the older woman. Just enough that she would be able to shift her hand behind her back and grasp the small knife in the dish. With slow, deliberate movements, Honoria tucked that blade into her sleeve just as the other woman turned back to her.

"My servants."

"All of them?" Mrs. Walpole asked.

No, but she didn't know that. "Of course. They are gathered below for their evening meal." It was a flimsy and obviously foolish excuse but it was the only thing that had readily come to mind.

Mrs. Walpole's disbelief was written plainly on her face. "It's a bit late for that, isn't it?"

Honoria shrugged, trying to give the appearance of nonchalance. "To maximize my time with Mr. Carrow, my schedule has shifted, as has the entire household's. Our days begin later and our nights last much longer. If you'd been watching us as closely as your son has been, you would know that."

"I will not tolerate impudence from the likes of you."

Honoria's eyes narrowed. "Impudence? You are in my house, uninvited and holding me at gunpoint, no less."

"And you are at my mercy!" Mrs. Walpole replied imperiously. "For you, I have none. It's people like you, people who support and aid those wretched creatures, that allow them to continue spreading disease and misery!"

Honoria's suspicions were proving true. The vitriol Mrs. Walpole expressed for the women they should have been helping was shocking. *Those wretched creatures. Spreading disease and misery.* She didn't even see the women as being human. Rather, she saw them as some sort of pest or vermin. Is that how she could have chosen to see them eliminated? Almost dreading the answer, Honoria asked, "All of those women who have been attacked in Soho . . . ?"

"They are not women. They are a plague upon this earth . . . a plague on my son! My poor dear boy detests them . . . as do I. But he is powerless to resist them," Mrs. Walpole went on. "So I help him. I help him to resist their lure."

"By killing them," Honoria said.

"Not personally," Mrs. Walpole snapped at her. "I'd hardly expend such efforts myself. No, I have hired someone to see to the task."

"You are a horrid woman. And your son—he is a horrid man.

You come here pretending to care about the plight of women in England. And all the while, he's patronizing the poor women we are supposed to be helping, exploiting their misfortunes while you conspire to have them murdered! And yet you take exception to *my* behavior?"

The woman's eyes narrowed. "Do not dare speak ill of my son. And of course, you do not have any interest in my son! You are as worthless as the harlots you choose to associate with! Amoral, grasping, opportunistic. A decent, God-fearing boy like my dear, sweet Maurice would never do for the likes of you. No. You want a criminal, a man who could never show his face in polite society!"

She did want him, Honoria realized. Terribly. And not just the pleasure he could give her. She wanted him. *All of him.* With his occasional bad temper and surly moods, his sarcasm and caustic wit, his very real vision of the world around them as neither black nor white but all the myriad shades of gray between. There was nothing about him that she would alter in any way . . . except his absence.

If there was one certainty in her relationship with Vincent Carrow, it was that he'd never lied to her. He'd kept his own counsel on certain matters, but even if he hadn't, it wouldn't have fundamentally changed anything that passed between them. Unlike the woman before her and so many others she'd encountered in her life, he'd never pretended to be something he was not. To her, that made him worth his weight in gold. And if she meant to tell him that, she had to survive the madwoman now brandishing a pistol in front of her.

Coolly and with complete confidence in its ability to provoke a reaction, Honoria uttered a single statement that was true and, in that moment, purposeful. "He's a better man than your wretched, spoiled boy could ever hope to be."

"Enough! I will not allow you to malign him so. This has gone on too long as it is. Climb the stairs, Mrs. Blaylock. We are going to your chamber," Mrs. Walpole demanded. "After all, most ladies who choose to end their own lives do so very privately."

So that was her plan. Make it look like the poor, lonely widow had taken her own life. Well, she wasn't about to cooperate on that front. "And why on earth would I want to do that? I will not make it easier for you to kill me. If you wish to shoot me, you will do it right here in the entryway where it will be obvious to one and all that there is a culprit to be apprehended!"

The woman blinked in surprise. She clearly had not considered that Honoria might be uncooperative. Apparently, for the past year, she had not been paying attention.

It was a stroke of luck, or possibly benevolent intervention, then that Mrs. Ivers, the cook, popped her head out of one of the concealed servants' doors. Mrs. Walpole whipped around to shoo the woman away. Honoria seized the opportunity. She untucked the blade from her sleeve and struck out, the knife slicing through the delicately embroidered sleeve of Mrs. Walpole's gown.

Red blossomed on the lilac-colored silk, and the small muff pistol fell from her hand, clattering loudly on the marble floor. The gun discharged, the pistol ball taking a jagged furrow out of a particularly ugly still life that had been hanging in the corridor.

Mrs. Walpole let out a tremendous shriek and lunged at her. Honoria shifted sideways, narrowly avoiding the woman's attack. She regretted the assumption that had led her to keep her sword in her coach. She'd mistakenly believed all the danger was outside, rather than within her home. Now she needed a weapon that would allow some distance between the other woman and herself.

The stick stand positioned behind the door was now in reach. From it, Honoria withdrew a hefty parasol. The frame and handle were constructed of such heavy wood that she rarely carried it. But that made it an excellent choice as a makeshift weapon.

Holding it aloft, she brandished it over Mrs. Walpole and, when the woman lunged at her, brought it down with all the force she could muster. The woman sank to the floor, wailing as she clutched her shoulder. But Honoria was taking no chances. She didn't lower her weapon but continued brandishing it high, ready to take another swing at the woman should she dare to get up.

And then the door burst open and Vincent rushed in, another man at his side. He drew up short, staring at Mrs. Walpole's fallen form, "Well, it seems you have everything in hand."

Honoria felt the overwhelming urge to simply throw herself into his arms. Would it be terribly inappropriate to climb him like a tree and wrap herself about him in the middle of the foyer? Yes, it would. But she was almost beyond caring. Instead, she simply let the parasol drop to the floor, and balefully asked, "Why are so many people determined to bring unpleasantness to my door?"

"I do not know, love. But for now, we have questions for Mrs. Walpole," Vincent replied. "Arliss, be so kind as to escort this woman to the drawing room while I discuss the most recent revelations with Mrs. Blaylock."

"Yes, Hound," Arliss agreed, and then hoisted the not insignificantly proportioned woman to her feet. If he was none too gentle in "guiding" her into the other room, no one felt compelled to urge more solicitous treatment.

"Where is Henrietta?" The question erupted from Honoria as soon as Mrs. Blaylock was out of earshot behind closed doors.

"The kidnapper was none other than Mrs. Walpole's nephew," Vincent explained. "Indirectly. A former footman fired from Ernsdale house for thievery was acting as their lackey."

Honoria blinked in surprise at that. "Oh. Oh, heavens. She said something . . . something about the other women. Apparently, her worthless son has been a frequent patron of the prostitutes in the very same neighborhoods where we have been conducting our charity work—there was a very good reason why I never wanted to admit men to the society!"

"Stay focused, Honoria. What did she say about the other women?"

Honoria was shaking. Trembling from a mixture of shock,

exhaustion, and fear. It was all too much.

***

VINCENT NOTED THE way she swayed on her feet and decisively swept her up into his arms. Carrying her into another room, far from Mrs. Walpole, he placed her on the sofa and went immediately to the bell pull.

Within seconds a rather flushed and portly woman—who did not look like a maid—stepped into the room. "Yes, sir?"

"Who are you?"

"Mrs. Ivers, sir. I'm Mrs. Blaylock's cook."

"I see. Well, Mrs. Ivers, Mrs. Blaylock requires brandy. It's been an especially difficult night," he explained.

"Yes, sir. I've already sent one of the girls to fetch it," she explained.

At that precise moment, a harried looking maid entered with a tray. "The brandy, sir," the maid said, bobbing a curtsy that set the whole tray to wobbling.

"Do not. Do not curtsy to me," Vincent said, uncomfortable with such a show of deference. It was not something he would ever get used to. Taking the bottle, he splashed a generous amount into the glass provided and then quickly placed that in Honoria's hand. "Drink that. Slowly. But drink it all."

He watched until she had taken several sips and then placed the bottle on the table. "That will be all, Mrs. Ivers. Thank you."

"Yes, sir," she agreed and then bustled the wide-eyed maid out of the room.

Alone, Vincent moved to the settee and eased himself down beside her. "Are you hurt?"

"No," she said, shaking her head. "I do not think she expected that I would fight back. Perhaps she truly believed that I would be some sort of docile creature she could order about. Of course, she's no experience with women fighting or even knowing how to. She never actually attacked any of those women herself but hired someone to do it for her. And Sally said it was a man."

"I spoke with one of Nell's girls who saw him—tall, thin, well-dressed in a dandyish way... I didn't make the connection when I saw him here earlier, but that is an accurate description of Maurice Walpole," he observed. "It might be an accurate description of his cousin, as well. We will know more later. My men are looking for the both of them now."

"I know that he was watching the house. He was watching me. He discovered the reform society because he chanced upon me in one of the rookeries when I was giving out baskets to the needy. I can only presume that he was there as a patron of one of those poor women." Honoria took a shaky breath. "Mrs. Walpole admitted that she ordered their deaths. She had someone else doing her bidding."

"There is one other possibility—the nephew. I do not think this is a straightforward issue with only one villain. I think there are many villains but they are all connected... quite possibly all related."

"You think Mrs. Walpole, her son, and nephew have all played a part?"

"What did Mrs. Walpole say her reasons were for wanting to kill you?"

Honoria frowned, wrapping her arms about herself as if she were chilled. "To protect Maurice... to save him from me as she'd saved him from other unsavory women. Or something to that effect. He saw me in one of the rookeries and became infatuated for lack of a better word. He joined the society to be closer to me and she joined to be closer to him. I think, ultimately, that no woman would have been seen as a good enough choice for her son. They have a unique attachment to one another."

"That's the motive, then. Even if the details aren't clear, there's no mistaking the fact that she is quite unhinged—unhinged and terribly possessive of her son."

"No. There's no mistaking it. But what does any of this have to do with Henrietta?"

He didn't wish to tell her that part, but there was no avoiding it. Honoria would not thank him for trying to shield her from the truth. "They never intended to take Henrietta. It was to have been you all along. When the nephew realized his mistake, he decided to work that to his advantage and ransom her."

She was silent for a moment, taking that in. He knew that if it had been up to her, she would gladly have sacrificed herself to save her sister. He was grateful that would not be a requirement.

"Where is she?" Honoria finally asked.

"On a ship at the St Saviour's Dock . . . near Jacob's Island. I've sent men to retrieve her."

Honoria leaned forward and put her head in her hands. "This is all my fault."

"No. It is not."

"I'm the one who insisted on doing this sort of charity work, and of doing it in such a personal manner instead of from a safe and reputable distance the way our mother always had. I'm the one who Maurice Walpole became obsessed with in the course of that work! Henrietta would never have been taken had—"

"Had the woman in your drawing room not been a lunatic," Vincent interrupted her. "Contrary to what you seem to believe, Honoria, you do not control everything."

She laughed bitterly. "Oh, you are not the one to cast that stone!"

"I am not casting stones. But I cannot allow you to labor under the burden of guilt that you have not earned. Walpole, his mother, and his cousin—that's who is to blame and all of this. And Ernsdale's bloody footman. You've done nothing wrong. You have, in fact, devoted your life to helping other people—even to your own detriment. This is not your fault."

"They know about us," she said softly. "They know and they will tell everyone."

Vincent walked to the window, hating the sick feeling in his gut at the thought that it might all be coming to a crashing end. "No one will believe them."

"I hope they do," she replied.

Vincent whipped around to face her. "What?"

Honoria lifted her head, looking at him in that way she had—straight into his soul. "I hope they do tell. And I hope they are believed. Because I won't hide it. I've nothing to be ashamed of."

"You have me to be ashamed of," he pointed out. *Criminal. Gutter rat. Blackmailer and extortionist.* The list was positively endless.

She smiled, slightly watery, a bit lopsided, and clearly full of so many different emotions. "Then I suppose Mrs. Walpole was correct in her estimation of me. I truly am shameless."

He might have laughed had the situation not been so weighted. "You are as mad as she is."

"No. If all of this has proven one thing to me beyond any shadow of doubt, it's that I know whose opinions I value. My sister's. Yours. My friends'—women like Sally Dawson. Those opinions matter. And all the fake smiles and practiced laughter in drawing rooms and ballrooms... that was never my place. I never wanted to be there. That is only where my father put me because he felt slighted by their exclusion of him—as if money earned were somehow dirty while money inherited or garnered through marriage were, by comparison, washed clean."

It was perfect. It was all that he wanted. And perhaps that was why he was afraid to reach out for it. Things he wanted had always required a battle. He'd had to fight for them. And she was simply offering herself to him. "You are in no condition to make such rash judgements. It's been a hellish day for you and these situations are still not resolved. Until your sister walks through that door, nothing is settled," he replied.

She nodded. "So we wait. And we settle it all after."

Chapter Thirty-Seven

THE WATER WAS unbearably cold. That was Henrietta's first thought. Then the significance of that thought hit her and panic soon followed. *Water.* She was in the water.

It was a mindless impulse to struggle, to fight against it. The fear from that horrible moment in her childhood came rushing back to her. Gasping for breath, flailing to stay above the water. But she was imprisoned once more in a pair of strong arms. They closed about her and a hand settled over her mouth. He shifted slightly in the water, moving them closer to one of the pilings, giving her something solid to hold on to. Instinctively, she reached out for it, wrapping her arms tightly about it. With the water rushing around them, to hold onto something still, something immovable in that swift current, was a blessed bastion of calm.

"Shhh," he whispered against her ear. "They are still scouring the wharf for you. Until they've moved off we must remain where we are. Nod if you understand."

Terrified for so many reasons, Henrietta managed to do as he'd said. Once she had, he removed his hand from her mouth. She dared a glance over her shoulder, but in the shadow spaces beneath the wharf there was no light. She could see nothing of this man, but the impression of mass was there. He was a large man, broad and incredibly firm, seeming somehow to tower over her even in the water. All of which was completely foreign to her. "Who are you?"

"My name is Joshua Ettinger. I'm a private inquiry agent—formerly of Bow Street. Your sister—indirectly—retained my services."

He'd answered one question and, in so doing, created a dozen more. She would have queried further but the loud thud of footfalls above them halted her. In fact, she dared not even breathe.

"Did you find her?" one of the men asked.

She recognized that voice. He was not the footman, but the other one.

"No. No sign of her. She likely drowned. Hobson told us she was fearful of water."

"Then I want a body," he growled. "I need one. She saw me. She knows my face. I'll not swing for this."

The second man sighed. "We don't have enough men to be scouring the city for a lone woman. Around here we'd as like get shot as not."

"Then hire more goddamn men!" The first man growled. "I will not dangle at the end of a bloody rope because that bitch managed to get past the men you trusted to be on watch, *Captain!*"

More heavy footfalls—one set heading to the ship and one set heading away from it—and then silence. There was nothing but the sound of water lapping at the pilings.

"You hit your head," he said softly. "You've been in and out for the last few minutes. I need to know if you're with me before we go ashore. If you're not fully conscious or if you're still unsteady on your feet I need to know. If I tell you to run, I need to be certain that you can and will."

With her heart in her throat, Henrietta considered it. She'd come this far, she thought, and she wasn't about to turn back. "I can do whatever it takes to get out of here." She took a steadying breath. "I want my sister. I just want to go home to her."

"All right. Let's go then. Quiet is better than quick. No thrashing about. We can't afford to disturb the water. Go piling to piling under the wharf."

She desperately wanted to just go, but the fear was still there. And she had to tell him. "I'm not a strong swimmer. I can barely tread water."

"That's all you need to do here. Hold on to me. I'll get us there."

As if it were the most natural thing in the world, Henrietta plastered herself to this stranger—to this mountain of a man—and let him guide her toward the shore.

At one in the morning, he had worried. At two in the morning, he'd sent Arliss and some of the other men out front to go in search of the others. It was three in the morning when word came. Arliss returned and the man's grave countenance revealed the dire nature of the circumstances they found themselves in.

"We'll speak in the entryway," Vincent said.

"No! I want to know what's happening," Honoria protested. "Please?"

After a moment's hesitation, Vincent nodded. "Go ahead, Arliss. Tell us what you've learned."

"She escaped, sir. How is anyone's guess. We found the ship, know where she was being held. She's not there now but one of the men from the ship told me she went in the water. There's been no sign of her since."

Honoria gasped. "Hettie hates the water. I can't imagine—she must have feared her abductors more than she feared drowning."

"And the other Mr. Walpole?" Vincent probed. All the while he kept his gaze on Honoria. She was pale. Her hands trembled slightly, and it was obvious to him that the entire ordeal was taking a toll on her.

"Mr. Gilbert Walpole, sir. He's fled into the Mint. But the men who were working with him are scouring the area for any sign of Lady Ernsdale. Our boys are hanging back, watching them. They know the area better and will have the advantage in finding her. Might as well let them do the legwork."

Vincent nodded. It was a solid strategy. "Thank you, Arliss. And Mrs. Walpole and her son?"

"Inspector Gibbs is here now. He talked to the son first. The man dissolved like sugar in water. Confessed to beating Sally Dawson. Confessed to beating all the others . . . but denied killing them."

It matched up well enough with what Mrs. Walpole had already confessed to earlier in Honoria's entryway. "Transportation for them both. Let Gibbs know."

"Won't there need to be a trial?" Honoria interjected.

Arliss' eyes widened and he looked at Vincent in shock. Vincent simply smiled and shook his head. The other man took his cue and left them alone once more.

Vincent turned and faced Honoria fully. "No trials. Not for any of them. It's a scandal that you cannot afford and one that calls into question my efficacy in my chosen and most profitable field. The fewer people who know the full details of the matter the better. But they will all be far, far from here. I imagine for those as soft as Mrs. Walpole and her son, New South Wales is a far more certain death sentence than anything the Old Bailey could dish out."

"And Gilbert Walpole? Is he to be transported as well?"

Vincent's hands clenched into firsts. "No. He's got more to answer for. I'll deal with him myself."

"Could . . . is it possible that Mr. Ettinger has found her?"

If there was a God in heaven, he prayed that was true. "Anything is possible. And I would never underestimate Joss Ettinger for any reason. With them being hunted by the others, he might well have holed up somewhere with her until they can safely make their way back here."

Honoria dropped her face into her hands. "And so we wait."

"We wait," he concurred. "I wish it were different. I wish—wishes don't mean a damn thing, do they? Nothing more than fodder for hopeless fools."

"Hopeful fools," she corrected. "And sometimes wishes and hopes are all that you have. They're what allow you to go on when things are at their bleakest."

"I'll leave by the dawn. I'll leave a few men outside and I'll send someone over who can wear livery and take up duties as a footman, so you'll have protection inside."

"No."

"No, what? I will stay until others are in place to assure your safety. This is nonnegotiable, Honoria!" He snapped. "You are not yet safe."

"No. If you leave at dawn, I'll be leaving with you. I'm not going to be left behind here while you try to pretend that—well, while you act like we are mere acquaintances. We are more than that and I have no intention of going backward. You, Vincent Carrow, the Hound of Whitehall, are stuck with me."

It should have sent him running. If any other woman in all the world had said such a thing to him, he would have laughed in her face and promptly put as much distance between them as the boundaries of England would allow. But this wasn't any woman—it was *her*. It was Honoria Blaylock, bane of his existence, tormenter of his dreams. The only woman in all of his life he'd even considered being in love with.

And quite possibly the only thing that might salvage his black soul.

"Alright. But we'll stay here. It's where Ettinger will bring your sister when he finds her." He gave her a searching look. "Are you prepared for what this will do to you?"

"No. But I'm even less prepared for what going on without you might do to me," she admitted. "We've tried. Heaven knows we have. For a year and a half, we've circled one another, we've hemmed and hedged our way around one another. But circumstances—or possibly fate—keep bringing us together. And when they didn't, I . . . well, I did something reckless that I knew would have consequences. I came to your rooms in the middle of the night. No woman, Vincent, is *that* naïve. I was creating a situation where I could have what I wanted without having to ask for it myself."

He wanted to go to her—to hold her and whisper pretty words. But he wasn't that man. In another life, perhaps he might have been. "I'm not the romantic sort, Honoria. I've never believed in love. It's just a word. Stuff and nonsense that people say to pretty up lust and mutually beneficial arrangements."

"I didn't ask you to love me," she protested, but there was hurt in her eyes nonetheless and pain in her voice.

"You didn't have to," he explained, a slightly bitter laugh escaping him.

Vincent walked toward the window and looked out into the darkened street beyond. Ornate architecture, opulence, waste, genuine wealth, and the mere sham of it existing side by side in elegant terrace homes. The view from his own windows was similar. but their worlds were vastly different. He would not compare their suffering. If he'd learned one thing in life it was that personal tragedy and the misery it brought could not be measured. They'd both had more than their share even if it had been in different fashions.

And being with him would cost her everything. No one in society would speak to her. She'd be given the cut direct by everyone she knew. The very fact that the most horrid thing that could happen to someone in that world was having a person deny them acknowledgement was proof enough of just how disparate their existences were. If he were the man she deserved, he'd walk away and live with the misery of wanting her, the misery of loving her, while she moved on with her life. But he was not that man. He didn't have it in him to be so selfless. He wanted her and damn the cost.

"I'm not even sure when or how it happened. Likely the first time I wanted to throttle you. Against every hard-learned lesson life has taught me, I love you."

"We barely know one another," she replied, harkening back to one of their earlier conversations, a question in her voice.

"I don't think that's true. I didn't really believe it the first time I said it. You know more about me than anyone in this world . . . well, other than Stavers. And I know more about you than anyone in this world except, perhaps, for your sister. And even then, it's not the same. Knowing someone physically when you also know their heart and mind—it's something different altogether. More different still when they know yours in return."

She pursed her lips thoughtfully. With her head cocked to one side she surveyed him with an assessing gaze. "And yet, every time I presume to tell you something about your heart or your conscience, you deny it and insist that I recognize you for the villain you claim to be. What are you then, Vincent? Hero, villain, or simply misunderstood?"

He shrugged, shoving his hands into his pockets. "Villain and hero depends entirely upon one's perspective in any situation. You would call me heroic for trying to find your sister. The Walpoles would deem me a villain for interfering in their schemes. You said I had a code, and while I never thought of it in those terms, it's true enough. I know what I can live with and what I can't, and I try never to violate those bounds."

"And bartering with me to help Henrietta? Did that violate your code?"

He regarded her thoughtfully for a moment, then answered, softly, "Yes, it did. But that breach of my code was preferable to going on without you. I couldn't do it then and I'm not certain, Honoria, that I can do it now."

He would have said more, but she simply flew from the sofa and launched herself into his arms. And he held her there without even a hint of remorse. She was his and he'd be damned before he let her go—for any reason.

Chapter Thirty-Eight

Sᴴᴱ ʜᴀᴅ ɴᴇᴠᴇʀ behaved with such a lack of decorum in all of her life. But the impulse had struck, and she wanted nothing so much as she wanted to be close to him. Needed to be close to him. With her world in a state of chaos and flux, he was rock solid. Regardless of what he'd said, she was fairly certain he would have worked to locate Henrietta even if she had not agreed to his terms. Perhaps not immediately, but it would have tugged at his mind and at the conscience he denied having most of the time, until he felt compelled to do something.

"I didn't mean to love you, either," she whispered. "In truth, I thought I was incapable of it. But you've shown me that many of the things I believed about myself were false—that Edwin poisoned my mind not just about men and marriage but about myself. I don't ever want to live in fear of what others think of me, Vincent. Never again. If it means being ruined, I'll be ruined. If it means living on the very edge of hell itself, I would—just to be with you."

She could feel him smiling against her cheek, could feel his arms tightening about her slightly. And then, against her ear, he whispered. "It's not exactly the edge of hell, but I do have a country house in Kent that I'm told is quite lovely."

Her eyes widened and she pulled back to meet his gaze. There was laughter in his eyes, something that was not seen very often. "Told? You've never been there?"

"It was given as payment for a sizable loan I had granted someone," he explained. "I'd intended to sell it, but I'm thinking that perhaps a bucolic existence might be nice. I don't know a damned thing about being a country gentleman, but I could probably learn."

"Do you want to? Really? You are London born and bred. It's your home."

"It's my vocation. Home will be wherever you are. Besides, I like the notion of trying my hand at the kind of life I ought to have led. Would have led, had the world been a slightly different place."

"What does that mean?"

"You could have been a duchess . . . the man who sired me was the late Duke of Clarendon. I just thought that was something you ought to know."

"Are you trying to dissuade or persuade with that bit of information?"

"Only to be forthcoming. I want no secrets between us."

"It doesn't matter," she said. And it didn't. He could have been heir to the throne and it would have made no difference to her at all. "You could be a chimney sweep or crown prince . . . I'm yours."

"I will spend the rest of my life trying to be worthy of your love . . . trying to deserve the happiness that you've given me."

"For someone who professes not to be much of a romantic, you are executing a remarkable facsimile of it." The banter was spoiled by an exhausted yawn.

"Go to bed, Honoria. Rest. I'll wake you if she arrives," he promised.

"I couldn't possibly! And besides, you've had nearly as little sleep as I have. You have to be exhausted, as well!"

"I am, but I'm much more used to it than you are. I often go days without sleep—one of the hazards of owning a club and having other business interests. Late nights are often followed by very early mornings. For an hour or so, even if you do not sleep, you should lie down and rest."

"Will you come with me?"

"Most assuredly not," he denied. "It would scandalize your poor Mrs. Ivers. And more importantly, if I get into bed with you, neither of us will rest."

Honoria shook her head. "I do not want to go upstairs alone. I want to be close by if she comes through that door. I'll rest on the sofa in here."

"All right. I want to have a word with Arliss anyway."

Before she could even ask what he meant to do, he'd scooped her up into his arms, carried her to the sofa and settled her on the cushions. Then he took a small blanket and tucked it in around her. "Sleep, Honoria. I will alert you the very second anything changes."

Her eyes closed and she was asleep before he'd even closed the door behind him.

"STRIP."

Henrietta would have balked at such a command, but she hadn't the strength of energy. Of course, she hadn't the strength of energy to comply, either. Every attempt to lift her numb fingers to the buttons of her coarse dress resulted in nothing more than inept fumbling.

"Damn it all!" He exclaimed and then, with more skill and grace than she would have expected from so large a man, divested her of the sodden garment.

"I'm sorry," she offered. Her voice sounded strange to her own ears, her speech slurred and indistinct. She sounded like Ernsdale did when he was foxed.

"It's the cold," the behemoth said. "It clouds your brain. It can drive you mad if you cannot get hold of yourself. But first things first, we need to get you warmed up."

The gown fell away. She wore nothing beneath it. Her chemise, stays, petticoat and stockings had all been taken along with the saffron silk dress that she so loved. The rough wool must have scratched her skin, but she was beyond feeling it. Almost every part of her was numb from the cold. Even her heartbeat seemed strange to her . . . sluggish and uneven.

She must have smiled.

"What is it?" he demanded, his voice quite gruff.

"I was afraid to drown," she managed. "But there are worse ways to die. Now I wonder if freezing to death might be one of them."

A word slipped past the firm, hard line of his lips then. It was crass and vulgar, and most men would never dare to utter such a thing in front of her. But he did. He said what wanted. He was strong and fit. There was nothing about him that hinted at weakness or fragility. And he stood there in dripping wet clothes, seemingly impervious to the cold. Impervious to everything really. He was immovable. What would it be like, she wondered, to be that strong and certain? She envied him that.

"You're not going to freeze to death. I won't allow it," he snapped.

She wasn't entirely certain he had a choice in the matter, but it seemed a foolish thing to point out to him when he already seemed to be in a rather foul mood. So she simply remained quiet and docile as he led her closer to the fire.

It was an odd thing, a box stove in the middle of a warehouse. But then it was odd to find such a well-appointed room in the middle of a warehouse, as well. The room also held a bed, several chairs, and a chest at the foot of the bed.

"What is this place?" She managed to ask as he led her to the stove and settled her before it. Immediately, he opened the door and shoveled more wood into it. She couldn't feel the warmth yet, but she could anticipate it and that offered her some comfort.

"It was the home of a dead woman," he replied.

"Oh, that's terrible. Did she die here?"

"No. She was already dead before she moved in," he explained.

He sounded funny. Funny enough that Henrietta turned her head in his direction, though even that small movement cost her dearly. She swayed and would have fallen over had he not had the foresight to position her with her back against one of the chairs. It was obvious to her, once she saw him, why he sounded so very strange. He was removing his own wet clothes.

Even in her present state, she could comprehend that it was a truly impressive sight. Broad shoulders, a chest that rippled with muscle and more heavy muscles still cording his arms. The light dusting of hair that covered his chest was something of a revelation to her. When it came to male nudity, ancient statuary was her only source of knowledge. While he looked very much like them in some ways, he was incredibly different in others.

His trousers fell to the floor. She had been mistaken. He was entirely different from the statues she'd seen. Henrietta wanted to look away—knew that she should look away. And yet her body and her mind were not yet in one accord. She could think something all she wished, but forcing her flesh to comply was another matter.

Then their eyes met. He cocked one brow. "Careful, Lady Ernsdale. You'll put me to blush."

"I don't think so. From what I can see you have absolutely nothing to be embarrassed about." Was she flirting with him? Inappropriately flirting, no less? Yes. Yes, she was. It had to be some sort of delirium brought on by the cold. Not because he was not worthy of the attention but because she had absolutely no notion of what she would do if he were to take those advances seriously.

He turned away from her then. As he positioned his clothing and hers in such a way that they would dry from the warmth of the fire, she was presented with his perfectly formed backside. Now that, she thought, definitely looked like the statues she'd seen. She imagined, if it were possible, it would be as firm—but it would not be cold marble that greeted her questing hand. It would be warm, supple flesh. And that was very dangerous, indeed.

He turned once more, but this time what she saw made her gasp not in appreciation but in horror. His shoulder was simply ravaged. There were two large divots, one in front and one in back. Deep, ugly scars where flesh had not simply been torn, but lost. There were other scars all around those. A pistol ball that had broken apart and had to be retrieved one fragment at a time—it was the only explanation.

"It's ugly as hell, but I don't have the luxury of covering it right now," he explained stiffly.

"Does it pain you still? The scars are still very red . . . and very new."

He let out a pained chuckle. "I'm learning, Lady Ernsdale, to ignore all manner of discomforts. Now lie down before the fire. I'll get us some blankets from the chest and we'll stay here until our clothes are dry and you've thawed a bit. Once day breaks, we'll make our way out of the Mint and get you back to your sister."

Henrietta did as he said. Moments later, he was lying down behind her, shrouding their entwined forms with a musty smelling and slightly moth-eaten blanket. His strong arms wrapped around her tightly, the warmth of his larger body surrounding her entirely. She could feel it seeping into her skin, melting her flesh and bones.

She hadn't drowned. And freezing was no longer a threat. In fact, she might very well go up in flames before the dawn came.

Chapter Thirty-Nine

It wasn't Vincent who awakened her. It was the joyous exclamation of Mrs. Ivers in the entryway. Sitting up on the sofa, the blanket falling away, she saw Vincent striding through the door. There was no triumphant smile on his lips, just grim satisfaction. One curt nod told her all she needed to know. Henrietta was home.

Jumping up, she didn't even bother to smooth her hair or her hopelessly rumpled clothing. She simply ran to the entry hall and was immediately brought up short. While kidnapping was certainly cause to look less than put together, she had never—not in all their lives—seen her sister in such a bedraggled state. Even as a child, she'd been impossibly fastidious with her appearance.

The roughly woven wool dress that draped her was the most hideous color—residing somewhere between brown, gray and some sort of muddy green. There was not a woman living or dead who could have been flattered by the shade. Henrietta's dark brown locks, normally so perfectly styled, were hanging about her shoulders in a tangled mass. And she smelled terrible, quite frankly.

"It was the river," her sister replied to a question that had not been asked. "I'm not even certain it could be classified as water given the degree of filth it contains."

"Mrs. Ivers, have a bath run for my sister, please, and have one of the maids get her something of mine to wear," Honoria requested. Even then she was stepping forward, pulling Henrietta into her arms.

"I'll make you smell, too!" Henrietta protested.

"I don't care," Honoria insisted. But she wrinkled her nose a bit. "Well, I care. But not enough to let go of you. Not just yet. I've never been so afraid in all my life."

"Where is my husband?" Henrietta asked.

"He's at his home . . . and you will stay here. This will be your home going forward," Honoria said. "Now, let's get you upstairs. We'll get you bathed, we'll get you some clean clothes, and then we'll sort it all out."

Stepping back so that her sister could actually walk, Honoria finally spotted Mr. Ettinger lurking just inside the door. It was a testament to how relieved she was to see Henrietta that she had not even noticed the massive, hulking figure of the man.

Leaving Henrietta, she walked toward him. He stiffened, his shoulders drawing back and an expression that could only be described as mutinous crossing his face. But it did not halt her. Honoria simply wrapped her arms about him, or as close as she could come to achieving that task, and embraced him warmly. *Like family*.

"Thank you," she murmured, hating the tears that threatened. "Thank you for bringing my sister home to me."

"You do not have to thank me. It's my job," he answered.

There was something in his tone, something that alerted her to the fact that all was not quite well with Mr. Ettinger. Honoria stepped back but didn't let go of him. "I do have to thank you. Whether it's your job or not, I am grateful. And if there is ever anything I can do for you, Mr. Ettinger, you have but to ask. It's yours."

"That's a dangerous sort of promise."

Honoria nodded. "Yes. So you know just how important it is to me . . . how important she is to me. And now, you are as well. You are no stranger here. You were family already to Mr.

Carrow, and now you are family to me."

He said nothing for the longest time. Then he stepped back, offered a single jerky nod and made for the door.

Honoria turned and headed upstairs to see to Henrietta.

⁂

"WHAT THE DEVIL has gotten into you?" Vincent demanded as soon as Ettinger had cleared the front door. He'd been waiting for the man on the front steps. He'd known him long enough to recognize that something was not right with him.

"It was a long night, and I spent half of it freezing my bollocks off in the sewer that is the Neckinger River," Ettinger protested. "The remainder of it was spent trying to avoid all the people who wanted to kill us and trying to keep *her ladyship* from freezing to death."

Vincent's eyes narrowed. He knew that look. He knew that sounded. And he felt immediate sympathy. After all, no one in the world understood as well as he did, what it was like to be marked straight to your soul by a headstrong and unmanageable woman. "How did you manage that? Keeping her warm that is."

"Lady Marchebanks' bolt hole in the old warehouse. No one else has yet discovered it, and the box stove and furnishings, as well as the blankets, remain relatively untouched," Ettinger answered.

"Mm-hm. I know the quickest and most effective way to warm a person who is half-frozen, Joss. It's not a fucking blanket, either."

Ettinger bristled visibly at that. "She's home, isn't she? I found her. You've got the ones responsible for the deaths and for her abduction now."

"In theory," Vincent replied. "Did you—prior to this abduction scheme, Lady Ernsdale was a virgin. It's not common knowledge, but it is a very important fact as she plans to seek an annulment from her shite husband. But if she's no longer chaste, if her virginity cannot be proven, then she'll have no grounds for it. And you know that bastard will not simply accept it quietly!"

Ettinger shoved his hands angrily into his pockets. "Whether or not the lady is a virgin is something you'll have to take up with her. My bit in all of it is done. And now, I'm going home. You'll be getting my bill soon enough. My very, very hefty bill!"

Vincent watched the man stalk away. There was nothing for it, he thought. If Lady Ernsdale was to get her annulment, he'd have to resort to bribery. Because he would have laid his very soul on the wager that Joss Ettinger and the lovely Henrietta had done much more than just stay warm together.

"Bloody hell," he muttered. "Bloody everlasting hell."

Epilogue

Two weeks later

SHE'D MOVED INTO the club. Well, into his rooms above the club. Honoria had been happy enough to leave the house that she had shared with Edwin, a house filled with terrible memories and the echoes of many, many tears. It was now her sister's. Henrietta had taken up residence there, living an openly separate life from her estranged husband while they pursued an annulment . . . mutually. Lord Ernsdale had agreed to concede that he could not bed his wife because he found her distasteful but only on the condition that it was made quite clear that he was capable of bedding other women. No one had objected since his cooperation would expedite the process.

But the rooms over the club were not to be their permanent home. Vincent was slowly getting his business affairs in order. With Stavers at the helm and a few trusted members of the inner guard to take over many of his duties, those endeavors would essentially run themselves.

The door opened and Vincent entered. As always, he was instantly stripping off his cravat, waistcoat, and shirt. He abhorred the smell of smoke that always settled on his clothes while he was belowstairs.

"I will not miss this," he said. "I'll implement a rule for our country home that there will be no smoking or snuff. Not of any variety. And minimal spirits. Sir Reginald Montrose spilled brandy all over me. I reek of it."

Honoria grinned as she sat up in bed, letting the covers fall away from the truly indecent peignoir that was her only clothing and had been delivered to her just that evening. "Joining the temperance movement, husband?"

His gaze flared with heat as it traveled over her. "God's blood, no. Never. But like battles, one has to pick their vices."

"And what are your vices?" She asked, lying back on the pillows in what she hoped was a seductive manner. From the way his gaze roamed over her, it appeared she had succeeded.

"You, wife," he all but growled. "You are my vice."

"We didn't have to marry," she said, eyeing the large diamond ring that winked on her finger. "I was quite content to be scandalous and live in sin with you."

"I'm trying to reform myself here," he complained, even as he shed his trousers and stalked toward the bed, quite proud and very, very naked.

"Not too much I hope. I rather like the criminal mastermind whom I fell so deeply, passionately, and—yes—foolishly, in love with."

He was looming above her, his face a mask of hunger. "Then by all means, let's break a few laws."

"But we're married! Nothing we do in bed is illegal, now," she protested.

"My sweet, innocent, naïve Honoria . . . who is the expert on criminal behavior here? Criminality is not determined by capture. The law exists whether it is enforced or not. The law I have in mind, in particular, is one that states 'you shall not break the peace'. Do you know what that means?"

As he'd asked his question, he'd taken both of her hands and lifted them up to the headboard. There were notches there that fit her hands perfectly and she had no wish to think about why the furniture had been designed in just such a way. "No. I can't say that I do."

He grinned. "It means, that if I can make you scream or moan or cry out my name to the heavens loudly enough to disturb our neighbors . . . then we are both in violation of that law. We are very much *breaking their peace.*"

"Our neighbors are very far away." It was said more in challenge than in doubt. She was quite eager for his attempts.

"Then I'll have to work doubly hard."

And he did. Several times. He didn't stop until she was hoarse from screaming and her entire body trembled and quivered with the aftereffects of the most exquisite release. Releases. In truth, she couldn't even count them. One blissful climax had simply rolled into the next until she was lost in a haze of pleasure and desire.

Against her ear, he whispered, "The real challenge will be whether or not we can still manage to break this law when we are in residence in Kent." He then simply collapsed onto the bed beside her, both of them utterly spent.

Honoria frowned. "How many acres comprise this property?"

"Twelve hundred acres, I believe. Roughly," he replied, his breathing beginning to even out once more.

"And you think you can make me scream loud enough to disturb our neighbors when we are there?" she demanded with a laugh.

"Darling, I think I made you scream loud enough that we might have disturbed them from here."

Honoria smiled. It was the smile of a very satisfied woman. Not just physically, though she certainly was that. No. She was blessed to be well satisfied in all ways. It only took letting go of the life she'd been forced into—the safe one, the respectable one—and seizing the slightly outlandish and entirely scandalous one that promised unbelievable happiness.

"And who am I to argue with that?" she replied.

The question fell on deaf ears. Vincent was already asleep.

The End

LOOK FOR THE STORY OF HENRIETTA AND MR. ETTINGER IN *THE LADY CONFESSES*. COMING SOON!

About the Author

Chasity Bowlin lives in central Kentucky with her husband and their menagerie of animals. She loves writing, loves traveling and enjoys incorporating tidbits of her actual vacations into her books. She is an avid Anglophile, loving all things British, but specifically all things Regency.

Growing up in Tennessee, spending as much time as possible with her doting grandparents, soap operas were a part of her daily existence, followed by back to back episodes of Scooby Doo. Her path to becoming a romance novelist was set when, rather than simply have her Barbie dolls cruise around in a pink convertible, they time traveled, hosted lavish dinner parties and one even had an evil twin locked in the attic.

Website: www.chasitybowlin.com

CPSIA information can be obtained
at www.ICGtesting.com
Printed in the USA
LVHW050715170723
752523LV00005B/73